EATING
NAKED

Stories

Stephen Dobyns

PENGUIN BOOKS

PENGUIN BOOKS

Published by the Penguin Group
Penguin Books Ltd, 27 Wrights Lane, London W8 5TZ, England
Penguin Putnam Inc., 375 Hudson Street, New York, New York 10014, USA
Penguin Books Australia Ltd, Ringwood, Victoria, Australia
Penguin Books Canada Ltd, 10 Alcorn Avenue, Toronto, Ontario, Canada M4V 3B2
Penguin Books India (P) Ltd, 11 Community Centre, Panchsheel Park,
New Delhi – 110 017, India
Penguin Books (NZ) Ltd, Cnr Rosedale and Airborne Roads,
Albany, Auckland, New Zealand
Penguin Books (South Africa) (Pty) Ltd, 5 Watkins Street, Denver Ext 4,
Johannesburg 2094, South Africa

Penguin Books Ltd, Registered Offices: Harmondsworth, Middlesex, England

First published in the United States of America by Henry Holt and Company 2000
Published in Great Britain in Penguin Books 2000
1

Acknowledgments are due to the editors of the publications in whose pages the following
stories first appeared: *Clackamas Literary Review*, for "Kansas"; *DoubleTake*, for "Devil's Island"
and "Part of the Story"; *Gettysburg Review*, for "Some Changes Coming"; *Many Mountains
Moving*, for "With Franz and Jane"; *Massachusetts Review*, for "Flaws in the Latex"; *New
England Review*, for "The Cedar Bungalow"; *North American Review*, for "Out on the Water";
Ploughshares, for "So I Guess You Know What I Told Him"; *Salmagundi*, for "Cynthia, My
Sister"; *River City*, for "The Chaucer Professor"; *Sonora Review*, for "Dead Men Don't Need
Safe Sex"; *Southern Review*, for "A Happy Vacancy" and "Eating Naked." "So I Guess You
Know What I Told Him" also appeared in *The Best American Short Stories*, 1995, edited by
Jane Smiley. "A Happy Vacancy" also appeared in the *Pushcart Anthology XX*, 1996. "Kansas"
also appeared in *The Best American Short Stories*, 1999, edited by Amy Tan.

The moral right of the author has been asserted

Printed in England by Clays Ltd, St Ives plc

For Michelle Blake and Dennis McFarland

CONTENTS

EATING
NAKED

A HAPPY VACANCY

There are perils in life so disturbing that we need to hold ourselves in a state of readiness, ever alert to exercise our outrage or disbelief. Yet even these events must be dealt with and understood. Worse than such events may be how the world responds to them. Consider the following.

Jason W. Plover, a poet with six books, was killed when a pig tumbled out of the sky and crushed him as he was crossing Massachusetts Avenue against the light at Harvard Square.

The pig was a seven-hundred-pound boar being used in a film about a bank robbery. A helicopter had been transporting it from a farm in Lexington to Memorial Drive along the banks of the Charles where a famous actress was waiting, as well as a Brinks truck rented for the afternoon. It was a key scene concerning the use of the pig as a porcine roadblock. The pig had been doped but not enough. It woke, saw daylight, heaved its huge frame toward the open door of the helicopter, breaking its bonds, and took a fatal step, a six-hundred-foot step with Jason W. Plover as its destination.

No telling what the pig thought. Its mind was probably a mass of question marks. The sky was blue, the weather mild, and the view of the Boston skyline must have been marvelous. It was late September and trees were turning color. An idea having to do with a possible mistake was perhaps being assembled in the pig's dim brain when it squashed Jason Plover to a splop of jelly.

One of the witnesses spoke of hearing a squealing. Another described a pig on a man's shoulders. A third spoke of seeing an angel falling out of the air. People paused, looked up, and saw what appeared to be a pink cloud dropping fast. Much was made of the fact that Jason Plover had been crossing against the light, that he had not waited. He had been on his way to a lunch meeting at the Harvest with his editor, Josie Kahn. A seventh book of poems was already in manuscript and he was eager to rush it into print. Jason Plover was someone always in a hurry. Had he been a tad less serious, a tad more casual, he might be with us still today.

But seriousness had amounted to Jason Plover's trademark. He had been a tall, heavyset man fond of wearing a thick tweed overcoat, which made his figure resemble a rolled-up mattress. When he walked he liked to set his entire foot flat upon the ground before lifting it for the next step. His heavy tread was well known in the halls of the English department at Tufts, where he had taught for fifteen years. He had had vast black eyebrows that he could wield as a samurai wields his sword. One position showed scorn, another superiority, and a third deep thought. There are many writers in the Boston area. Toss a stone in a public place and you are likely to hit one. But for seriousness—sheer, bullying, heavy-lidded, I'm-the-most-important-poet-on-God's-green-acre seriousness—Jason Plover had the rest of the writers beat.

Now all was changed.

The headline in the *Boston Herald* read PLUMMETING PORKER PULVERIZES POET.

In the same way that Jason Plover had taken liberties with the truth when alive, so had the headline writer at the *Herald* taken liberties with the truth in announcing Plover's death. He wasn't pulverized, he was squashed.

No matter.

Plover had had a wife, Harriet Spense, who was an associate professor of Feminist Studies at Tufts. She too had a deep seriousness, but, lacking her husband's physical mass, her seriousness was qualified by the weight difference separating her from her departed spouse. Additionally, she had a certain lightness of soul and imagined herself someone who could take a joke. She was an attractive forty-year-old woman, tall and statuesque, with dark red hair.

She first had a glimmer of the changes that lay before her when she entered the faculty room at Tufts the day after her husband's death. A friend was covering her classes and Harriet had stopped by briefly to pick up a book. She assumed that one of her colleagues was telling a funny story because the eight or nine faculty members were laughing with an abandon she had never before witnessed within these walls. Harriet Spense loved her husband and grieved over his death. Yet she also looked forward to whatever might distract her from the awfulness of his passing, meaning that she hoped to share in the joke. However, when her colleagues caught sight of her, they clamped their mouths shut, turned away, and began to make coughing and choking noises, as if it were not something amusing but acrid smoke that was responsible for their condition. Although suspicious, Harriet didn't quite catch on.

Then at the funeral home, as she spoke to the director, whose face was bright red, she found herself distracted by chuckling from a farther room, as if corpse preparation held charms the nature of which had so far escaped her. Indeed, the director himself began to stammer as he tried to enunciate with proper seriousness the word "reconstruction." At the church, the minister wouldn't meet her eye and again she heard distant laughter, as if the church workers found extraordinary delight in their daily tasks.

There were other small signs that need not be fully recounted: the attentiveness of the press, people staring at her on the street, neighbors behaving with inappropriate heartiness. Actually, it was at the funeral that all became clear and Harriet caught an unpleasant glimpse of her future. There were a lot of TV cameras. The Episcopal service was conducted with appropriate solemnity yet there were occasional giggles, even guffaws. Sitting in the front row with her two embarrassed sons, Harriet Spense realized that the oddity of her husband's death might wipe out the accomplishments of his life. It is hard for six serious books of poetry, with a seventh on the way, to compete with the burden of being killed by a falling pig. Put the seven books on one end of a teetertotter and the pig on the other and there is no contest. We read in history that the Greek poet Aeschylus was killed when a turtle dropped by a passing eagle struck his head and split his skull. Aeschylus's reputation has long since recovered but presumably in Athens there was a period of furtive laughter. It was wartime and people needed a joke.

Jason Plover was now the poet who had been killed by a falling pig. His books immediately disappeared from the stores and new printings were planned. Years earlier he had written a poem entitled "The Pig and I" that had appeared in his second collection, *Household Mysteries*. It was not a great poem but it detailed those differences in thought, generosity, and humanity that separate the human being and the pig. A human being cares about his or her brothers and sisters; a pig does not—such was the poem's theme. It was astonishing to Harriet Spense how many requests she had over the next few months to anthologize this poem. It was as if Jason Plover's death were an example of how the animal kingdom can strike back; as if the falling pig had been on a revengeful kamikaze raid. And, too, the anthologizing of the poem allowed the editors, mostly other poets, to write a biographical note detailing the manner of Plover's death. In this they had a lot of fun.

Plover had been a moderately well-known poet and it was not uncommon for literary magazines to ask him for work. Now Harriet was swamped with requests. Her husband had had about twenty unpublished poems, which he intended to include in his seventh volume. These poems were actually fought over; editors called Harriet Spense day and night. Many said they would be happy to publish material that had already appeared in other magazines. These were magazines with circulations between five hundred and two thousand copies. With Plover's name on the cover, their sales would triple.

The editor of a famous poetry magazine in the Midwest was particularly insistent. Some years earlier he had begun devoting himself to theme issues, which let poets feel that their work was being rejected because it wasn't sufficiently about "Fatherhood" or "Nature" or "Cemeteries" or "Home Owning" or "Buying a Dog." This editor called Harriet Spense a dozen times. He was planning a "Pig" issue and it wouldn't be complete without a poem by Jason Plover. In vain did Harriet say that her husband had no other poems about pigs. "Any kind of poem will do," said the editor. Not even its quality was important. He would take an unfinished poem, even rough notes. The editor offered to pay double the rates and was offended when Harriet refused to send

7

him anything. He seemed to think she was attributing a serious-ness to poetry that his theme issues were hoping to deny.

Harriet Spense's life became increasingly difficult. Not only had her husband been transformed into a figure of fun, but she became amusing because she had been married to him. There was a facial expression that Harriet learned to recognize as the Oh-you're-the-woman-whose-husband-was-killed-by-falling-pig expression. People would try to be sympathetic, yet giggle at the same time. They would cover their mouths and look away and their eyes would water. Because her husband had really been killed and because people like to think they possess some shred of decency, very few made jokes to her face, yet when they saw her coming they were clearly prepared to be amused. Even the most serious of us seek out chances to partake of the long slide into laughter. There is a sweetness to that wonderful forgetting that makes us crave it. Had Jason Plover been a plumber or a post-man, the humor would not have been so great. But as a poet with a deep seriousness he was especially vulnerable.

Jason Plover had had a characteristic gesture. First he would join his thumb to the fingertips of his left hand. Then he would draw back all five digits toward the palm, pause, and shoot them forward as he opened his hand wide, duplicating, as it were, a miniature explosion. It was a dismissive gesture. Something small and inconsequential was being blown away. He would make this gesture at the end of summing up another poet's work or dis-cussing an inferior poem. He would make it after discussing another writer's intellect or chance of true success. No telling who made it first after Jason Plover had been squashed by the falling pig, but soon Harriet Spense began noticing it all over Cam-bridge. And she came to understand that the gesture—the little outward puff of fingers—now referred to Jason Plover himself: events had conspired to blow him away.

Harriet's sons were deeply depressed. Frank was a junior at Boston University. Charles was a senior at Harvard. Three weeks after their father's death they dropped out of school. They spoke of needing to visit the West Coast to see what was going on. They regretted that their name—Plover—was sufficiently unusual to remind people about that poet—their father—who had been squashed by a falling pig. They discussed new names: Jacobs and Wellerby and McBride. They were intelligent young men who had had a clear vision of a bright future. Now they felt their lives were finished unless they renamed themselves and moved to another part of the country. They needed something like the FBI's witness protection program. Harriet tried to dissuade them, but in her heart she couldn't blame them. Her own teaching had suffered greatly from the particulars of her husband's death. For one thing strangers began sitting in on her classes. There was always a whispering, and once she heard an "oink-oink" from the back of the room.

"Perhaps you should take a leave," her chairman told her. He was a tweedy bearded man who liked to rub his stomach as he talked.

"It's all so ridiculous," said Harriet.

"It is, rather," said the chairman. "Think of being killed by a falling pig." And the chairman covered his mouth with his hand.

"No, I don't mean that," said Harriet. "I mean people's response to his death."

"I would have given my foot to have seen it," said the chairman. "No offense intended."

And so Harriet Spense took a leave. The dean made no problems. Actually, when she sat waiting to see him, she heard gales of laughter from his office, and when several men came out they refused to meet her eye.

Harriet had a fairly large amount of money from Jason's

publisher owing to his increased sales and the rights to his poem, "The Pig and I." His new book was to have been called *Transcendent Moments in the Spiritual Veldt*, but the editor, Josie Kahn, wanted to change the title to *Pigging Out* or *Pork Thoughts*. Harriet refused, even though Josie said it might mean an extra ten thousand dollars. "To think," said Josie, "I was so *close*. Just my luck that I didn't see it happen."

One night at the beginning of November while Harriet was boxing up Jason's clothes to give to the Tufts Impoverished Students' Fund, she thought, I'm sick of Jason's poetry. I'm sick of the life we had together. Then she glanced around guiltily, as if afraid her thoughts had been overheard.

Harriet had never until now questioned her life with Jason. Her husband had been a highly respected poet and she was a highly respected feminist thinker whose book on gender issues in the workplace was used in classes at more than thirty colleges and universities across the country. They had often been invited out to dinner and were much in demand for the quality of their conversation. Jason Plover's high seriousness and Harriet Spense's moderate seriousness were given a value that was almost monetary. It paid for a lot of meals. When Jason's opinion was asked, other guests fell silent. Jason would rub his jaw, manipulate his black eyebrows, and enter his sentence much in the way an icebreaker enters a frozen sea. He had liked to make *hrumphing* noises and clear his throat. He liked to make that little exploding gesture with the fingers of his left hand. And while Harriet's own ego was not so tied up in her conversational abilities, she also liked being someone to whom people listened.

This too had changed. People now listened to her because her husband had been killed in a ridiculous manner. She could have said nothing but "Doo-dah, doo-dah" and her listeners would have been equally pleased. She could have done no more than whistle. And if she had grunted like a pig, oh, how happy people would have been.

As a result Harriet Spense came to question the value of her former life. Had it ever been the content of her speech that people appreciated? Was it not her serious manner and her husband's even more serious manner? Was it not to their curricula vitae, rather than their voices, that people listened? And now her vita was radically altered. This led her to an awareness of the shallowness of her life and the superficiality of what she valued. She saw that the deep seriousness with which her life had been swaddled was simply a buffer. It had existed to keep people at a distance. It indicated that she had a certain importance and needed to be treated with respect. It had been a strangler of spontaneity and impulse. It had rigidified her life as if she had been dipped in concrete. These realizations caused her a chagrin that was even greater than the embarrassment she had felt because of how Jason had died. Indeed, she now saw that the manner of her husband's death was almost fortunate because it revealed the lie she had been living. She had loved her husband and had forgiven him his foolishness, but she saw that his final gift to her had been the absurdity of his death, because it opened to her a new life, a new way of living.

So it was that eight weeks after her husband's death, Harriet closed up her house in Cambridge and moved to Ann Arbor. Her two sons had already disappeared; she knew of them only by brief postcards from California signed Magillicuddy. Harriet's undergraduate degree had been in clinical psychology and she got a job at a hospice. She was drawn to the idea of people dying in bed surrounded by others who loved them, or at least who had deep respect for them as human beings and for the whole experience of death. For her, death had become a joke, a dreadful *buffo*, and she needed to make it big again.

"The process of dying," Harriet told a cancer patient, "is a process that begins with birth. It continues while we occupy ourselves with what is important in our lives: our careers, our families, our pleasures. Our death accompanies us all through our years, gradually taking our place until it exchanges itself for us completely. The event that will soon occur in your life has been preparing itself for every moment of your life."

But mostly she didn't counsel anybody, mostly she helped with small embarrassing chores like bandages and bedpans, and she liked to read to people: she would read Dickens and Thackeray and Tolstoy, great long books that gave the dying the sense that enormous expanses of time stretched before them.

Each day she would have conversations with the men and women whom she thought of as her patients. The elderly, especially, had had long and interesting lives. They had traveled and witnessed events Harriet had only read about in history books. "I didn't know Lawrence of Arabia personally," said one old man, "but I often saw him from afar when I was in Damascus."

"I was a freshman at Clark when Freud presented his lectures," said an ancient lady. "Dr. Jung was there as well. He had a very pointed head."

There was something about these stories that made time seem causal, and Harriet realized she was attempting to repair her sense of causality. Her husband's death appeared to lie outside causality. The malignant Demiurge who hangs life's carrot before our eyes had been having his or her little joke. What do we do with an extremely serious poet? We kill him with a falling pig. Those people who had laughed at the manner of her husband's death: shouldn't they have been terrified? Didn't Jason's death indicate an awful truth about the cosmos—that if it has a divine direction, then its prime mover is whimsy?

There was a doctor of about Harriet's age who came to the hospice. His name was Robert Chase. He was a tall, willowy figure with a mop of graying blond hair. He never stood completely straight but kept shifting as if the wind were tugging him this way and that. He would sway with his hands in the pockets of his white coat and look at Harriet with his deep blue eyes.

"Do you ever read poetry?" Harriet asked him one day in the staff lounge.

"Absolutely not," said Robert. "Did you hear about that poet in Boston who got killed by a falling pig?"

"I read something about it," said Harriet.

"You wonder how many times something like that misses us. You know, the truck that would have run us down if we had been just a little faster."

"He had crossed against the light," said Harriet.

"Probably one of those stress-ridden Type A personalities," said Robert. "I wonder what he did to relax."

Harriet nearly said Jason had collected first editions and had been her husband, but instead she closed her mouth and shrugged. "Whatever it was," she said at last, "it wasn't enough."

After a few of these conversations, Robert Chase invited Harriet out to dinner. They went to a small Italian restaurant on the road to Ypsilanti. Robert kept looking at her, not out of curiosity or as if expecting anything from her, but just to rest his eyes upon her.

"I think people try to make their lives too serious," said Harriet, as they shared a medium-sized antipasto.

"Is that why you work at the hospice?" Robert wore a blue denim shirt and a yellow tie. Harriet liked how undoctorly he appeared.

"I think I work there in order to see just how serious life can be. If you stare long enough at the most serious thing that life has in store for us," said Harriet, "perhaps you can come out on the other side."

"You mean on the side of laughter?"

"Why not? I mean, I don't intend to laugh at the people at the hospice. My job is to help them and make their departure more comfortable and less fearful. But me, what damage does such solemnity do to me? So I look at it and study it and perhaps with time I'll grow accustomed to it."

Robert kept moving the salt and pepper shakers across the red-and-black checkerboard squares of the tablecloth as he listened. "Do you think that seriousness is connected to fear?"

"I expect it's influenced by fear," said Harriet. She thought of her husband's seriousness, how he wore it like a garment. Most often his laughter had been ironic or sarcastic or superior. His laughter had been judgmental and, as a result, all his laughter had been serious. Was it possible to laugh without any element of judgment? Jason Plover's life had been an edifice built to demonstrate the solemnity of his endeavor. Poor Jason, killed by a falling pig; his death had overturned the premises of his life.

"Seriousness," said Harriet, "often exists as something we want to show other people. We want others to think us serious, which suggests a fear of not being sufficiently respected, of not being taken seriously. What does seriousness get us? It neither delays our death nor makes it easier to bear."

"And what is the opposite of seriousness? Frivolity?"

"Most literally, perhaps, but I think the opposite of such a seriousness is love, because love accepts all possibilities, whereas seriousness only accepts what it sees as correct. Perhaps I work at the hospice for purely selfish reasons. I work to improve the quality of my love."

"That seems pretty serious," said Robert.

"I'm not against seriousness. I'm against the earnestness of seriousness. I want to go beyond it. I want seriousness to be an element in my life and not its reason for being. Look at the unexpected changes that life can force upon a person. Surely life's intrinsic definition—that is, constant change—argues against rigidity. Seriousness may be no more than self-protection, and life can come along and just brush it aside."

"And how can it do that?"

"It can drop a pig on your head from a great height."

Harriet saw Robert more and more often, and she came to realize that they would probably begin a romance. This made her happy. She didn't tell him about Jason; she didn't want to muddy the romantic water. She knew she would tell him sooner or later but she wasn't afraid of doing so. She also knew she would eventually leave the hospice and return to teaching.

There was an old man at the hospice named Franklin, who had long ago been a high school principal in Bloomfield Hills. Now he was ninety-five. Harriet read him *Bleak House* and was even nearing the end of the book. One afternoon in spring, she asked him, "What is the funniest thing you can think of?"

Franklin lay back on his pillows and looked out the window. It was a sunny day and the cherry trees behind the hospice were in full flower. Franklin's gray and spotted hands lay on the counterpane and trembled as if they were getting ready to start up and go someplace.

"The funniest recent thing I can think of," said Franklin, "was something I read about last fall. A fellow was crossing the street in Boston and a pig fell out of the air and crushed him. It had fallen out of a passing helicopter. The man was a poet, I forget his name. He was hurrying someplace important and this seven-hundred-pound pig fell on top of him. It dropped like a rock and hit him right on the noggin. I don't know, it's probably not funny, but it tickles me. I mean, I got to die here in this darn bed. Why couldn't I have been killed by a pig falling out of the sky? Nobody would forget it. I'd be famous forever. This poet, what an opportunity! Some people have all the luck."

Harriet Spense considered how Franklin yearned for the fame that had resulted in her husband's ultimate trivialization. She found herself laughing. She put her hands on her knees, leaned her head back, and gasped for breath. It was neither a guffaw nor the hysterical shriek of nervousness. It was the laugh of someone whose solemnity has been overthrown, the laugh that erases every other concern. Our plans, our memories, our fears are all replaced by a peculiar yet distinctive hooting. To some it sounds like a mob of crows; to others, a donkey's bray. In fact, it is the sound of the world disappearing as all the content is sucked from our heads, to be replaced—briefly, oh, too briefly—by a happy vacancy. And doesn't this sustain us? Doesn't it provide the strength to let us bear up our burden and continue our mortal journey?

EATING NAKED

When Bob Frankenmuth hopped down from the cab of his Chevy pickup, he saw the deer lying back on the road with its head twisted around like somebody saying goodbye. He had hit it on the curve. It was dusk and the shadows were strange. The deer had come down out of the pines. First it wasn't there, then it was: sudden and jittery. Bob had been thinking about Roxanne and the various ways he might leave her: divorce or simple desertion. He had hardly been watching the road at all. The deer was a doe; it was bound to be a doe. Fucked up one more time, Bob thought.

The right front fender of the pickup was crumpled and the headlight broken. Bits of fur were embedded in the grille. Bob kicked the bumper, then walked back toward the deer. It was spring, and deer had begun to come down out of the hills. Bob was trying to get back to Kingston from Delhi and had taken a short cut. Now he would be late.

The body of the doe straddled the yellow line right at the curve. Bob knew he should drag it to the shoulder before another car came along. If he wanted, he could keep it. The law said it was his. He could put it into the back of his pickup and take it home for supper. But there was no way he could get Roxanne to cook it, given her present attitude toward domesticity. She had given up cooking when she decided to go back to college last fall. Bob and the two boys had had to fend for themselves.

Another car was coming and Bob ran forward to warn the driver. He could hear the tires squealing on the curves. The car was going too fast, given the two-lane road and the decreasing light. Bob saw the car's headlights and he began waving his arms. The dead doe was just a brown lump on the pavement. The driver slammed on the brakes and swerved around it. Then the car went out of control, swinging in a full circle with its tires shrieking and going sideways into the trees. It was a black Taurus station wagon. When it swung around, its brake lights made a flashing red arc. The crash against the tree trunks was a deep sound, a metallic crunch, joined with a crumpling and rattling. Bob stopped in the roadway. Where one moment everything had been noise and running, now it was silent.

"Christ," said Bob. He ran for the Taurus, which had come to rest against a tree and was tilted up on its side. One headlight was broken, the other shone into the pine branches. He got to the driver's door and pulled it open. The driver was alone in the car: a woman, leaning forward over the steering wheel. At first Bob thought she was unconscious; then he saw her shoulders heaving and thought she was crying. Then he realized she was laughing. She was blond and young-looking.

"You all right?" asked Bob. He wanted to run back and drag the deer off the road before another car came along.

The woman looked up at him. A pretty face with no marks on it, straight blond hair, and a little stub nose. She was laughing but there were tears in her eyes. "Nothing goes right, does it? Just nothing at all." She laughed some more.

"Hang on a moment," said Bob. "I got to move that deer."

Bob ran back across the road. Crazy women made him nervous; you never knew what they might do next. The front fender of the Taurus was bent back into the tire, puncturing it, meaning the car wasn't drivable, which also meant Bob would have to give the woman a ride someplace. No telling when he would get home. Oddly enough he felt good about this. His life with Roxanne felt like a tunnel he'd gotten stuck in, and here was a sudden veering in another direction. He grabbed the doe's hind legs and began to pull. The creature was still warm. Maybe it weighed a hundred and fifty pounds. The body wasn't cut up or gory. Maybe its neck was broken, that's all. Bob thought again about taking the doe with him. "If you were a real wife," he could say to Roxanne, "you'd cut this up and cook it." He thought how stupid that sounded. Even so, he began dragging the deer toward his pickup.

"You put that thing in the road on purpose?" asked the woman. She had climbed out of the Taurus and was walking after him. She moved unsteadily. First, Bob wondered if she had been drinking; then he guessed it was shock from the accident.

"I hit it about a minute before you came along." He stared at the woman, trying to determine if she was serious. She was more of a girl. Bob doubted she was twenty-one. She was tall but still a few inches shorter than he was. Her blond hair hung past her shoulders. She wore jeans and a thick blue ski sweater that hid her figure.

"What're you doing with it?" she asked.

"I'm going to put it in the back of my pickup."

"You going to eat it?"

"I might."

"My car won't go," said the woman.

Bob kept dragging the deer. "Your car's messed up, all right," he said. "I'll take you to a garage."

"My boyfriend wants to kill himself," said the girl. "I need to get to his place in a hurry. Can you take me there? It's not far."

Bob stood holding the hind feet of the deer. He could feel the sharpness of its small hooves: a weapon that hadn't helped it any. The girl had a small flat face. He thought how she had been laughing and crying when he found her bent over the wheel of her Taurus.

"Give me a hand then," he said. He had begun to feel proprietorial about the deer's corpse. If he didn't take it, some trooper would. Besides, he wanted to give it to Roxanne. He imagined dumping it right down on the kitchen table and saying, "Here!"

The girl took one of the rear hooves and they pulled the body toward the pickup. Bob snuck a look at her, trying to judge her figure under her thick sweater. Up until Roxanne had gone back to school, Bob had thought of himself as settled down. His sons were eight and ten. Bob built summerhouses for rich yuppies from Manhattan and invested his profits. His life had been proceeding perfectly smoothly until Roxanne decided she needed her teaching certificate.

"Why does your boyfriend want to kill himself?" asked Bob. He didn't take the girl's problem seriously. He couldn't imagine anybody having really serious problems until they were over thirty.

"He thinks I don't love him." The girl spoke without looking up at him. They were both into pulling the deer.

"Do you love him?"

"I can't tell anymore."

"You think he'll kill himself?"

"I don't know, but he's got a gun."

They reached the pickup and Bob let down the gate. He had a stepladder in the back. His tools were in the tool case.

"You take the front hooves," he told the girl. They both took hold. Bob counted to three and they heaved the deer up into the bed of the truck, where it landed with a *thunk*. Its head hung back and its large brown eyes seemed to stare at them in the last of the light.

"There," said Bob. "At least that's done." He had a sudden thought of how the deer had probably been off to someplace specific, and he wondered if there were other creatures that had begun to miss it.

"I'm Bob Frankenmuth," he said to the girl. He wiped his hand off on his jeans, then offered it to her. She shook it firmly. A lock of blond hair fell across her eye and she tossed her head to the side.

"Laura Spalding," she said.

"Let's go see your boyfriend," said Bob. "You think he's dangerous?"

"He just can't relax. I tell him to chill out but he can't. He's a jerk." She stood with her hands shoved in her hip pockets and her head tilted to one side. On her feet were big Timberland boots with the laces untied.

"Sounds like you love him," said Bob. He climbed into the cab. The girl climbed into the passenger's side. Several empty beer cans were on the floor and the girl's boots bumped against them. It was seven-thirty and almost dark. Bob started the engine. His one headlight pointed down the road toward the next curve. "Where do I go?" he said. He didn't like it that the kid had a gun.

"Go straight for about three miles. I'll tell you where to turn."

Bob released the emergency brake and the pickup rolled forward off the gravel. A breeze came down from the hills, cold with the feel of the last snow up in the gullies. Even in the dark, the pine trees had a green smell.

"So," said Bob, "you think your boyfriend constitutes a serious problem?"

"If you're scared, you can drop me off at the turning."

"What's the guy's name?"

"Chuckie Phelps."

"I'm not scared of anyone named Chuckie," said Bob. He tightened his jaw. He disliked how he liked to sound tough. He was tired of all his actions and reactions. He was sick of always knowing what he would do next.

"You been screwing other guys?" asked Bob.

"Not really," said the girl. She gave him a quick glance, then stared straight ahead. The one light swung across the trees at the curve. They had passed no other cars.

"So this guy thinks you don't love him, and he's going to shoot himself? Why doesn't he just go out to L.A. or find himself another girl?"

"He's an artist." She said this with some exasperation.

"What's he do?"

"He makes pots."

"I call that a potter, not an artist." Bob began to think about L.A. Why don't I go out there myself? he wondered. Then he thought of his two sons. He couldn't leave them and he didn't see how he could take them. "I guess life's just fucked up," he said. "Your artist pal wants you and you want more. Nothing's ever an even fit."

"How come you know so much about it?" said the girl. Her voice was sarcastic. Bob realized that she saw him as an older man. This surprised him.

"I don't. I'm just making talk." He had entered a parenthetical stretch at the end of his day and it felt pretty good, as if he were on vacation. He was on his way to take a gun away from a potter, and he had a dead deer in the back of his truck.

"What kind of gun does Chuckie have?" asked Bob.

"He's got a nine-millimeter, a couple of rifles, and a twelve-gauge." The girl was leaning against her door, looking at him.

"Is he a religious nut or something?"

"No, he just likes guns."

"Is he dangerous?"

"I never know what the hell he's going to do."

"So who's the other guy?" asked Bob.

"There is no other guy," said Laura. "There's just the idea of another guy. I mean, I like the idea of guys other than Chuckie. But he thinks I'm blowing him off. I'm sick of him trying to make me his property so I told him to fuck himself. I said I didn't want to see him anymore. So he called me up and said he was going to shoot his head off. I told him to cut it out. Then he fired the gun right by the telephone so I could hear it. I jumped about a foot. What a jerk."

"But you were going out there," said Bob.

"I like him. I mean, I want it over, but I don't want him dead. He'd be killing himself to make me feel bad. It makes me angry even thinking about it. So I want the chance to yell at him and tell him he's being a jerk. I tried to tell him on the phone, but he hung up."

"So you're going to yell at him and he's going to wave his guns around," said Bob.

Laura kicked one of the beer cans on the floor. Bob could see her white face in the dash lights. "I said you don't have to come," she told him.

But when she pointed out the road where he had to turn left,

Bob slowed and swung the wheel but didn't stop. He again told himself he wasn't afraid of anyone called Chuckie. Besides, what would happen if he let the girl off at the corner? He would have to return to his own life. The kids would be asleep by the time he got home. Roxanne would ask where he had been. He would tell her about the deer. She would ask why he hadn't been able to miss it, as if he had hit it on purpose. He could almost see how she'd look at him, as if she had caught him in a lie. He could see the whole evening like seeing a movie. Chuckie and his nine-millimeter was a more interesting alternative, full of unknown choices that Bob could make and choices he could refuse. Bob had been married for twelve years and it had never been easy.

"He's got a red mailbox," said Laura. "It's about a mile up on the right."

"A farm?"

"A run-down place with a barn where he throws his pots. It's a wreck but it was cheap."

"He sounds like a hippie," said Bob.

"No," said Laura, "he's just confused."

The driveway was bordered by old maples, sporting small, adolescent leaves. Beyond the trees were dead-looking fields with bushes and small pines. No one had done any farming here for quite a while. The driveway was about one hundred yards and on the left was a ragged stone wall. Bob could see a small white house. A dark Econoline van was parked in front. He pulled up beside it and cut the motor. Lights were on in the downstairs of the house but Bob didn't see any movement. There was a front porch and a peaked dormer over the front door. The porch sagged and the house needed paint. Wooden crates and two-by-fours and old tires littered the yard. Bob opened his door and got out. The air smelled musty and damp. Laura got out on the other side. There was still no sign of anyone.

Suddenly there was a rifle shot. Bob ducked behind the truck. What the hell am I doing? he asked himself.

"Get out of here!" shouted a voice.

"It's me!" called Laura. "We need to talk."

"I don't need to talk to your boyfriend," came the voice.

"He's not my boyfriend," called Laura. "I had an accident. He hit a deer and I swerved to avoid it."

Bob stayed crouched down by the hood. He wondered if this made any sense to the guy with the rifle.

"You're lying," came the voice.

"The deer's in the back of the truck," said Laura. "And his truck's banged up. Come and see, won't you?" She spoke as if to a child.

There was movement by the side of the house and a heavyset man came into view. Bob guessed he was about twenty-five. In the crook of his arm he carried a rifle, maybe a 30.06. His shoulders were hunched and he walked slowly. He kept his black hair in a ponytail and wore jeans and a jean jacket. He looked like a guy who hadn't heard any funny stories for a long time. Bob wondered what it would be like to be sunk that far into yourself.

"So who's your friend?" asked Chuckie, stopping about ten feet away. There was a glint of an earring in his right ear.

"I don't know," said Laura. "He's just a guy. His name's Bob. I never met him before."

"Why doesn't he come out where I can see him?" said Chuckie.

Bob didn't like this but he came out anyway. He stood near the front of the truck so he could jump back if Chuckie made any move with the rifle. Bob's knees felt funny and he guessed his body was scared. It didn't really bother him. He hadn't experienced anything interesting for a long time.

"You hit the deer?" asked Chuckie.

"It's right here in the truck," said Bob.

"What'd you take it for?" asked Chuckie.

"I plan to cook it," said Bob. "You got a grill?" Even Bob was surprised at his question. He hadn't known he was going to say the words until they popped out.

"A grill?" asked Chuckie.

"Sure. So we can cook the deer. I'll field-dress it and string it up on that tree. We can be eating venison steaks within the hour, hot off the beast." Bob hitched his thumbs in his back pockets and tried to look relaxed.

"Jesus Christ," said Laura, somewhere on the other side of the truck. "Now I'm stuck with *two* crazy guys."

"You mean you want to cook it here?" asked Chuckie, coming forward. He hadn't shaved in several days and his cheeks looked shadowy. He held the rifle loosely with one hand.

"Why not?" said Bob. "You got any better plans?" Other than shooting yourself? he thought. "As a matter of fact, I'm starving."

"I got an outdoor grill," said Chuckie.

"Well, there you are," said Bob. "Help me drag it out of the truck." He walked to the back of the pickup and let down the gate.

"I don't know," said Chuckie.

Bob felt engaged in a piece of theater and he saw no reason not to play it out. "You eaten already?"

Chuckie stood by the cab. "A couple of doughnuts, that's all."

"Then what's the problem?"

Chuckie glanced over at Laura, who had climbed up on the hood of the truck and was sitting Indian style. Her thick sweater made her body look like a tent. "She tell you I wanted to kill myself?"

"She said something about it. How come you want to kill yourself?"

"Everything's fucked up, that's why." Some of the anger came back into Chuckie's voice.

"So we might as well eat the deer," said Bob. "You got potatoes, any wine, maybe some beer? Something for a salad?"

Chuckie was looking down at the ground. "I guess I got some stuff."

"Let's do it!" said Laura, jumping down from the truck. "I like the sound of this."

An hour later the deer was hanging by its rear hooves from the branch of a maple near the kitchen door. Bob had skinned it and gutted it. He had turned his truck around, and the one headlight illuminated the deer's corpse. Now it hung pink and clean with the chest cavity and belly gaping open and a heap of pink intestines steaming nearby on the ground. Bob had never gutted a deer before but he had gutted fish and chickens and rabbits and he didn't think a deer could be much different, only bigger. But pulling out the intestines had almost finished him. His clothes were blood-splattered and his arms were bloody to the elbows. But it was all different. He was engaged in a series of actions outside the circle of criticism and complaint that dominated his life. He had cut the deer's heart from its chest and held it in his hand. It was warm and bloody and the body itself glistened in the cool evening air.

Chuckie had built a fire, feeding it with logs, and he brought a big grill down from the barn. He had never gutted a deer either, nor had Laura, who was digging through the kitchen for stuff to eat with the venison. There were no potatoes, but she had found macaroni, and then pesto in the freezer. She had also found four bottles of champagne left over from Chuckie's twenty-sixth birthday in March, and there was plenty of beer. Bob's bottle of

Budweiser had gotten so slippery, when he had been hauling the guts out of the deer's belly, that he could hardly hold on to it.

"You got to go out to L.A.," Bob was saying, as Chuckie put more wood on the fire. "You could have a whole new life out there. Or Portland or Santa Fe or Miami. What's the point of shooting yourself over a girl?"

"It's not just the girl," said Chuckie. "It's everything."

Their tone was slightly joking, slightly hip. They could have been talking about cars.

"Sure. You got this place, you got all your stuff, but it's not working out. So instead of selling it or leaving it, you decide to kill yourself. I bet lots of people kill themselves because they don't know what to do with their boxes of stuff. It's like not wanting to pick up. Let someone else deal with it, they say."

"How come you know so much about it?" asked Chuckie. He had taken off his jacket and wore a black T-shirt. A strip of his white belly was visible over his belt buckle.

"I don't, I'm just making talk. But right now my marriage is messed up about as much as it can be, so I'm thinking Other as well."

Chuckie poked the fire with a stick. A mass of sparks rose into the darkness. "What d'you mean?"

"Other lives, other alternatives. Something's not working so you think of Other. Kingston's not working, so you think of New York or Boston or L.A. You think of other women, other jobs, other children, other cars. And *you've* been thinking about the biggest Other of them all: death. Me, if I have to pick, I'll pick a smaller one. Why kill myself when I can go to L.A.?"

"You said you had two boys. What about them?"

"They'd prefer me in California than dead."

"What's wrong with your wife?"

"Nothing, except we had one sort of marriage and now she wants another, and I don't feel there's enough room for me in the new life. She wants to be a grade-school teacher. It's a fine profession, but I'll take L.A." Bob bumped against the deer and it swung on its ropes. His nostrils felt full of the smell of smoke and bloody meat.

"So you think she's choosing the teaching over you?"

"It's just change, that's all. Isn't that why you want to shoot yourself? To make a protest against change?"

Chuckie turned back to the fire. "I don't want to talk about it anymore."

"Things refuse to stay the same so you're going to refuse to move forward."

"I said, I don't want to talk about it."

"Or is it just Laura? You want to hurt her and make her remember you sadly all her life? There're lots of girls."

Chuckie turned back again. "Don't make me mad," he said.

"Yeah, you're the guy with the guns." Bob began slicing chunks of meat off the deer's loins and flanks and stacking them on a tray. "You know," he continued, "I first came up here after college. I bought a wreck of a house, fixed it up, and sold it for three times what I paid for it. Then I bought two houses. Soon I had five guys working for me. I did that for a few years; then I started designing houses. But sometimes I think what I really liked was going into a wreck, ripping out the plaster, and making it pretty. Take this place. It's a dump but it's got potential. So, what if we switched? I fix this place up, and you go to Kingston and move in with my wife. We just swap lives and get happy again. How does that sound?"

"Crazy," said Chuckie, but he was smiling.

"Why? You're not a bad guy. My wife would probably like you

after a while. I could visit my kids. We'd both wake up in the morning with a whole new set of expectations."

Chuckie scratched the bristles on his cheek. "And you'd get Laura?"

"She's not my type," said Bob, "but if she comes with the property, then I guess I'd have to put up with it."

"This is really crazy," said Chuckie again, but he seemed to be thinking.

Bob wiped the blood off his hand, then tilted the bottle of Budweiser up to his mouth. It seemed people spent their time trying to make their lives unchanging whereas change was the medium in which they moved. As long as one avoided death and injury, did the changes matter as much as how one responded to them? Laura had gotten interested in other men, so Chuckie wanted to shoot himself. Roxanne was spending all her time taking courses, so Bob was thinking of moving out. Both men were saying no.

"Or I could stay here with you," said Bob. "We could become gay lovers. I've never had a gay experience, have you?"

"I don't like that kind of stuff," said Chuckie, letting the stubbornness back in his voice.

"You're too serious. I'm just saying anything's better than putting a bullet in your head. You need to respond with positiveness, like if we switched lives or were lovers or became missionaries in Africa. If something's wrong with my truck, I don't junk it. I fix it."

They cooked the meat on the grill. There were about two dozen thick slices. Bob sprinkled them with salt and pepper. The meat sizzled and hissed, and little beads of blood glistened in the light of the fire. Bob threw the cooked slices back on the tray. It made a pile bigger than they could ever eat. Chuckie carried the

tray inside. Bob washed his hands in the kitchen and then followed him. Laura had set the dining room table with a white
sheet. Daffodils from the garden had been arranged in a blue
vase. The plates and dishes were also blue and Bob realized that
Chuckie had made them. There were green beans and macaroni
with pesto, bread, and butter. Bob set the tray with the meat in
the center of the table. On a desk by the front window were
Chuckie's two rifles, a shotgun, and the nine-millimeter pistol.

"Your friend Bob thinks he and I should become lovers," said
Chuckie. "Either that or I should move in with his wife."

"Why not do both?" asked Laura. She was twisting the cork on
one of the bottles of champagne. There was a loud pop and the
cork shot across the room. She hurriedly poured the champagne
into three wineglasses, which were also blue pottery.

Bob finished his beer and put the empty on the desk with the
guns. He had lost track of how many he had drunk. "This is a special occasion," he said, holding up his hands to get their attention.
"We should eat naked—just take off our clothes and eat naked."

Chuckie and Laura stared at him.

"I mean it," said Bob. "We have this great feast. We should
make it one hundred percent memorable. Stick it in our minds
forever. A couple of hours ago we were all stressed out in a hundred different ways and now we're happy."

"I'm not completely happy," said Chuckie. "There's still all
kinds of stuff I don't like."

"That's because you want everything to go on being the same.
I say we take off our clothes, eat this deer, and afterward we'll
do whatever the god of change wants to have happen. I mean,
aren't you sick of doing what you've already figured out you're
going to do?" He began unbuttoning his shirt. It didn't bother
him to get undressed in front of them. The room was warm from

the woodstove. He had entered one of life's time-out periods, and as long as he didn't hurt anybody or get hurt himself, the rest didn't count.

"I don't mind eating naked," said Laura; then she laughed. "I've never done it before, except for snacks in bed." She pulled off her heavy blue sweater. Underneath she wore a red bra. Bob had already removed his shirt, and he kicked off his boots. The venison was steaming on the platter in the center of the table. It formed the center of their circle, the hub of their wheel. The lights from the porch shone through the dining room windows, casting the shadows of the curtains on the white walls. Laura had put four candles on the table, and their flames shifted and flickered.

"This is crazy," said Chuckie, as he watched Laura and Bob get undressed.

"You keep saying that," said Bob, "but you're mixing up peculiarity with craziness. It's peculiar to eat naked, but not crazy. What's crazy is to shoot yourself. You've got to get these things in perspective." Bob began taking off his jeans, then he took off his socks and jockey shorts. In another minute both he and Laura were standing naked. She had small breasts and hips and Bob liked the look of her. He worried that he might get an erection; then he didn't care if he did or didn't. Bob nodded to Chuckie. "Care to join us? Better hurry before the meat gets cold."

Chuckie looked from Bob to Laura. Being clothed in front of them was also a form of exposure. He began pulling at his black T-shirt. "Oh, I might as well," he said. He pulled the T-shirt up over his head.

"Great," said Bob. He stepped to the table so Chuckie wouldn't feel he was watching.

"I've never done anything like this," said Laura. Her voice was at the very edge of laughter, almost a giggle.

It was a rectangular table and she sat down across from Bob. Her bare foot brushed against Bob's foot, then she moved it away. She had sharply defined shoulders and her collarbone shone in the candlelight. Her breasts were slightly uneven: her left nipple pointed to the left while the right one faced Bob directly. Chuckie took his place at the head of the table. He was chubby. His uncircumcised penis poked out of a mass of black pubic hair. As Chuckie sat down, Bob noticed an appendicitis scar. The hair on Chuckie's chest was in tight black curls. Bob began to put his paper napkin in his lap, then stopped. Using the napkin was like wearing clothes. He didn't feel cold but he was aware how the straw seat of his chair scratched his bottom.

"Let's dig in," said Bob. He waited as Laura took some venison, then took several slices for himself before offering the tray to Chuckie.

"We should say some sort of grace," said Laura.

"Are you religious?" asked Bob.

"Not particularly," said Laura, "but I like that Higher Power idea they have in A.A."

"We should say grace to the deer," said Chuckie, "to the spirit of the forest. He or she made it all possible."

They bowed their heads. "To the spirit of the forest," they said in unison. Laura laughed.

Bob raised his glass of champagne. "To the deer," he said.

Laura and Chuckie raised their glasses. "To the deer," they repeated.

"I hope the deer's spirit is watching us," said Laura, glancing toward the window.

"I hope none of my neighbors show up," said Chuckie.

"I wish I could call my wife and tell her what I'm doing," said Bob. "She'd think I'd gone right around the bend."

"Would she be mad?" asked Chuckie.

"Or jealous?" asked Laura.

Bob couldn't get over how the candlelight flickered on their nakedness, making their skin shine. Laura had turned off the kitchen light. "She'd think it was wacko," said Bob. "I don't know. I've been so mad at her that when I imagine her saying anything, it's always something I think is wrong."

"Too bad she's not here," said Laura, with her mouth half full. "We could loosen her up. What's her name?"

"Roxanne," said Bob. He wondered if she would loosen up. He wondered if he wasn't the one who should loosen up. At the moment he felt about as loose as a pail of water splashed on the floor. He raised his glass. "Another toast. To Los Angeles. To the world's great escapes."

"I don't like L.A.," said Chuckie. "The driving's fucked up."

"And what they make you pay for venison," said Laura, "is off the charts."

They laughed. The venison was moist and tender and crisp from the grill. Gradually, they grew silent as they ate. Chuckie's big stomach pressed against the edge of his plate. Bob wiped the grease from his mouth with his bare arm.

He grinned and drank some champagne. "Isn't this better than being dead?"

Chuckie grinned, then scratched the bristles on his cheek.

"You should call your wife," said Laura. "Are you really going to leave her?"

"I guess I thought that if we had a fight, the fight would make me leave her."

"That doesn't sound very brave," said Chuckie.

"Don't get heavy on me, Chuckie," said Bob. "We need to tell some jokes."

"Potter jokes," said Chuckie. "You know what they call a potter with an I.Q. of one hundred and fifty?"

"What?" asked Laura and Bob in unison.

"An art school."

Laura laughed and toasted Chuckie with champagne. Bob began opening the second bottle. The cork exploded across the room and they laughed some more.

"I could have shot the deer with a champagne cork," said Bob. He filled their glasses.

"Here's another," said Chuckie. "Did you hear about the potter who was also a terrorist? He tried to blow up a bus but he burned his lips on the exhaust pipe."

Laura laughed again; then she began to make a rasping sound in her throat. She bent forward over her plate and her hands gripped the table. It took Bob a moment to realize she couldn't breathe. Even in the candlelight he could see that her face had turned color. She looked up at him and he was startled by the fear in her eyes. Bob jumped up and his chair fell over behind him. Chuckie jumped up as well.

"She's choking!" said Chuckie. He began hitting her on the back. His hand against her bare skin made a thunking sound. His penis bumped against her shoulder. Laura kept choking and gagging. She knocked over her wineglass and the champagne splashed across her plate. Laura's hands were gathered at her throat as if she were strangling herself.

Bob shoved Chuckie out of the way and dragged Laura to her feet. Standing behind her, he put his arms around her, linking his hands under her breastbone. Her blond hair got in his mouth. Then he heaved hard. She struggled against him, still choking. He heaved again. He was afraid of breaking a rib, of giving her internal injuries. His penis was pushed against her buttocks and Bob could feel himself getting an erection. He was shocked by this. He heaved again.

"Get a knife!" he yelled at Chuckie. "I'll have to put a hole in her throat." He stepped away, struck Laura hard on the back, then again took hold of her and yanked upward. Chuckie ran back into the room holding a paring knife. Bob heaved a fifth time and the piece of venison lodged in Laura's throat broke free. She gasped for breath.

"Oh, God," she said, and sat down on the floor. Bob sat beside her and put his arm over her shoulders. She put her arms around his neck and wept. Her blond hair brushed his face.

Chuckie stood over them, a glass of champagne in one hand, the paring knife in the other. His bare belly was like half a basketball. "She could have died," he kept saying. "She could have died."

Bob took the glass from Chuckie and drank a little. Then he gave it to Laura. She drank quickly, then coughed and drank some more. Her left hand rested on Bob's thigh. Chuckie sat down on the other side of her and put his head on her shoulder. "You could be dead," he said.

Bob reached up for the bottle of champagne and refilled the glass. Chuckie drank some too. All three were drinking from the same glass. Laura continued to weep, but she was trying to laugh as well. "I thought I was over," she said.

"Are you all right?" Bob kept asking. He recalled how he had been pressed against her. The mixture of passion, desperation, and fear still made him wonder. Laura put her arms around them, gripping their shoulders. Their heads bumped together. Bob wiped Laura's nose with a napkin. She patted his shoulder.

On the wall Bob saw the shadows of the dining room curtains being blown in the breeze from the window. They jumped and leapt about. They moved as in a dance, like creatures bound by the music to which they listened. It had significance yet also seemed without significance. They seemed to follow a pattern but

Bob could understand no pattern. He couldn't stop looking at their flickering motion.

In later years, this kind of movement, this kind of shadow, would recall that evening at Chuckie's farm. Briefly Bob would feel himself sitting on the floor again with his bare skin against Laura's. He could almost feel her warmth. Bob would see the curtains twisting. He would remember how he had felt himself at the edge of some important articulation and then it had slipped by. They had gotten to their feet. They had drunk more champagne. The world had begun to reassert itself. Soon they had gotten dressed. They grinned sheepishly and spoke of how much they had drunk.

Over the next few months Bob had seen Chuckie once or twice but he hadn't seen the girl again. He didn't forget Chuckie's name; it was too boyish to forget. But in later years he couldn't remember if the girl's name had been Laura or Lauren. He would ask Roxanne, but she had forgotten as well. They had stayed married, although Bob couldn't explain why. The fissures dividing them had closed once again. His life had gotten back on track. The word Bob used to explain it was "priorities." And that too was because of the dinner at Chuckie's farm. It had helped him to be clear about his priorities, although he found it hard to say exactly what that meant.

But as the details of the evening continued to blur, what Bob remembered most clearly was how the girl's breasts had pointed in slightly different directions and how her face had turned blue. And he remembered how warm her skin had felt. "In any case," he would say, when he and Roxanne went out with some new people for dinner, "she was the one who nearly died. Not the guy who wanted to shoot himself, not Chuckie." It was a way of making sense of the strangeness of his actions and then of the surprise, the sudden change in the evening's direction, or what he had thought was its direction. Then he would recall the shadows of the curtains, like a message rendered in a language of which he had no understanding. Fluttering shadows against a lighter wall. But at last there came a time when even those shadows vanished from memory.

For Howie Michels

PART OF THE STORY

There were days when Lily Hendricks would look from the picture window of her mobile home for an hour or more, watching the clouds making round, hopeful shapes in the air. What was hopeful for Lily was anything ongoing: clouds moving west to east, birds keeping busy, progress being made. But mostly the western Michigan sky was overcast and life didn't care squat. Mostly life tried to pen you up within its chain-link fence. Lily had a little dog named Joyce that would bring her the box of Kleenex whenever Lily cried and the tears spilled onto her lap. The dog, half cocker, half beagle, would yip and wag her tail. Joyce was always upbeat. Lily had also tried teaching Joyce to fetch the bottle of Old Crow, but Joyce could only manage a pint bottle and Lily liked to buy her bourbon by the gallon.

Lily was sixty-three. She had had five children and she had given all five up for adoption. But that was long ago. In those days whenever she was with a new man and she asked herself should she or shouldn't she, the wildness always won. Maybe two of the children had had the same father, but Lily wouldn't put money on it. She hadn't played the field, she'd played the county. But that was history. Now she had Burt on Saturdays and Herbert on Wednesdays, and weeks would go by when neither of them could get it up. They were older men who liked their quiet and they did what they were told.

In the past year Lily had thought more about her five children than in the previous twenty-five. This was not a result of awakened conscience; they had tracked her down. Robbie had been first. He was forty-five and taught high school in Monroe, outside of Detroit. Lily felt proud that one of her children was a schoolteacher. He had phoned and she was a little cool until she realized that he didn't want money and he wasn't going to complain. Robbie's father was one of three possible men, all dead now. Maybe it had been that time she had done it in the hayfield, or maybe that time in the back seat of a Plymouth. She had asked Robbie, "What color's your hair?"

"Brown."

"Curly?"

"Straight."

"And your eyes?"

"Brown."

She had asked more questions. Maybe Robbie's father had been Jerry Lombardi, who died in Jackson, where he had been serving ten to fifteen for armed robbery. Somebody had stuck a knife in his back. When Lily heard the news, she thought that Jerry probably deserved it. He had always been a mean man, someone who'd cross the street just to kick a stray dog. She wanted to ask Robbie if he had a mean streak, but she didn't feel it was something she could discuss over the phone.

In that first conversation she had told Robbie about his four half-brothers and half-sisters. It was just chitchat as far as she was concerned. She would have told anybody. Now, however, she felt he had wormed the information out of her; he had asked questions and she'd been too truthful to lie. She had given him the dates of their births, more or less. She had used the same Catholic agency in Lansing with each adoption. She'd call up Sister Mary Agnes to tell her she had another little parcel on the way. Sometime later Sister Mary Agnes would give her a new name to remember in her prayers. Not that Lily did much praying, but it was more convenient to have a name to think about than Baby X.

If Robbie was the oldest at forty-five, Marjorie was the youngest at twenty-five. Five babies in twenty years. And lucky she was to have had only five. After the last, Lily had had her tubes tied.

Robbie had contacted them and one by one they called. They had hushed voices as if talking to somebody important. They didn't want anything, seemingly, except to hear her voice and let her know they were okay. But she knew that was only part of the story, and for months she had been expecting the next install-ment. "I'm waiting for the other shoe to drop," she told Burt and Herbert. "It's going to be the big one."

The next installment had come in spring, the middle of April. Robbie had called on a Sunday—one of those gray, bourbon-drinking Sundays. He said he'd been talking to his brothers and sisters, and they had decided to take a big step. They wanted to make her acquaintance. When would be a good time to visit?

"All of you?" asked Lily.

"That's right, all five. We want to meet our mom."

"Won't that be too much trouble for you?" asked Lily.

"Nope, we've been talking about it. I've met Gwen and Frank, but this would be a good time for all of us to get to know one another."

Lily wanted to ask why, but she kept silent. She didn't see why they wanted to meet her, and she didn't see why they wanted to meet each other. She wished them well; she hoped they had happy lives, but she didn't want to get to know them. They were mistakes, bloopers. The rubber had broken or the man hadn't used a rubber or she had stopped taking her pills or they had been in too much of a hurry. She had opened the door a crack, and one by one her children had snuck into the world. They were like ghosts, but they were living. She was glad they were living. She even liked it when they called. But she didn't want to meet them.

"I got a pretty tight schedule during the next few months," said Lily. The lie sounded so obvious that she felt bad about it. Twenty hours a week she worked at the Rex Diner and that was about it. Sometimes she played cards with a couple of the girls. Then on Saturdays and Wednesdays she had Burt and Herbert. She considered saying that she was off to Disneyland or Indianapolis, but the prospect of a whole string of lies exhausted her. It was not that she felt any allegiance to the truth. God knows she had cheated on too many men for the truth to be more than a stumbling block. But sometimes falsehood took more strength than she could summon up.

"What do you have to do?" asked Robbie patiently.

"Oh, it's nothing I can't get out of," said Lily. "You come whenever you want and I'll make the time. But there's no room in the trailer. You'll have to stay at the motel." Lily felt it was only right that they should stay where at least one of them had been conceived.

Robbie handled the arrangements. He was practical and efficient, which made Lily think he probably wasn't Jerry Lombardi's kid after all. Jerry was a fuckup. In the afternoons, Lily would sit staring at the clouds through her picture window and she would know that right at that very moment Robbie was pushing his plans forward. It frightened her. It was like what she had heard about soil erosion or the ice caps melting. Bit by bit it was going on even while you slept or brushed your teeth. There was nothing hopeful about such activity, nothing upbeat. The negatives were rushing to get a leg up on the positives and someday soon she would be knocked for a loop. Little Joyce would lay her furry head in Lily's lap and stare up into her eyes. Even the dog knew trouble was coming.

A week later Robbie called back. "We want to come in May," he said.

"Just don't make it on Mother's Day," said Lily. "I don't think I could stand it."

They settled on the Saturday after Mother's Day. Many phone calls were made. Robbie took care of the reservations at the motel. Lily thought of these five adults and their expectations. In her imaginings they had question marks instead of faces. Soon those question marks would be exchanged for specific features. Would they have her straight nose? Her brown eyes? She felt anxious and hopeful. She would give them pancakes for breakfast. She was afraid they wouldn't like her, that they would feel disappointment.

Most likely the weekend would have been pleasant, even slightly dull, if events hadn't conspired to make it otherwise. Lily had known something would go wrong. She had even ticked off the possible disasters on her fingertips, but she had never thought of this one. She had never thought that Burt would cash in his chips right in her own bed. Kicked the bucket, bought the farm—whatever Lily called it, the whole business took about ten seconds from beginning to end. Maybe it was a stroke, maybe a heart attack. In days to come, Lily would think of his death and want to blame Burt for the trouble he had caused, as if his death had been an act of petulance.

Burt was a retired hardware salesman, and he was soft. That was the problem. No exercise. Too many sweet things over a lifetime on the road. Jams and jellies. Thick butter. He felt hurt that he had to miss his Saturday just because Lily's children were coming to visit. He grew sullen and made remarks about how things should stay where you put them and not come back to plague you. So at last Lily said, "Then come Friday night, but you have to be gone by eight o'clock Saturday morning." Which, in a manner of speaking, he was.

And when Lily blamed Burt for dying, what she mostly blamed was his appetite, that on this particular occasion he had wanted to have sex more than once. "Burt had a greedy streak," Lily would later tell the girls over cards without bothering to explain herself. Often Burt didn't want to have sex at all and they played gin rummy instead. But because Lily's children were coming, Burt must have felt a need to assert himself. He got himself all inspired again around seven-thirty that morning, and fifteen minutes later he was dead, lying naked on the sheet with his mouth open and his teeth still on the dresser. Lily had scrambled away and watched as Burt had seemed unable to catch his breath. He had choked and gasped, and his face reddened. Then he was gone.

"For crying out loud!" Lily stared at Burt, waiting for him to do something. He lay on his back with his arms flung out. After a minute she leaned forward and gently slapped his face. "Burt, Burt." Lily was so used to him doing exactly what she said that she felt some exasperation when he failed to respond.

Once she realized he was dead, she hurried to the phone. She could call the rescue squad or she could call the police. She glanced at her watch. It was eight o'clock. At eight-thirty her five children were due to arrive to have breakfast with their mom. She stood with the receiver in her hand. She thought of her children, the accidents of their births. Late nights in parked cars. Twice in the diner on the kitchen counter after closing. And here was Burt, the last of them, or at least the most recent, sprawled naked on her bed. The rescue squad would have to come from town. Most likely they would arrive at the same time as her children. She imagined Robbie and Frank and Gwen and Merton and Marjorie standing by the door watching Burt being removed from their mom's bedroom. What she saw on their faces was disappointment. Their mom was up to her old tricks again. Sixty-three years old and still having fun. Lily hung up the phone. Burt was in no hurry. He could wait. Lily returned to the bedroom to get dressed and make herself look pretty. Then she'd get started on the pancakes.

Robbie arrived at eight-thirty on the dot and brought Gwen with him. Robbie was a tall man wearing a blue plaid sport coat, and Lily could see something of her face in his, like looking at her own face through several inches of water. Gwen, who was forty-one, didn't favor her at all: a stout black-haired woman who would look like she was crying even when she was laughing. She wore a dark green suit with some lace at the collar and glasses with thick black frames. Little Joyce barked and barked. Lily kept nudging the dog with her foot and telling her to shush. She would have shut her in the bedroom if she hadn't been afraid that Joyce would take a bite out of Burt's nose. Lily had dressed Burt, even putting on his shoes and socks. There was an easy chair in the bedroom, and she had dragged him over to it. She had stuck a *Reader's*

Digest in his lap, put in his teeth, and shut his mouth. She brushed his hair and set his reading glasses on his nose. Now he looked as if he had just happened to die in the bedroom. Maybe he had reached an exciting part of the story and popped his ticker. His death didn't look sex-related; it looked reading-related.

Gwen stood just inside the door with her arms folded, looking around the trailer. "This is really very nice," she said.

Robbie was trying to keep the dog from jumping up on his trousers. "Active little fellow," he said.

"It's a girl," said Lily, with a smile that hurt her cheeks. "Her name's Joyce. But come in. Have some coffee. It's almost ready." She had put on dark slacks and a beige turtleneck sweater. On a chain around her neck was a good luck medallion showing a rainbow in four colors and a little pot of gold.

"Do you have any decaf?" asked Robbie.

"I'll check," said Lily, who knew she didn't.

"It must be nice living in a mobile home," said Gwen. "Everything's always within reach."

Lily sat her two children down at the kitchen table. It was a red vinyl booth, just like the booths at Rex's Diner. Lily had even taken one of the diner's chrome napkin dispensers and a glass sugar shaker with a chrome screw top. "What about tea?" she asked her son. Both her children were glancing around while trying not to appear nosy. They kept making sideways looks.

"That would be fine," said Robbie. When he spoke, he leaned forward and opened his mouth more than was necessary. His teeth reminded Lily of a wolf in a story. The front ones were as big as postage stamps. They didn't look like her teeth, nor did they look like Jerry Lombardi's. She couldn't stop staring at her children. Her fascination with their faces almost frightened her.

Lily poured coffee for Gwen. Her daughter's mouth was puckered as if a drawstring had been pulled tight. She wore no makeup and her eyebrows were dark and shaggy. Lily herself plucked her eyebrows, and she liked to wear the brightest lipstick she could find. That morning she was wearing one called Passionate Appeal.

Joyce kept jumping up on Robbie's knees. "You can just whop her if you want," said Lily. "She's used to it." Then she thought of poor dead Burt and hoped he wouldn't topple onto the floor. She hadn't even had time to grieve yet. She put the kettle on the stove. "So you're from Toledo?" she asked Gwen.

"That's where my adopted parents lived," said Gwen, "and that's where I was raised."

Lily wondered if she heard a note of complaint in her voice. Gwen was an accountant. Numbers were her life, she said. It amazed Lily that all her children did things. She took down the flour and baking powder and began to prepare the pancake batter as Gwen talked about Toledo. There was more to it than met the eye, she said.

A few minutes later Lily heard the rumble of motors and glanced out the kitchen window. A Ford pickup had drawn up behind Robbie's Chevrolet, and a little green Toyota was right behind it. Two men and a woman got out. The woman would be Marjorie, her youngest. She had been riding in the Toyota with one of the men. Marjorie was pretty, with strawberry-blond hair, but nervous-looking, and she fidgeted with her hands. The two men were Frank and Merton, but Lily didn't know who was who. For a second Lily felt she lacked the strength to open the door.

Frank was the taller one; he was thirty-six. Merton was pudgy and soft; he was thirty-two. Soon all five were crowded around the kitchen table. Lily was struck by how different they were from one another. If she had shoved a pencil blindly into the phone book she couldn't have found anyone more different. They were as different from one another as she was different from a

Chinaman. Lily couldn't recall having sex with a Chinese gentleman, though she might have had she known one.

"I can't tell you how long I've hoped for this happy event," said Frank. He was a lay Baptist preacher in Marshall. He wore a dark brown suit and had elaborate sideburns that curved forward and ended in points. His face was long. It didn't seem thin so much as squished, as if something had squeezed his head at the ears. He wore black shoes and white socks.

"I've been waking up early every morning just from excitement," said Merton. He was a druggist in Flint and still unmarried. He kept fooling with red spots on his face. His hands seemed swollen and soft. He wore a baby-blue corduroy sport coat, a red plaid shirt, and no tie. His jeans were white.

"Sometimes I start to weep," said Marjorie, "and I don't know why. I've been dreaming of this moment all my life." She was a dental hygienist in Saginaw. There were tears in her eyes. She kept pushing her hands through her blond hair, which would rise up and float back down like a cloud. When she spoke, she never looked at the person she was speaking to until the very end of her sentence. She wore a light-green summer dress with a full skirt that rustled when she shifted in the booth.

The five of them had gotten acquainted over dinner the previous evening, but Lily could tell they were still strange to one another. They kept looking at each other as if seeking resemblances. Lily stirred her pancake batter; it seemed the one safe thing. Gwen poured coffee and made tea for Robbie. Then she began hunting for dishes. She was short but efficient. Like her mother, she seemed to take comfort in activity.

Later Lily decided there was never really a specific moment when she felt it wasn't going to work. Rather, she had experienced an increasing dread. Her children's collective grievances were like a sixth person in the room. Lily could almost see his face: a real troublemaker. She thought of Burt sitting in her bedroom getting stiffer and stiffer. She almost envied him.

"I can't tell you what a special occasion this is for me," said Lily. It seemed her only hope lay in falsehood. "Seeing you together is like having all my eggs in one nest." She cracked two eggs into the bowl and stirred vigorously.

Gwen gave a tight smile. Marjorie's eyes welled up. Robbie gave the dog a push. Frank lowered his head and nodded. Merton scratched his face and stared at the breadbox. Their neediness oppressed her.

"The pancakes will be ready in a jiffy," said Lily. The bacon was already sizzling on the grill. Once they started eating, they would be occupied. But what would they do after that?

Frank said grace and they bowed their heads. Her children's mouths filled with food seemed a reasonable alternative to silence. Chewing, after all, was akin to talking. They all sat crowded at the table and bumped one another with their elbows. Lily had real maple syrup. She kept sneaking furtive looks at her children and she felt them taking quick looks at her as well. It was barely nine o'clock. The day stretched ahead like an alp.

She was struck by how they chewed in similar ways: slowly and methodically. Frank ate with the tines of his fork pointed up. Robbie ate with the tines of his fork pointing down. Lily asked them about sports and Merton was talking about dart games. Marjorie said she played bingo at her church. Lily considered the passion that had sparked their lives into being and wondered where it was now. Robbie, Frank, and Gwen were all married, with children, which made Lily a grandmother. Even this surprised her. She imagined generations proceeding into the future just because Jerry Lombardi had gotten her drunk in the back seat of his old Plymouth. She found herself suddenly yearning for actions without consequences, simple routines like taking food orders or wiping off tables with a clean white rag. She remembered all those nights when some faceless man had had his way with her. She had thought of those actions as having clear beginnings, middles, and ends, but she had been mistaken. There weren't any ends. Never were, never would be. There was only a dull ongoingness, as if she had taken it into her head to walk all the way from Grand Rapids to Detroit. But even that journey would end, while this one didn't seem to. It was just one foot plopped in front of the other for the duration. She had had these children, and they had had children, and those children would have more children. Again she thought of Burt propped up with his *Reader's Digest*—the lucky devil.

Her children went on to talk about things they had recently read in the newspaper: troubles in Russia, troubles at home. Frank told about a circus elephant that had rampaged through a shopping center in Cleveland and had to be shot. Marjorie spoke of how Boy Scout leaders seemed to be getting in trouble almost everywhere. Lily felt touched by how they were trying to be conversational and civilized. They stumbled between one subject and the next while the subjects closest to their hearts remained lurking to the side. Lily wondered how long it would take them to speak their minds. If things got too far out of control, she thought, she could always walk into her bedroom and scream. Then they would find Burt and that'd be that. In the midst of Burt's death, her children wouldn't have the courage to ask their mother embarrassing questions about her life.

After breakfast when the dishes were washed and put away, they moved into the small living room. Her three sons sat in a row on the sofa. They were crowded and leaned forward with their elbows on their knees. Whenever they did anything in the same way—scratched their noses or wrinkled their foreheads—Lily wondered if it was genetic. Marjorie sat in the easy chair and Gwen sat on the arm. It seemed affectionate but they weren't touching. Lily stood in the entrance to the kitchen.

Robbie glanced around at the others and cleared his throat. "We were wondering," he said, "if you could tell us anything about our fathers?"

Even as the question was articulated, Lily had an image of their fathers. Oh, she didn't know who they were exactly but she visualized a row of men who might have been their fathers: a rogue's gallery of male longing. The dim-witted and lustful. The mean-spirited and carnal. Lily doubted there was a high school graduate in the bunch. And their accumulated jail time approached triple digits. Think of the beer and whiskey these men had consumed, the cars crashed, the women beaten or bullied, the jobs lost. In her imagination the men peered at her, leering and moronic. They had wanted her and she had been unable to say no.

"Your fathers were all grand men," said Lily at last.

"Were they all different?" asked Frank. "I mean, are any of us full brothers or sisters?"

"Five fathers for five children," said Lily. "They were all different, yet they were men you'd be proud of."

"Can you tell us their names?" asked Merton.

Lily had been afraid of this. In her bedroom stood a tall bookshelf packed with paperback romances: intimate tales to soothe her solitary hours. Now she called on them for inspiration.

"You have to ask yourself why we never married," she began. "Love was experienced and exchanged. Deep truths were shared. These were men with families, with positions in the community. In their youth they made mistakes. They had married the wrong women. As the years passed they came to realize the error of their ways. It was then we met."

"And this happened five different times?" asked Merton.

"More than that, but only on five occasions was a child conceived. In fact, three times I had miscarriages. Somewhere your little heavenly half-siblings are circling the globe. But if you could have known your fathers, then how proud you'd be."

"You mean they're dead?" asked Gwen in a whisper.

"Every single one." Lily covered her eyes with her hand. She was thinking hard. In her mind's eye she saw the dark-haired, bare-chested men on the book jackets, the women whose torn gowns were kept in place only by the magnitude of their bosoms.

"What was my father like?" asked Robbie.

"The colonel," said Lily. "He disappeared during Tet. Missing in action. He had sent me a note from Saigon saying he was going underground. Without doubt, he was one of the bravest men I've ever met. They never found his body. Could be he's still in some dank jungle cell, chained to a post."

"And my father?" asked Frank. "What about him?"

"He raced cars. He was no stranger to Indianapolis. He was at home on a thousand tracks. Your father was one of the great ones. How ironic that he should be burned to death at a small county fair in Tennessee. He swerved to avoid a child who had strayed out onto the track. His wife was a strict Catholic and dead set against divorce."

"And mine?" asked Merton.

"The priest," said Lily. "The only one who wasn't married. He looked just like Gary Cooper."

The others pressed forward with their questions.

"Your father," Lily told Gwen, "was a state senator. One of the grand old men of Michigan politics. When we were together he was over seventy, still vigorous and full of life. Had he been a younger man we'd have married. He was eighty-five when he passed away. He knew you lived in Toledo. He kept his eye on you."

"I got a scholarship to the Brothers School," said Gwen.

"That was the senator's doing," said Lily.

"And your father," Lily told Marjorie, "was a navy stunt pilot. You remember that crash over the fairgrounds in Detroit twenty years ago? No matter. He was about to tell his wife he wanted a divorce. I've carried his picture in my heart. Compared to him, other men were flotsam in the wind."

Now her children were perking up. Their faces were developing lively expressions. Lily brought out the bottle of Old Crow, and Gwen got ice and glasses. Marjorie no longer wept and Frank no longer looked dour. Robbie sat a little straighter. Even Gwen began to smile. Merton stopped picking at the red spots on his face.

"But how did you happen to be with my father, the colonel?" asked Robbie.

"It was shortly after the Miss Michigan contest," said Lily. "He had seen me on television."

"You were Miss Michigan?" asked Robbie respectfully.

"No, no. Only a runner-up. The colonel called me at my parents' farm in Okemos. We agreed to meet at the state fair. One thing led to another and we ran away together. I've always been a sucker for a uniform. Then the colonel was sent overseas. After that, life was very hard. Of course I never inherited a penny."

"You must have met the senator shortly after that," suggested Gwen, pouring her mother a little Old Crow.

"He saved me. I was sitting on the lawn outside the capital weeping and he found me. Without him, it would have been the white slavers or worse. He had a shock of pure white hair that nearly reached his collar. And a white mustache as well. Can you blame me for going with him? He had a stretch limousine with a smoked glass partition. Even the chauffeur couldn't see us."

"You did it in the limousine?" asked Gwen.

"Not only was the senator impetuous," said Lily, "he was forceful. He wanted to take my mind off my troubles. He swept me away." Lily was beginning to enjoy herself, but then she thought of Burt, how he was becoming stiffer in death than he had ever been in life.

"My father must have come next," said Frank.

"The dentist," said Lily.

"You said he raced cars," said Frank.

"Yes, a dentist who raced cars. I was hitchhiking out of Lansing and he picked me up in his Jaguar. He drove like the wind, and he fixed my teeth as well."

Her children's eagerness propelled her forward. To Merton she told the story of the priest who had given her confession and how she had become his housekeeper. The first domesticity she had ever experienced. She had cooked him sweet things, but in the end his temptation had been too great and he had thrown his clerical collar to the floor. To Marjorie she described the amorous excesses of the stunt pilot and how they had once had sex parachuting over Sleeping Bear dune. "When we hit the sand, we were still coupled," said Lily. "His organ was black and blue for weeks."

Their willingness to believe drove her to further excesses. But as she spoke she remembered how it really had been, with high school dropouts pulling her down between parked cars. She visualized how the sleeves of their jean jackets had been cut off at the shoulders and how they wore little silver chains across the instep of their motorcycle boots. They kept packs of Luckies in the rolled-up sleeves of their T-shirts. They had flat bellies and freckles, and they chewed toothpicks. Although they had seemed tough and virile, they were lousy lovers. Had they stayed around, they would have been lousy fathers, slapping their children just as they had slapped her. With them in the house, none of her children would have found a profession. Robbie wouldn't have been a teacher, Gwen wouldn't have become an accountant.

Lily had a hunger that overswept her and she had squandered it on riffraff. It was only as an older woman that she had begun to exert some control over her male companions. There had been Burt and Herbert and others. If they weren't all kind, they were at least obedient.

But hadn't Burt been kind? He got her a new TV and had her refrigerator fixed. He talked to her about her life and told her she was a good woman even when he got nothing out of it. Again and again she had kicked him out, calling him a sorry brute and a worthless dead sausage. He had been a salesman from Illinois, a childless man who had wandered into western Michigan and took a part-time job with the hardware store. "My biggest regret," he often told her, "was I never had kids." Now he was dead in the bedroom armchair with a *Reader's Digest* propped in his lap. And at that thought Lily, who had been laughing and joking with her children, burst into tears.

Her little dog Joyce was sitting beside her. When Lily began to cry, Joyce trotted out of the room. Lily didn't stop to think that Joyce was off to fetch the Kleenex and the Kleenex was in the bedroom.

"I've been a bad mother," said Lily, sobbing.

"No, no," said Marjorie.

"I have. I've been with men it was wrong to be with, and I've been irresponsible with my body."

"You were following your inner needs," said Merton.

"I've cheated and I've done what I shouldn't."

"But we're glad to be alive," said Frank. "We're grateful for that." Her five children stood in a semicircle around her. Their foreheads all wrinkled in the same way.

It was then that Joyce began her ferocious yapping. By the time Lily got her thinking in order and called to Joyce to stop, it was too late. Gwen had gone to see what the trouble was and screamed. Then she came running back to the living room. Little Joyce trotted after her with the box of Kleenex.

"There's a dead man in the bedroom!" Gwen said. "And he's reading the *Reader's Digest!*"

"How can you tell he's dead?" asked Merton.

Frank and Robbie went to look. The others stared at Lily.

She covered her eyes with her hand. Truth and falsehood stretched ahead like two roads. But truth was a dark and muddy track compared to which falsehood was all fresh macadam. "I've been a terrible liar," she said.

"But who is it?" asked Gwen.

Lily buried her face in a wad of Kleenex. "That man's your father," she said.

"You mean Gwen's father?" asked Merton.

"No," said Lily, with her face still in the Kleenex. "That's Burt. He's the father of all five of you."

There was silence. Lily looked over her wad of Kleenex and saw she was alone. From the bedroom she heard the hushed voices of her children. Little Joyce jumped on Lily's lap to have her neck scratched. Lily wondered if she could escape while her children were occupied. But where could she go? She had to see her story through to the end.

Robbie was the first to return. The others trailed after him. Their faces showed surprise, grief, and confusion. It gave them a family resemblance.

"But how?" said Robbie. "Are you sure he's our father? Who is he?"

"That's Burt," said Lily, "Burt Frost. He drove out to meet you. He lives just this side of Grand Rapids. The excitement was too much for him. All night he talked about you, talked about seeing your dear faces. He got wound up tighter and tighter. He died just before you arrived."

"He's the father of all five of us?" asked Marjorie. Her children began to sit down again.

"That's right. You're full brothers and sisters. Burt and I were lovers for forty-five years. His wife wouldn't give him a divorce. He was a salesman and she was a rich woman. She didn't want children and he yearned for them. I wanted you to think you had grand and important fathers. Burt never did a mean thing in his life. He was gentle as a kitten. When his wife died, he didn't get a penny. He moved here from Illinois to be near me."

"But why didn't you get married?" asked Merton.

"By that time it seemed too much like locking the barn door after the horse was gone," said Lily. "We were companionable, but we didn't want to tie the knot."

Lily recounted the history of her sexual escapades, and it wasn't far from the truth. She described how and where each of her children had been conceived. But instead of Jerry Lombardi or Bobo Shaw or Leftie Meatyard, she inserted Burt. She had loved only one man, and she had been faithful. Now they were still together in their twilight years, but the fire of sexual passion had cooled. They were companions over cards and the checker board. They discussed their children's careers with pride.

"But he sounds like a wonderful man," said Marjorie.

"He was," said Lily. She was struck by the eagerness of their belief. They had a mother, but they wanted a father too. And wouldn't Burt do? Lily's story was leaky, but it would float. Out-side, it began to rain.

All during their talk, one or another of her children would go into the bedroom to take a look at their new dad.

"I was going to wait till you'd gone," said Lily, "then take him back to his place. He's got a little house. It would embarrass him to be found here. If Burt had a fault, it was his love of privacy."

"I'm like that myself," said Robbie.

"You favor him in more ways than one," said Lily.

"People are going to wonder why you kept him here so long," said Frank. "You could get in trouble with the authorities."

"I figured I could take him home, then call the rescue squad," said Lily, "but I just don't feel I could do it now."

"Maybe we could take him," said Robbie. "Is it far?"

"Not far at all," said Lily.

And so it was settled. There were loose ends but Lily snipped them off. There were doubts but Lily slowly rubbed them away. She drew a map to Burt's house. She made sandwiches for every-body. They drank more whiskey. Frank said Baptist prayers over Burt and they had a little service with all six of them crowded into the bedroom. They stared at Burt fondly. Lily felt how glad Burt would have been had he known. She found herself happy.

Around dusk, they put Burt into the back of Frank's Ford pickup, chair and all. They couldn't bend him; it was best to keep him seated. The rain had stopped and there was a red glow in the sky.

"We'll buy you a new chair, Ma," said Merton.

Robbie, Gwen, and Marjorie sat in the back of the pickup to keep Burt from toppling over. Merton followed in his Toyota. They were only going about ten miles. In the dim light Burt didn't look dead. He looked fatherly and alert. His new children sat at his feet as if Burt were telling them a story. And perhaps, in a way, he *was* telling them a story, because weren't they learning the story of their lives? What did it matter that it wasn't a true story? They would commit it to memory. They would embroider it and pass it along to their children and grandchildren. It would be a bright color in a dim world. And wasn't that more useful than a sentimental allegiance to a series of events called truth?

Lily stood by the window and watched. She held little Joyce in her arms so she could watch too. Lifting the dog's right paw, Lily moved it up and down. From outside it would seem that the little dog was waving goodbye.

THE CHAUCER PROFESSOR

It was not a bar where the chairman regularly went—a bar in a motel near the campus—and that was the point. It had been a burdensome Friday, with an acrimonious tenure review followed by his cultural rhetoric class with the students inattentive and already concentrated on their weekends. Here in the bar he could sip his martini and give himself a half hour before he went home to face some small domestic crisis. He would have time to regulate his breathing.

So when the chairman saw a man he recognized, his immediate reaction was annoyance. He couldn't put a name to the face, and he dreaded those conversations when the other person knew him while his own mind drew a blank. Perhaps the man was a former graduate student; perhaps he taught in another department. He sat by the window looking out at the snow. He wasn't drinking, and his table was bare except for a book that lay open by his hand—a thin man about forty with long sandy hair in need of brushing, wearing a red-and-black plaid shirt.

The chairman asked the bartender for a dry Tanqueray martini, straight up, with two olives. Few people were in the bar, presumably because of the snow, which was supposed to fall all night, the first snow of the season. The chairman put his hand to his short beard. Who was the man at the table? He didn't think he taught at the university, but there was something special about him, as if he were connected to the university in some way. The man continued to stare at the street, where cars were moving slowly with their lights on. Occasionally there came the whine of tires spinning on ice as a car had trouble on the grade. The man's profile was to the chairman: straight nose and a square chin. He tried to identify the book but it was too far away, at least thirty feet; it was a thin book and it looked worn. Perhaps it was a critical monograph or a book of poems.

As that thought occurred to him, the chairman at last remembered. The man was a writer, someone who had read for the department about two weeks before. The chairman had only been able to attend the reception. The man's name was Boyd, but the chairman wasn't sure if that was his first or last name. And he was from Phoenix or Tucson. The cost of his travel had been equal to half his fee. Strange to see him again. Was he a poet or a fiction writer? The whole idea of contemporary literature seemed rather irrelevant, given the current critical climate. Even the most avantgarde writers were hopelessly out of date.

The chairman's thoughts returned to the difficulties of his job: quarrels among faculty, schedule conflicts impossible to resolve. His term as chair had another year to run and it was conceivable, because of the financial advantage, that he would let himself be elected again. And of course he could continue to oversee the philosophical direction of the department, urge one or two of the diehard traditionalists toward retirement, bring in another Young Turk from Yale or the West Coast.

The chairman looked up to see Boyd walking toward him. At first he thought Boyd had recognized him, but he was simply leaving the bar. The chairman was torn between speaking or pretending not to see him. But it was too late. Boyd glanced over, although still, the chairman thought, without recognition.

"Hello, Boyd, back in town again, I see." .

The other man seemed startled, then recovered himself. "Yes," he said, "yes. What a coincidence."

Instead of pausing, Boyd appeared to speed up. He gave the chairman an uneasy smile and passed into the lobby.

The chairman wondered if he had the name wrong. Perhaps it was a name like Lloyd or Floyd. He had meant to go to the reading, to show the flag, as it were, although he was just as glad when the dean had called to discuss curriculum changes. But the question of the name was annoying. The chairman prided himself on his accuracy, that and his heartiness even when he didn't feel hearty. When he finished his martini, he stopped by the front desk.

"What's the name of that tall fellow who's staying here? He has a cowboy look about him. Is it Boyd?"

The receptionist was a young woman in a blue dress. "That's right," she said. "Robert Boyd."

"Does he stay here often?"

"No, this is his first visit."

"But wasn't he here about two weeks ago?"

"That's when he arrived. He's working temporarily at the university."

"Aha," said the chairman. "That's convenient."

"Yes, he has his meals here and everything."

A buzzer sounded on the switchboard and the woman turned

to answer it. The chairman continued through the lobby, then paused. Had Boyd really been here for—what was it—fifteen days? Who was paying for it? The English department had picked up the tab for one night, but who was paying the rest? The chairman glanced around for a telephone. A sign directed him to a small alcove where a row of six phones was attached to the wall.

Boyd had been invited to read by a poet in the department, Harry Rostov. The chairman decided to call him. But even as he dialed the number, he cautioned himself. Rostov drank too much and he was a gossip. Also, because of committee assignments and obligatory freshman composition sections, there was no love lost between them.

Rostov's girlfriend answered and then went to get him. What did the chairman fear? He could hardly articulate it.

"Harry," he said, after cool greetings had been exchanged, "I've been going over the receipts and we haven't received a bill from the motel where that Boyd fellow was staying."

"You're doing that on a Friday night?"

"I'm just tidying up." It was like Rostov to deflect any conversation into anecdotal material. "Were we supposed to receive one?"

"The motel should have sent one after he left." Rostov's words were slurred as if he had already had too much to drink.

"Was he doing work for any other department?"

"Of course not. It was a one-day gig."

"And you took him to his plane?"

"A cab was coming to his motel. What's this about anyway?"

"Just curious about the receipts," said the chairman.

"Doesn't the secretary take care of that?"

"I like to stay on top of things."

The chairman returned to the front desk.

"Is the English department paying for Mr. Boyd's stay, by any chance?" He wore what he hoped was a charming smile. Even so, he felt his face getting hot.

"Why, yes, it is," said the young woman.

The chairman's mind was full of numbers as he reentered the bar. The motel was at least seventy dollars a night, then food and drinks. Boyd's bill could be two thousand or more. Where would the money come from? The chairman ordered another Tanqueray martini. The tiny creative writing budget was already committed, as was his own discretionary fund. He would have to go to the dean, a man whose preferred emotions were scorn and indignation. Then there was Boyd himself. How long did he intend to stay?

The chairman went back to the alcove to call his wife. She answered on the fifth ring. Something had come up and he'd be late. In the background he could hear his children wrangling. His wife's voice was toneless, as if he were talking to an alert answering machine. That morning they had discussed the possibility of going to a movie but that would have to be canceled. The chairman hung up and returned to the bar. It was empty except for two women leaning toward each other over a table. Outside he could see the snow swirling against the streetlights. A plow rumbled by and the yellow light on top of the cab was briefly reflected across the white landscape.

The chairman suddenly felt furious with Boyd. He hated how these writers inflated themselves and assumed a ridiculous sense of privilege. It could take weeks to sort this out. He finished his martini and returned to the front desk.

"Could you tell me what room Mr. Boyd is staying in?"

The young woman typed several keys on her keyboard. Her monitor flickered. "Room Two-fifteen. Shall I announce you?"

The chairman smiled. "I want it to be a surprise."

As he walked down the hall he found himself thinking of lawyers, police, and unpleasant scenes. It seemed impossible to hope that a scandal wouldn't result. He imagined the jokes from the other chairs. History especially was always on the lookout for what he called a good laugh.

He knocked on the door and heard a chair scrape inside the room. "Who is it?" Boyd called.

"I need to talk to you," said the chairman.

The door opened slowly. The chairman was struck by the fear in Boyd's eyes. Until that moment, he had hoped for a reasonable explanation. Seeing the fear, the chairman's own anxiety increased as well.

The chairman introduced himself. "We met briefly when you were here to read."

Boyd's fear gave his face a tightness and his eyes seemed bigger or maybe the whites of his eyes were bigger. He had taken off his plaid shirt and wore a blue T-shirt. It was hot in the room and there was a smell of men's cologne. Boyd had a small blond mustache and he kept smoothing it back with his thumb and forefinger. "I guess you better come in." He stood back to let the chairman enter. The room was neat and half a dozen books were stacked on the television. The top book was a volume of Boyd's poetry called *Loaves of Unleavened Bread*. The pretty Chardin reproduction on the cover showed a piece of flat bread on a wooden table with a silver knife beside it.

The chairman looked at Boyd expectantly as Boyd closed the door. "Sorry to bother you, but I was curious about your room."

Boyd kept smoothing back his mustache. "What do you mean?"

"I mean, who is paying for it?"

"The English department invited me."

"That was for one night. This is your sixteenth night."

Boyd assumed a boyish smile, but the fear in his eyes didn't go away. "I don't have any money."

"Surely there's the check from your reading."

"That's pretty much gone. I needed some clothes. Taxis, dinners." Boyd held up a small yellow cassette recorder. "I got myself a Walkman."

The chairman felt his teeth close together in a way his dentist had warned him against. "Isn't there your job in Arizona . . . ?"

"I'm not teaching this semester. Anyway, I'm an adjunct."

The chairman himself used adjuncts, part-time faculty who were paid as little as possible and had no benefits. He thought of them as the hoplites of the university system. "But how do you support yourself?"

"My wife's a lawyer. We live mostly on her salary."

"Can't she send you the money?"

"I'm afraid that's impossible."

Boyd said this so forcefully the chairman didn't doubt it. The two men faced each other. The chairman could see his own profile in the mirror: gray beard, short gray hair, dark overcoat. Boyd was the taller by five inches but the chairman was probably heavier.

"And how long do you plan to remain here?"

"I don't know. I don't have any plans."

"We can't pay." The chairman felt his teeth clamping together again. He lowered his voice. "The department has no money. How could you put us in this situation?"

Boyd stared at the floor. He seemed to be concentrating so intensely that the chairman began to feel hope. Then his expression changed to irony. "Believe me, you were the last thing on my mind," he said at last.

The chairman began to swear, then caught himself and took a

moment to regularize his breathing. He disliked any slippage of control. "But why didn't you go back to Arizona? Rostov said you were supposed stay only overnight."

"I was afraid I was going to kill my wife," said Boyd.

The chairman thought he had misheard. "Say that again?"

"I'm afraid I'm going to murder my wife."

"Good grief," said the chairman. He sat down on the end of the queen-sized bed, then abruptly stood up again. After all, it wasn't his room. No, he thought again, it *is* my room. That's the trouble. He was torn between asking more or just turning the matter over to the dean. He was hot and he could feel his undershirt sticking to his skin. Walk out, he told himself. Just walk out of the room. But he was unable not to ask the question. "Why did you want to kill your wife?"

"Do," said Boyd calmly. "Present tense. I still want to kill her."

"But why?"

Boyd pushed his fingers through his hair. He had a high narrow forehead with a strip of white skin at the top which the hair normally covered. "You want me to order a drink? And food? They make a good turkey club. I'd like the chance to talk."

The chairman started to say no, then reconsidered. After all, he had to find out what was going on. But again, he told himself to go home. His wife and kids were waiting. No telling what problems their day had produced. There was even time to call the sitter and get to the movie. He wiped his palms on his overcoat. "Sure," he said. "That would be nice of you." Then he asked himself, Why am I thanking him? It's the department's money. Removing his overcoat, he folded it and put it on the bed. Then he sat down beside it and waited. Boyd was talking into the phone, telling room service what he wanted. When he hung up, he leaned back against the edge of the bureau with his legs stretched in front of him. He wore black cowboy boots with gray lizard skin across the toes. They looked expensive. The chairman found himself wondering what Boyd could get for them.

"My wife moved out," said Boyd. "We have a daughter, a two-year-old. She took her as well. I called home after my reading. There was a message on the machine. 'Bob,' it said, 'you're a lousy lover and lousy husband. I've moved in with Jack. Why don't you solve a lot of problems and not come home.' " Boyd had turned so he was standing next to the mirror, making it seem as if there were two of him: two images of confusion. "She'd never had any complaints about me as a lover. I mean, she'd never said anything against me."

"Had you been quarreling?"

"Everything seemed fine. No objections as far as I could tell. I bet people are calling the house just to hear that message. My students, my friends. . . ."

"Who's Jack?"

"A partner in her firm. Jack Marshall. I knew she liked him, but I didn't think it was sexual. They often had to be together. You know, late evenings. I'd take care of Amy—feed her and put her to bed. Hang on a minute."

Boyd got up to go to the bathroom. He didn't bother to shut the door. The chairman listened to the sound of his urine splashing in the toilet. He was aware of his impatience changing to irritation. By hiring people like Boyd, universities only made themselves vulnerable to potential problems. Surely, it was the job of any good search committee to weed out the unstable types. Even Rostov had been a mistake. Boyd whistled a few notes of a song. The toilet flushed.

"But why kill her?" asked the chairman when Boyd returned. He disliked how his questions led him deeper into Boyd's story, as if each new fact heightened the suggestion of his interest and consequently his complicity. He considered his own marriage. His wife's name was Ruth. She had been a graduate student in history when they met nine years ago. They'd had two children in three years, a son and a daughter. Ruth's Ph.D. thesis on women organizers in the I.W.W. was put on hold. She even joked about it: she'd gone wobbly on the Wobblies.

"At first it was the anger," said Boyd. "The kind of anger that comes when something totally awful happens. I just wanted to strike back. Don't you ever have anything like that?"

"No," said the chairman.

"Well, I had this flash of anger. I mean, I'd no idea anything was wrong. She seemed eager to go to bed with me. Of course I'm often busy. I like to write at night when the house is asleep, and at times she resented it. And that phone message. There's no way she didn't mean it to humiliate me. I bet even the plumber heard it. Sure I was angry, but the idea of killing her didn't occur to me till I called her."

"You called her at Jack's?"

There was a knock on the door. Boyd opened it and a young black man in a white jacket wheeled a cart into the room. On it were four bottles of Beck's and a tray covered with a white cloth. Boyd signed the check and gave the waiter a five-dollar bill. The man snapped the bill together and slipped it into his shirt pocket.

The chairman thought of how Harry Rostov had come to him a year or so ago, wanting to talk about his divorce, and how he had told Harry that it really wasn't any of his business. But the questions he was now asking Boyd were not personal questions. They were not motivated by curiosity or a wish to meddle; he was representing the department. Indeed, he was representing the university itself.

Boyd pushed the cart to the table by the window and moved the tray onto the table. Taking an opener, he pried off the caps of two of the Beck's and handed one to the chairman. "Have you ever been fantastically in love?" he asked.

The chairman took the bottle, almost missing it as he abruptly looked up at Boyd. "Love?" he asked.

"I mean fantastically in love, hopelessly, passionately."

"That sounds like the poet talking."

"Come on, tell me."

The chairman poured his beer into a glass. It foamed up and he took a drink to keep it from spilling. Then he glanced at the sandwiches. The turkey was chunks of fresh turkey breast. The bread had been toasted a golden brown and was still steaming. "What does this have to do with your call that night?"

"I want to know if you'll know what I'm talking about."

"Everybody's been in love," said the chairman. He walked to the table and sat down. He felt impatient with the subject. It was the sort of thing that students talked about. The chairman was in love with his wife. He loved his kids. He had been in love with his first wife as well, at least for a time. And there had been a girl in high school he had loved—oh, nearly twenty-five years ago.

"Not everybody," said Boyd. "You read much poetry?"

"My training was in the eighteenth century. I've read lots of poetry." The chairman loosened his tie and undid the top button of his white shirt.

"Any contemporary poetry?" Boyd took a drink of beer from the bottle, holding the neck between his finger and thumb.

"It seems to me," said the chairman, "that we were talking about your fear of murdering your wife and your refusal to vacate this room: a room that is being charged to my department. We had gotten to the point where you said you had called her the night of your reading."

Boyd made a dismissive gesture with his hand. "My wife's name is Joanie. Did I say that? I met her when she was right out of law school. I had an instructorship in Tucson. This was ten years ago. We had sex all the time. She was like a meal I couldn't get enough of. I even hated to go to sleep because then she'd be out of my sight, out of my thoughts. When we slept together I wanted to tie her to me so I'd be aware of her every movement. She was seeing someone else, a guy she was actually engaged to. I rode right over him. If he'd been aggressive or to some degree uncivilized, he would have fought me. He was a lawyer too. I went over him like a steamroller over hot macadam. By the time he figured things out, Joanie and I were already sleeping together. He just wandered off. Like he was roadkill. I've even forgotten his name."

"Did you feel badly about that?"

"What was I to do? It was like I'd taken out my heart and shoved it deep inside Joanie's body. Either my heart was going to bust or this other guy's. Then there was the hunger. You never ask if it's right or wrong. You just want to feed, to fuck her in any way possible. Have you ever felt like that?"

The chairman lifted one quarter of his turkey club, pinching it between his fingers to keep it together. In its center was a large toothpick with a red cellophane frazzle. "Perhaps not to the extreme you describe," he said.

"Why not?"

"Perhaps that's my manner. My sympathies tend to be with the young lawyer."

Boyd made another sweeping gesture with his hand. "Fuck him! What does he matter? Haven't you ever had anything completely obsess you?"

"You mean you wanted to kill your wife because you had this obsession with her?"

"No," said Boyd. He moved to the table and sat down. "The obsession was gone. We liked each other, even loved each other.

71

And our sex was still good, but the hunger was gone. Either it just wore out or we wore each other out. A passion like that pushes everything else out of its path. You can't be married and have jobs and children and work and write and have something like an emotional bubonic plague."

"What happened to the man she'd been engaged to?"

"Who cares what happened to him? He disappeared."

The chairman took a bite of his sandwich and wiped the mayonnaise from his lips. The turkey was very moist. He took a drink of beer. "I don't see why you want to kill her."

Boyd held a quarter of his sandwich as well. He motioned to the chairman with it. "It was when I called her. The bitch."

"Why?" said the chairman. "What did she say?"

"She said she was in love, fantastically in love. The same obsession we'd had, she now had with this asshole. If she'd just fucked him, that I could forgive. She took our lives and threw them in the trash. What she liked was the hunger, the devouring. Even when I was talking to her they were fooling around. She'd put her hand over the mouthpiece and speak to him. I could hear her. 'Don't,' she kept saying, 'don't, I'm on the phone, don't touch me there.' Then she'd laugh. Not at me, at him. And I stood right here like an idiot and kept saying, 'You mean it's over, it's really over?' And I thought, All I want is to put a bullet in her head."

"You're being foolish," said the chairman. He felt surprised as soon as he said the word.

"Why? Because I don't like the way she betrayed me?"

"You said yourself you had no passion for each other anymore. So she and this Jack character are pushing you aside just like you pushed her fiancé aside. What did you call him? You're a roadkill just like he was."

"Nobody makes me roadkill," said Boyd. He bit into his sandwich and looked at the chairman. He had light-brown eyes, almost a rust color. They both ate for a moment. The chairman patted his lips with his white cloth napkin.

"What's your wife like?" asked Boyd.

"She's fine."

"Are you crazy about her?"

"I said she was fine."

"Is she your first wife?"

The chairman sipped his beer. "Why do you want to know?"

"Jesus, guy, I only asked if she was your first wife."

"She's my second," said the chairman. He took another quarter of his sandwich and drew out the oversized toothpick with the red cellophane frazzle. The toothpick slipped from his hand and he leaned over to pick it up from the floor.

"What happened to your first wife?" asked Boyd.

"We were divorced."

"Did you leave her or did she leave you?"

"I don't see that it's any of your business."

"Hey," said Boyd, "it's your call." He opened the last bottles of beer and gave one to the chairman. The sandwiches had come with fat deli-style pickles. The chairman bit into a pickle; the vinegar was sharp on his tongue.

"You ever read any of my poetry?" asked Boyd.

"I'm afraid not."

"How come you didn't come to my reading?"

"I had to see the dean."

"She left you, didn't she. Your first wife. She's the one who left you."

"I don't want to talk about it," said the chairman. He put the remainder of the pickle on his plate.

"Did you love her?"

"I don't want to talk about it."

"The first couple of years Joanie and I were together we still had that craziness. She was an assistant D.A. then. I'd go to her office and we'd fuck on the floor. Right in city hall. She was a screamer, she'd make a lot of noise, and the secretary would start knocking on the door, really hammering on the glass. But we wouldn't stop. We wouldn't stop till we were done."

"And now she's screaming with Jack," said the chairman.

Boyd looked at him with his rust-colored eyes. "Aha," he said, "an unkind cut."

"I'm sorry," said the chairman.

"When your first wife left you," said Boyd. "What did you do? Did you hate her?"

"People get used to things," said the chairman. The room felt hot. He removed his tweed jacket, folded it, and put it on top of his overcoat. The blinds were down, but through a crack he could see snow swirling around a light in the motel parking lot.

"You're right, you know, she *is* screaming with Jack." Boyd slapped his hand down on the table so the plates jumped. " 'Do it to me!' she screams. Then she makes this moaning noise. Can't you see why I want to put a bullet in her head? I want to stop that voice. I've heard it every night I've been in this motel."

"You're a dog in the manger," said the chairman.

"And you're a shit."

They ate in silence. The bacon broke to pieces between the chairman's teeth. He watched how Boyd ate, how he took big bites and then chewed a long time. The chairman realized that he himself took small bites and swallowed more frequently. He poured the last of his beer into his glass.

"You want me to order some more beer?" asked Boyd.

"I don't mind."

"How about dessert. They've got a good carrot cake."

"No, I shouldn't."

"Coffee or decaf?"

"Just the beer's fine."

Boyd went to the phone. The chairman pulled back the blind and looked out at the parking lot. The security light made the snow appear yellow. Nearly a foot had fallen. He would have to shovel it in the morning, but perhaps he could get his wife to do it. The chairman's first wife had been a classmate in graduate school at Cornell. They had met in a Chaucer class in the fall and were married in June. Then they moved into married student housing. Her name was Priscilla. He was just finishing his master's degree and still had three years to go for a Ph.D. He'd been teaching comp and writing his dissertation. Some nights he hadn't gotten back from the library till midnight. Priscilla became involved with one of the professors, an associate professor actually. The chairman had returned home early one night and found them having sex in his own bed. The professor had just laughed. He said he'd been giving her an independent study. Even Priscilla laughed. The chairman hadn't known what to do. The next day he moved out, leaving Priscilla with the bills. It had been the only revenge of which he had been capable.

"I don't think you'd really kill your wife," said the chairman, when Boyd got off the phone.

"Why not, professor?"

"You're an imaginative type. You've become enthusiastic about the idea of revenge and it frightens you. I understand your anger, but surely there's counseling available, people to talk to. If you kill her, you'll only go to jail."

"Sometimes jail is worth it."

"I doubt it," said the chairman. "I've taught classes in prison. It's violent and noisy, and the sex is unpleasant. You wouldn't be able to write."

"Maybe, maybe not, but I'd have a lot to write about."

"Is that why you want to kill her? To give yourself a topic for your sonnets?"

"I don't write sonnets," said Boyd. "You want me to read you one of my poems?"

"No, thanks."

"Are you one of these English professors who hates English?"

"Not necessarily."

"Then why don't you want to hear a poem?"

"The occasion seems inappropriate."

On the middle finger of his right hand Boyd wore a silver ring with the head of a bull. Its eyes were tiny red stones. Boyd kept turning it around his finger. "You've got a funny idea of what's appropriate," he said.

This time it was the chairman who had to use the bathroom. He shut and locked the door, then peed into the bowl just above the water line so as not to make a splashing noise. He told himself that he couldn't let himself be bothered by Boyd's questions. After all, he had to make Boyd vacate the motel room. That goal rendered his personal feelings irrelevant. The chairman turned on the cold water, then quickly looked through Boyd's travel kit. At least there weren't any pills. He washed his hands, dried them thoroughly, and returned to the bedroom.

A few minutes later came a knock at the door. The young black man entered with a cart. The chairman saw four bottles of Beck's, two brandies, and two pieces of carrot cake. He thought, The department is paying for this. The waiter collected the empty bottles and dishes and Boyd gave him another five-dollar bill. Snapping the bill between his fingers, the waiter put it in his shirt pocket. Boyd opened two bottles of beer.

"I got you carrot cake anyway," he said. He put a plate in front of the chairman. The carrot cake had white frosting and in the center was a tiny carrot of orange frosting. The chairman poured beer into his glass. Boyd put a brandy snifter next to the plate of carrot cake.

"When your first wife left you," said Boyd conversationally, "you didn't want to kill her?" Boyd sat back down across from the chairman. He rested his left arm on the back of his chair and dangled his beer bottle between his thumb and forefinger, letting the bottle swing back and forth like a pendulum.

"I was finishing my dissertation. There was no point in killing her."

"What was your topic?"

"Alexander Pope."

"Coolly classical, is that how you see yourself? Your first wife runs off with some guy and you just shrug and say 'So what'?"

"I didn't say 'So what.' "

"Did your guts hurt?"

The chairman picked up his glass. "My guts hurt."

"But you didn't say anything?"

"I moved out. I took my books and clothes and was gone the next day. She even got the cat."

"Why the hurry?"

"I caught her having sex with someone."

"Someone you knew?"

"The Chaucer professor."

Boyd leaned back and laughed a great guffawing laugh.

"I don't see what's so funny about it," said the chairman. He set down his glass without looking and nearly missed the table.

Boyd was still chuckling and smoothing his mustache, as if his laughter had ruffled it. "It's just the Chaucer. D. H. Lawrence wouldn't be so bad. Did she seem to like it?"

"I didn't stay long enough to find out."

"Oh, come on."

"It's true. I left right away." Actually, he had watched from the doorway. The Chaucer professor was a somewhat portly man. He had pulled up Priscilla's skirt, a long peasant skirt with rings of brightly colored cloth. He had his hands pressed against Priscilla's buttocks, making white marks on her flesh. At first the chairman had thought that Priscilla was trying to shake him off, then he realized that she was shoving herself into him. She kept saying "Oh, oh," in a high, almost childlike voice.

The chairman puffed out his lips, then picked up the fork and took a small piece of carrot cake without frosting. It was moist and still warm, as if just baked. He took a larger bite. He looked at Boyd and wished he could do something to hurt him.

"So you were pretty young when that happened?" asked Boyd.

"I was twenty-eight, so it was sixteen years ago."

"Is your ex-wife still with the Chaucer professor?"

"I have no idea. I lost track of her after the divorce."

"Do you still hate her?"

"I have no feelings one way or the other." The last he heard, Priscilla was teaching at a community college in West Virginia, some dreary place. He felt it served her right. Actually, he had hardly thought of her for years. Is that really true? the chairman asked himself. Surely sometimes he dreamt of her. He felt he had to turn the subject back to Boyd and the motel room.

"Don't you have friends in Phoenix?" asked the chairman.

"Some. More in Tucson."

"Can't they help you?"

"They're people we knew together. I can't contact them without them all knowing, and either feeling sorry for me or not sorry for me."

"I felt more or less the same way," said the chairman. He had spent one last year at Cornell, and for the entire year he had been certain that everyone was laughing at him. And probably they were. It had been an amusing story.

Boyd leaned forward over the table, holding the edge with both hands. "Didn't it make you angry?"

"There's no advantage in anger."

"Hey, you got to take a stand. Somebody hurts you, you have to hurt them back."

"You've been in the West too long," said the chairman. "There's your daughter. She must miss you."

"Jesus, she may not even be mine," said Boyd. He raised the beer bottle to his mouth, then saw it was empty. He drank some brandy instead.

"Of course she's yours."

"You have kids?"

"Two."

"And you're sure they're yours?"

"Of course I'm sure, what a foolish question."

"If you're so sure, then why get angry?"

"I'm not angry."

"Were you crazy for your second wife as much as the first?"

"I was older," said the chairman. He realized he had had a lot to drink. Two martinis, three bottles of beer, and half a brandy. He rarely had two drinks in a single evening and most nights he had nothing. He watched Boyd open the last two bottles of Beck's. The room seemed even hotter.

Boyd leaned back in his chair. "Do you punish your present wife for what your first wife did?"

"What do you mean?" The chairman had been pouring the beer into his glass.

"You caught your first wife fucking the Chaucer professor. You ran away with your tail between your legs and never saw her again. After a while, you met someone else, got married, had a family. Don't tell me you don't imagine catching your present wife with someone. What's her name?"

"Ruth."

"Sure, Ruth. Don't tell me you haven't come home and imagined catching Ruth with the Milton professor or the Dickens professor or the Derrida professor."

"That's ridiculous."

"Why? You've already got the picture in your head. All you need to do is transfer the faces. I bet every time she takes too long to get to the phone you start wondering."

"She has all the freedom she wants."

"Was she a student?"

"History. She's still completing her thesis."

"Why hasn't she finished it?"

"Well, you know, the family . . ." The chairman took a drink of beer, then wiped his mouth on the back of his hand. He disliked how uncertain he sounded.

"She hasn't finished it because you keep her on a short leash. You've seen what women are capable of. The hungers and betrayals. The weaker sex, right? I bet you've turned her into a depressed little mouse."

"Dammit, Boyd!"

"Aha, so you do get angry."

The chairman tried to lower his voice. "You're being purposefully objectionable."

"I'm just trying to get the picture. I bet you're the tyrant of your household: one of those guys with a schedule up on the refrigerator, the whole day broken into ten-minute segments. They're probably glad you haven't come home."

"That's ridiculous!"

"Who knows what pleasures they engage in when you're gone."

"What're you saying?"

"When the cat's away . . ."

The chairman stood up, pushing back his chair and knocking over a bottle of beer so the foam poured out.

"Do you know what Ruth's doing right at this minute?" asked Boyd. "I mean, do you really know? Jesus, can you blame her?"

"You've a filthy tongue!"

"Not only do you get angry, but I bet you could kill someone. You remember your first wife moaning and groaning under the Chaucer professor and you crack the whip at Ruth and the kids. You're their fucking chastity belt."

"Stop it."

"Is Ruth a screamer or do you make her stop?"

"Shut up!"

"What about sexy underwear and handcuffs? Do you make her talk dirty? Do you make her your slave?" Boyd was getting to his feet and the chairman pushed him, shoving his hands against Boyd's chest. Boyd fell back against his chair, tumbling across it so his feet kicked the bottom of the table, making the plates jump. His shoulders struck the floor hard and his head hit the corner of the heating unit. He rolled over on his side and lay without moving.

"Jesus," said the chairman. "Jesus Christ." He scrambled around the chair and bent down beside Boyd. He had to clench his hands together to make them stop shaking. Boyd lay with his eyes half open but not looking at anything. He didn't appear to be breathing. The chairman began to touch him but was afraid to. A trickle of saliva dribbled out of the corner of Boyd's mouth and down his neck. "Boyd!" he said, then he stood up. "Jesus Christ, what have I done?" Boyd's brandy was still on the table. The other glass had spilled into the chairman's carrot cake. The chairman lifted Boyd's glass and drank it off. I've killed him, he told himself.

He thought of the dean and others at the university—all their talk and eagerness to pass judgment. And his own explanations? What would they be?

He would have to call the police. He couldn't pretend this hadn't happened. The black waiter had seen him in the room. But as he began to move toward the telephone, the chairman paused. Perhaps it didn't have to be like that. Couldn't it appear that Boyd had fallen on his own? If the chairman just left, then who knew when Boyd would be found? Certainly not until the cleaning women showed up in the morning. Then, if the police didn't come to him, he could go to the police, after the death had been made public, and say he had been the man in Boyd's room but that Boyd had been fine when he had departed. Why shouldn't he be believed? After all, the chairman held a respected position in the community.

The chairman turned back to Boyd. He was sitting up cross-legged and his face was bright with suppressed laughter. The chairman was so astonished he stepped back and stumbled against the TV.

Boyd guffawed. "If you could only see your face. You look like someone out of a monster movie." And again he began laughing, a loud hooting noise.

The chairman took a step toward him and Boyd scrambled to his feet.

"Be careful. You don't want to do it. Remember? It was bad enough just thinking you'd done it. 'Jesus!' you kept saying. Your fucking face! I wish I'd had a camera."

"You bastard."

"Hey, Professor, I've shown you that you could kill someone. Isn't that worth knowing? You should pay me. You should pay me what this room's going to cost for two weeks. You want another beer? Maybe a nightcap?"

"I'm glad your wife left you. I'm glad your guts hurt."

"Tut, tut, Professor, who says it's true. Remember? I'm an imaginative type. I might have made up the whole thing. Maybe I've just been hiding out working on my sonnets."

The chairman grabbed his coat and overcoat from the bed. Had Boyd been lying about his wife? Had he really believed him? But sure, he believed him. He had believed everything. He yanked open the door.

"I want you out of here by tomorrow," said the chairman.

Boyd stood by the mirror, studying a bruise on his chin. He didn't look at the chairman or appear to be listening. After a moment, he picked up a brush and began brushing his long sandy hair.

The chairman forced himself to turn away. He needed to get a grip on himself. As he walked down the hall, he heard Boyd laugh; then he heard the door close with a click.

The chairman passed through the lobby. The clock over the front desk said ten-thirty. Through the windows he saw it was still snowing. He noticed the alcove with the phones. Perhaps he should call his wife. His wife. He tried to summon up her face but all he could see was her yellow hair. For a moment he didn't even remember the color of her eyes. Boyd had been right. He liked how his wife wouldn't act without consulting him. He liked how his children always knocked at the door of any room he was in. He stood by a phone and leaned his head against it, feeling the cold metal against his forehead. He reached in his pocket for a quarter.

But when he picked up the telephone it wasn't his own number he dialed. He found himself dialing the dean's home number. He listened to the ring. Seven times, eight times. Then the dean picked it up. His voice sounded thick with sleep.

The chairman identified himself. "I'm sorry to bother you so late, Jessup, but we've got a problem with a visiting poet."

The chairman gripped the phone as the dean stormed at him. Didn't he know how late it was? What kind of business couldn't wait till Monday morning? At other times the chairman might have been offended. Tonight he felt reassured. Something that had gone off the tracks was being set back on course. His life and the business of the university were inextricably entwined. And as the chairman listened to the dean's anger, he felt that both were beginning to go right again. He would have another drink at the bar just to settle himself, and call his wife later. There was no hurry.

THE CEDAR BUNGALOW

Luigi Travelli had been in his grave three days when Chuck received the package from Luigi's wife. It was more than a package, it was a large box. If it had come one day later, Chuck wouldn't have been there to get it. He and June were splitting up and she was getting the house.

Chuck hadn't gone to Luigi's funeral. They lived in cities nearly three thousand miles apart. Chuck and Luigi had been best friends back in the seventies when they both lived in Bellingham. Then Chuck had moved to Albany because of a job offer. It had been more than fifteen years since he had laid eyes on Luigi, although they talked on the phone and sent cards at Christmas.

They had last talked just a day before Luigi's death. Luigi had colon cancer and knew it was coming. "The Big C," he said, making a song out of it, "is coming to get me." It was bad luck, he said, no more than that. "Fuckin' cancer just grabbed me out of the air," he said.

Chuck was ten years younger and they had both worked construction in Bellingham. To Chuck's mind, Luigi was a guy who never let the world knock him flat. Nothing could make a dent in how he saw himself. Self-image or self-awareness—Chuck wasn't sure what to call it but he was certain it was a feature he didn't possess himself. "He was *consistent*," Chuck would tell June when they were still talking. For Chuck, consistency was a mystical quality like inner peace or karmic transcendence. He himself was like cloud or shifting colors, uncertain who he was from one day to the next. "Flaky," June would tell Frankie, her new lover.

The five years that Chuck and Luigi worked together Chuck saw as his education. "Like he was my university," he told June. "He was the B.A. I never got." He still kicked himself when he thought how he left Bellingham to be a crane operator in Albany. Why had he left his best friend? Think of the talks he'd missed! Chuck would strike his forehead with the flat of his hand. Then he would ask himself, But isn't that my problem? Never being sure of the value of anything? Never knowing if he wanted something or didn't want it? Maybe that was what happened to his marriage. Chuck would be off scratching his head in a bar or an all-night diner, wondering about his place under the stars, while June focused her sights on Frankie. June herself had a precise sense of value. She knew what she wanted and what she didn't, and after a while Chuck had been transferred to the negative column.

It was Chuck's special gift—despite his uncertainty—to link up with people who knew what should be done and how to do it. "The work's better in Albany," June had told him. "You'll never be a full-fledged crane operator if you stay in Bellingham. Albany's the state capital. They're building all the time."

So they had packed up their house. They packed up their two kids, Molly and Pete. They packed up their dog, Hank, and their cat, Bouncy, and even the three goldfish. They jammed everything into a big U-Haul and drove east.

"I'll miss the good times," Chuck had told Luigi.

Luigi had tapped Chuck on the beefy part of his arm with his fist. He had been a solidly built short man, going bald, despite his black hair, so that his pink scalp took the shape of a horseshoe. "You'll visit," said Luigi. "There'll be more good times. Maybe I'll come east. I want to see Niagara Falls."

But they hadn't visited. They had never seen each other again. They had only talked on the phone.

"You wouldn't recognize me anymore," Luigi had told him about four weeks before his death. "I lost all this weight."

Chuck had shuddered. He hated how death just reached down and plucked people off the face of the earth, like a hand plucking grapes from a bowl.

"You'll gain it back," Chuck had said.

"No, this is the end of the ride." Luigi had laughed. "I got the figure of a tap dancer. What's the guy's name? Fred Astaire."

During the weeks that June kept telling Chuck their marriage was over, Chuck thought of Luigi dying in Bellingham. He wanted to visit him, but he was afraid of what he looked like: a scarecrow gone bald from the chemo. And he felt if he stayed with June and told her ten times a day that he wanted to put the magic back in their marriage, maybe he could convince her.

"I want to be with you," he kept telling her. "We'll make everything electric again. I love you."

June would sit on the other side of the yellow kitchen table swirling the coffee in her cup so roughly that it sloshed over the side. "Don't you understand that I don't care if you love me anymore? I love someone else."

June did aerobics and her body was hard. Chuck felt the hardness was part of the trouble, that it had driven the kindness right out of her. He thought if her body was softer, she would still love him.

"I'll do everything right from now on," Chuck promised. "I won't mess up."

"I don't care what you do," said June. "I don't care if you do it right, I don't care if you do it wrong. We're history. Why can't you accept that? Get with the program, Chuck."

Frankie was a weight-training instructor at June's health club. Already he was moving his stuff into Chuck's house. He was a forty-year-old body builder who wore baggy shirts and baggy pants. Carrying a box into the house, he would pass Chuck in the hall. Frankie smiled affably. "What goes around, comes around," he would say. Then he made a clucking sound with his tongue, the kind of sound you make when you want a horse to move faster.

Chuck didn't tell Luigi his marriage had fallen apart. He figured that with cancer and impending death Luigi had a pretty full plate. "I can't keep food down anymore," Luigi told him. "They got so many tubes into me I look like a machine."

"Are you in pain?" asked Chuck. He often worried about pain. Both physical and emotional. Maybe even spiritual pain. There seemed a lot of it: balloon-shaped clouds of pain drifting through the skies searching for somebody vulnerable to snag on to.

"Nah, they don't have pain these days. They just give you a little shot and you dream the hours away."

Maybe I need a little shot, Chuck would think. His emotional pain was like a pulled muscle in his chest. His spiritual pain was like a flickering TV set after the station has gone off the air. Chuck would look from the window and his mind would drift away. He would think of new scenarios, escapes that show up in the nick of time.

Chuck loved his job with the crane. He loved picking up heavy things and moving them to the top of a building. He would look down from his great height, and the world seemed manageable. He'd pick up a load of lumber like picking up matchsticks. The only trouble was you had to be alert. You had listen to the directions that came over the radio. Chuck would sit in his cab and stare toward the horizon where the clouds were building and dispersing across the sky. He would think of being with June on a beach or camping in the Adirondacks. He would think of ways to put the magic back in their marriage or awful things that might happen to Frankie. Shortly he would grow aware of his name being squawked out of the radio's little speaker.

His boss, Ernie Petrocelli, liked him all right but couldn't cut him a lot of slack. "We got a schedule," Ernie would say. "You could get somebody killed. Maybe you should take a leave."

"No, no, I'll be okay. My mind wandered, that's all."

But it scared Chuck. It was as if his life was coming apart like a tissue in a tub of water.

His kids were grown up and his daughter was married. "Life has different stages," Molly said one evening when she stopped by to visit. "This is just the end of one of the stages."

"I don't want it to end," Chuck answered.

Molly was pregnant. Her whole mind was focused on her belly. She couldn't imagine an imperfect system. She lifted her hands toward her father, then dropped them in her lap. "Life moves on," she said.

And his son Pete said, "Maybe you should beat the guy up." Pete sold men's clothing at Sears and worried that it kept him from having a masculine image.

"He's a weight lifter."

"You could come at him from behind, really nail him."

"Violence doesn't solve anything."

"But it would feel good," said Pete. "Look at Steven Seagal. He's always got a big smile. You need to power-thrust the guy, time-warp him out of existence."

One evening when Frankie's red Ford Probe was parked in his driveway, Chuck took his house key and made a two-foot scratch on the driver's door. He was so startled by what he had done that he tried to rub it away, which made the scratch even more noticeable.

The next day June asked him, "Did you put that scratch on Frankie's door? You're really losing it. I'd hate to get the cops to put you out of here."

"Do you remember our honeymoon in Seattle?" asked Chuck.

"Water over the dam," said June. "I want to get moving."

His last conversation with Luigi took place on a Sunday night. Luigi's voice was very faint, just a whisper over the wires. Chuck thought of all the distance it had to cover, all the night sky and cold prairie. It was early November, and each morning there was frost on the grass.

"I'm sending you something," said Luigi.

"I don't want you to die," said Chuck.

"Pay attention," said Luigi. "This thing I'm sending you, I put a lot of time into it. Don't just junk it, okay? Like I'm trusting you with it."

"What is it?"

"I can't talk anymore. I'm feeling sick."

"Is it the pain?"

"It's the whole shebang. The whole kit and caboodle."

The line went dead.

Chuck had held on to the phone, as if by cutting the link between them he was putting Luigi into his grave. He kept speaking into the mouthpiece. "Hello? Hello? Luigi?" There were long-distance noises: water rushing, the twinkling of stars, maybe an animal howling on the dark plains of Wyoming. Then the phone began to beep.

"What are you doing?" asked June, coming into the kitchen.

"I'm talking to Luigi."

June listened to the beeping. "He's gone," she said.

The next day Luigi's wife called to say that Luigi had died. "It's a relief from all that pain," she said.

Chuck realized he had been expecting a miracle. "I can't believe it," he told Luigi's wife.

"He was very sick," she said. "You knew that, didn't you? The cancer was in his body like vanilla bean specks in vanilla ice cream. It was everyplace. I'll mail the package after the funeral."

Chuck hadn't even asked about the package. He hung up and went to the refrigerator for a Budweiser. He stared into the refrigerator and thought how cold it was and how cold death must be. There were tears in his eyes. June came into the kitchen.

"Luigi's dead," Chuck told her.

"You knew it was coming, right?"

"It knocks the wind out of my sails."

"My lawyer says you've got one week to get out of here. Then he's serving papers. Come on, Chuck, life doesn't stand still. By the way," she added, "that's Frankie's beer."

Chuck packed but his heart wasn't in it. He went to bars in the evening. He was late to work. Instead of looking for a place to live, he thought about Luigi's death. He felt comfortable thinking about the death because it kept him from thinking about June and Frankie. The death was like an ugly oasis in a desert of ugly thoughts. He was sure it would be better to die of cancer than to have a hammer fall on him from the top of a construction site. Lots of people died of cancer. To die of cancer was like belonging to a group.

When the package arrived from Luigi's wife, Chuck had

forgotten all about it. He had been wandering through his house looking at the stuff he and June had bought over the years. It all had memories attached. They had had sex on the couch; they had fought on the rug. He collected up some baby pictures, a chair, some of his clothes, the other television, some odds and ends belonging to his parents, three silver spoons, his father's favorite screwdriver. He put them in a pile in the living room. It didn't amount to much. He was still looking around for something else when the UPS man rang the doorbell.

The package looked heavy but it was more bulky than heavy. It was a cardboard box measuring three feet by three feet. "Looks like you got a present," said the UPS man.

It was only when Chuck saw the return address that he realized this was the package that Luigi had talked about, the thing he was trusting him with. Chuck got a knife from the kitchen and began to cut away the tape. Inside the box were thousands of S-shaped bits of Styrofoam. He tried to put the Styrofoam in a garbage bag, but soon it was all over the floor.

When he unpacked the box, Chuck saw that Luigi's gift was a miniature bungalow covered with tiny cedar shakes: a house a little over two feet long, two feet deep, and two feet high with working windows and doors. It wasn't a dollhouse, it was a serious house. Chuck knew what it was because he'd been hearing Luigi talk about it for ten years over the phone. It was a model of Luigi's house in Bellingham, a house that Chuck had visited, where he had eaten dinner and where he and Luigi had sat on the screened-in back porch drinking old-fashioneds. And, look, here was the porch with real screens and tiny rocking chairs. There was the stone chimney with a scroll metal *T* for Travelli. Through each of the windows Chuck could see furniture. There was even a tiny doorbell. Chuck pressed it gently with the nail of his little finger and jumped when he heard a faraway *ding-dong*.

Not that the bungalow was perfect. Some of the windows were crooked. The shingles on the roof were uneven and in places the cedar shakes made wavy patterns. Still, it was pretty good. Better than Chuck could have done. And clearly it had taken a long time to build. Upstairs it had three bedrooms. Downstairs was the living room, dining room, kitchen, and den. Each room held a memory for Chuck: jokes and conversations and shared meals. Luigi's wife had made a great stuffed manicotti, and some kind of eggplant dish as well. Besides the screened-in porch off the back, there was a front porch that ran the width of the house. Some of the tiny furniture had been bought from places that sold dollhouse supplies; some had been carved or sewn from bits of cloth. The fireplace was made from real stone, little pebbles cemented together. The braided rug was actually braided. There were gutters at the edge of the roof, even drain spouts. No, it wasn't perfect but it was passionate and determined. More than that, it was Luigi Travelli's house, the house where Chuck Malone had been a welcome guest. Crouched over it, Chuck tried to explore every corner. There was no basement but underneath was a false bottom and a panel that revealed wiring and four batteries. As Chuck peered through the tiny windows, his eyes kept welling up with tears, and other than this cedar bungalow he felt there was not much else in this world that he liked.

June found him lying on his belly staring into one of the little bedroom windows while all around him on the carpet were S-shaped bits of Styrofoam. She looked at him as if this scene summed up everything she had come to dislike about her husband and she meant to fix it in her memory.

"You're going to have to clean this up," she said at last.

"Look what Luigi sent me," said Chuck. If she felt as strongly about the bungalow as he did, then perhaps they could fix things. For a moment, he felt hopeful.

"A dollhouse," said June.

"No, it's a replica of Luigi's house in Bellingham. Remember? It's even got a doorbell."

"It's still a dollhouse," said June. She wore slacks and a dark sweater and stood with her arms folded. Standing above him, she looked ten feet tall.

"Come and see," said Chuck.

"I don't have time. I got to make Frankie a sandwich. You better take your dollhouse with you tomorrow. Otherwise it winds up in the fireplace."

The next day Chuck had a room in the Econolodge right downtown. Two suitcases of clothes were in the closet, two boxes of odds and ends stood by the door, and on a table by the picture window rested the cedar bungalow. Chuck had gotten a special rate by renting the room by the week. Yet that very arrangement seemed final proof that he and June were finished. Already Frankie was lying in Chuck's bed. Frankie was using Chuck's blue coffee mug and sitting in his place at the kitchen table. Frankie was watching Chuck's favorite TV shows and laughing at the same jokes that Chuck and June once laughed about.

The desk clerk at the Econolodge had helped Chuck carry the boxes to his room. His name was Bob and he stopped to look at the cedar bungalow. Bob was a thin middle-aged man with threads of white hair, and his hands shook.

"Most dollhouses are made in Japan," he said. "You can tell this isn't a Jap dollhouse because it has flaws."

"This isn't a dollhouse," said Chuck. "My buddy made it. It's a copy of his house in Bellingham. He's gone now. Cancer. We'd sit on that back porch and laugh. I got a hundred stories."

"Cancer," said the desk clerk. "I done my time with cancer. There's a shop on Clark Street that sells dollhouse stuff. I mean, if you want to add some little people."

"I don't want little people," said Chuck.

That evening Chuck put the cedar bungalow into the back of his Dodge and drove to the Myrtle Lounge eight blocks up Western Avenue where he did his drinking. By his own estimate he wasn't much of a drinker, but he saw himself as going through a rough period and felt he needed liquid encouragement. Besides, he wanted to show the cedar bungalow to some guys he knew. He didn't want to spend the evening in the Econolodge waiting for the phone to ring.

Chuck carried the bungalow from the parking lot to the front door of the lounge. Then he had to maneuver the door open with his foot. The bungalow wasn't heavy but Chuck didn't want to bump it against anything. Maybe eight men were drinking and watching TV. Chuck carried the bungalow across the red tile floor and set it on the bar. "Give me a Budweiser," he told Louie the bartender. "I got a thirst."

"Where'd you get the dollhouse?" said Louie. He was a chunky gray-faced man with short gray hair who had paid his drinking dues years before. Now he drank nothing but Sanka, so his breath had a sour coffee smell.

"It's not a dollhouse," said Chuck. "My best buddy sent it from Bellingham. He's dead now. Cancer got him just last week. This is a living replica of the house he lived in."

"I been in Bellingham," said Louie. "I drove out to Mount Baker National Forest and saw a bear. You ever seen a bear? I mean a real one, not one of those bears in zoos."

Chuck said he didn't think he had.

"They're a whole different kind of bear," said Louie. "More alert somehow. Say, Chuck, you'll have to move that dollhouse outa the way if we get crowded later on. It blocks the TV."

Reg Schultz came in around nine-thirty. Reg and Chuck had known each other five years and worked construction together.

Reg had a tattoo of a hula dancer with a grass skirt on his left bicep that he could make dance. His face always looked tanned, but it was from high blood pressure rather than the sun. He was a welder and had scars on his hands. Maybe he was forty. Chuck showed him the bungalow. By then he had had four beers.

"You could put gerbils in it," said Reg. He wore a white cowboy shirt with red stitching on the pockets.

"I don't want to put gerbils in it," said Chuck. "It's my friend's house, an exact replica. Luigi, maybe you heard me mention him. He's been in his grave only four days. See these little windows? They go up and down."

"I got a problem with the windows in my place," said Reg, getting a Miller's. "Fuckin' wood's rotten. What I couldn't tell you about carpenter ants would fit in a thimble."

There was a basketball game on the TV, the Knicks and somebody else. Several men were putting down bets. Chuck found that by bending over and peering through the front windows of the bungalow and out the back, he could see a tiny piece of his own face reflected in the bar mirror. It was like being actually inside the bungalow. He bought Reg a beer and then Reg bought him one.

By the time Tony Sanchez showed up at ten-thirty, Chuck had had six beers. Sanchez was an electrician. He was a dark-haired guy with a belly. In the lapel of his jean jacket he wore a red carnation. "Where'd you get that funny little house?" he asked.

"My friend Luigi sent it to me. He's dead now."

"His buddy died of cancer," said Reg. "It's all he can talk about. For Christ's sake, he hasn't seen him for fifteen years."

"I had an aunt that died of cancer," said Tony. He sucked his teeth and looked philosophical. "I guess we all got our special way to die."

"Look at this," said Chuck. "The doorbell works." He pushed the button, but there was too much noise for the bell to be heard.

"I got a friend that makes cathedrals outa toothpicks," said Tony. "He says it keeps him from drinking too much."

"You feel like getting a pizza down at the bowling alley after a while?" asked Reg. "I'm developing a hunger. You hear my stomach growling?"

"Did I tell you my wife kicked me out?" asked Chuck. "She's got a weight lifter."

"When me and my old lady split up," said Reg, "I never looked back. Say, Tony, where'd you get that red carnation?"

"A girl at the mall was giving them out with cracker samples," said Tony. "I already ate the crackers."

"You know, that's what Louie should have in this place," said Reg. "Crackers and cheese. I hate a place that calls itself a lounge but don't have food."

"The weight lifter put all his weights in the basement," said Chuck.

"That's the best place for them," said Tony. "Otherwise they fuck up the floor."

"I still think June'll give me a call," said Chuck, bending over to look into an upstairs bedroom of the cedar bungalow. "I mean, what's a weight lifter after twenty years of marriage?"

Chuck's friends had nothing to say to that.

By one-thirty Chuck was ready to go home. Reg and Tony had left to get a pizza. Chuck was swaying a little at the bar. "Time to hit the road," he told Louie. The basketball game was over and the bar was clearing out. Chuck didn't know who'd won.

"You driving?" asked Louie.

"I'm parked in the lot." Chuck began pulling on his jacket.

"Let's see your keys."

"Sure, how come?" asked Chuck, handing over his keys.

Louie put the keys in his pocket. "You're loaded, pal. I'll get these back to you tomorrow. You want me to call a cab?"

"Come on, Louie, give me my keys."

"The cops would put my ass in a sling if they pulled you over. I'll stick 'em in your mailbox when I go home. I go right by your place. You want a cab or not?"

Chuck pushed his hand across his forehead. Was he drunk? Maybe a little woozy. On the other hand, maybe the night air would clear his head. "Just hold the door, will you? I don't want to bang up my bungalow."

Out on the sidewalk Chuck heard the door to the lounge shut and lock behind him. He had already gone half a block when he realized that he didn't live in his own house anymore. He was at the Econolodge. Louie would be dropping off his keys at the wrong place. He started to go back, then stopped. He could get the keys tomorrow. He was tired of telling people he lived in the Econolodge. He was tired of talking about Frankie the weight lifter. He was tired of hearing jokes about the cedar bungalow. He glanced around for a cab but the streets were empty. The night was cool but not freezing. He even saw a couple of stars. Chuck got a better grip on the cedar bungalow and decided to walk. After all, it was only about seven more blocks to the motel. He thought of Reg and Tony eating pizza. He sure hadn't wanted to take his cedar bungalow into some pizza joint.

Chuck set off along Western Avenue, stumbling a little but not badly. The bungalow didn't weigh much. He held it to his chest and looked over its roof. The small shingles scratched his chin, but it wasn't a bad feeling. At the corner he waited for the light, although there weren't any cars. He liked how drinking beer made him feel. Like right now he didn't feel like much of anything.

After four blocks a patrol car pulled up beside him and the officer rolled down his window. "Where're you going with that dollhouse?" asked the cop. The cop's voice wasn't friendly or unfriendly.

Chuck considered saying it wasn't a dollhouse. He considered telling the cop about Luigi and how he was dead. He considered saying how his wife had kicked him out.

"I'm staying at the Econolodge," said Chuck carefully. "The name's Chuck Malone, Room Two-ten. I was just showing this to some friends."

"Don't stay out on the street too long, Chuck," said the cop, rolling up his window.

Chuck walked another block, then sat down on a bench. He put the bungalow on the bench beside him. In the dark, it looked like a house in which people were sleeping. He imagined Luigi and his wife in bed. Luigi had had a dog. Maybe its name was Mike. Maybe it was Mack. The dog would be sleeping in the kitchen by the back door. A street cleaner whooshed by. There was a siren a few blocks away.

Chuck bent down to look inside the screened-in porch. His fingers touched the false bottom under the bungalow. He felt some switches, each one not much bigger than the tip of a toothpick. He moved the first one and a little flashlight bulb lit up on the back porch ceiling. Chuck got down on the sidewalk so he could see better. There were the two little rocking chairs where he and Luigi used to sit. Between them was the table where they had put their old-fashioneds and sometimes a bowl of chips, sometimes a bowl of peanuts. The floor of the back porch was covered with dark green linoleum. It seemed to Chuck that the chairs were even rocking back and forth, slowly and comfortably, the way they rock when two men, two old friends, are discussing the serious business of this world.

"Luigi," said Chuck in a whisper, "my wife kicked me out. You remember June? She does aerobics now."

As he leaned closer, Chuck understood that the little house was empty and there was no one to listen. He thought of the days to come when there would be no one to help him with the big decisions, no one to say what to do or how to do it. And those days seemed to stretch ahead without conclusion. But it was too late in the night for such thoughts. He'd drunk too much, and when he bent down and got his eye up to the screen door of the back porch, it seemed he could really see the little chairs move.

"Luigi, June's taken up with a weight lifter. How can I compete with that? She doesn't like who I am anymore. She looks through me like I'm a cracked pane of glass. I'm in the Econolodge. Luigi, what do you think I should do?"

Chuck waited. The chill in his knees from the cold concrete had begun to travel up his legs. Clouds moved across the last visible stars. It would rain later, and in the morning there would be puddles in the parking lots. Each would contain a splash of oil, a small prism. Hung over and short of sleep, Chuck would notice such a puddle around 7 A.M. when he left the motel for coffee and a doughnut on his way to work. The puddle would seem to hold an imprisoned rainbow, and Chuck would worry about all the disappointed and unfortunate and confused who had made wishes on that particular rainbow and how those wishes would now go undelivered.

THE PITY OF IT

I don't know, I've done some things I shouldn't have done and not enough things that I should. But some stuff sticks in your throat no matter how much you try to cough it up, no matter how much you spit.

I was fucking this woman. Her husband was out of town for a week and I meant to see her a lot. He had just left, like he wasn't even an hour out of the house and already I had hopped on his wife. He was a black guy, but I didn't know that then. His wife was white enough. She had a big belly, and I liked how it felt against mine. I liked how it got to feel greasy. It was February, a day or two before St. Valentine's Day. The snow was old snow and the weather seemed stuck somehow. You'd look out the window and the New Jersey sky was a dead color. The snow was littered with frozen dog shit: the brown flowers of dead winter. It was the middle of the afternoon, that's how eager I was to fuck her.

I'd met her two weeks before at a gas station. She couldn't make out the self-service directions, like the pump wouldn't work and she was telling it to go screw itself. So I offered to help. I mean, I was getting gas myself. She looked me over in that appraising way and we got to talking about how gas stations rip you off and why don't they have a kid pumping the gas like they used to. She didn't say anything about any husband. The way she acted I figured her options were open. She had black hair that was all tangled, and I imagined what it would be like to have it caught up in my fingers. Talking to her, I could almost feel it. It felt like my body was aimed at her, and I could see her twitching toward my attentiveness. No, not twitching, she was just alert. So I pumped her gas and she watched me. I asked if she felt like a cup of coffee. These moves, they must be written down someplace. That evening I fucked her for the first time. By then I knew she was married but so what? Her belly against mine was like greased latex.

So this day that her husband had gone on a trip, I stuck it to her right in the middle of the afternoon; and when I was done, we were laying there and she was talking about how she would like to be someplace warm, some beach with palm trees and coconuts. She'd been to Venezuela once and she talked about that. I was only half listening. She was a woman with a lot of complaints, like the room was too hot or too cold or she had a headache or someone had cheated her. My right hand was under the pillow and I felt a piece of paper. I drew it out.

It was a valentine. Her husband had written her a valentine and left it under her pillow in a square white envelope. It had a red heart made out of aluminum foil with a bunch of lace around it, and inside was written *To Carolina, my dearest and sweetest. You are always in my thoughts*.

Folded inside the valentine was a fifty-dollar bill so new you could almost smell the green. I rolled off Carolina's belly and showed her the valentine. "Hey, look at this," I said.

She took it, glanced at it, put the fifty on her night table, and gave the valentine a toss. "What a jerk," she said.

"He's stuck on you."

"Like chewing gum," she said. She reached for a cigarette and gave me one as well.

He had signed the card *With all my love, Sam.* I asked her, "How long you been married to Sam?"

She blew some smoke toward the ceiling. "Too fucking long. Eight years."

"He must still be hot for you."

"Why shouldn't he be? I'm good to him." She started playing with my prick, trying to get it cranking again.

"What's he do?" I said. "I mean, for a living."

"He sells computers to high schools," she said. "What do you care?"

"I don't. I'm just talking."

"Well, tell me how you like me instead," she said, giving my prick another crank. "How do you like what I'm doing?" Then she stubbed out her cigarette and got busy.

But I was lying. The valentine had put the guy in the room. The lumps in the mattress came from his body. I could see his suits in the closet. And I thought what it was like for him, being married to a woman who fucked a lot of men, because no way was I the first. Carolina wasn't like that. She had an appetite.

"Does he know you fool around?" I asked.

"Jesus," she said, giving me a shove, "you're no fun at all."

"I'm curious about the guy," I said.

"He doesn't know shit," she said, pushing back her black hair, "and neither do you."

Later, as I was getting dressed, I looked at their wedding

picture. That's when I saw he was a black guy. It showed Sam as about six feet with glasses in black frames, curly hair, and big lips. Blow-job lips, we called them. They were standing in some room as fancy as a funeral parlor. Carolina was cuddling up to him and he was looking proud. The guy looked familiar. I didn't think I'd seen him before. But maybe he'd come into the garage when I was working or maybe I'd seen him around town.

"Hey, he's a black guy," I said.

"So what, you racist?"

"I don't care if he's pink and got spots. Does he have an extra big dong?"

"Big enough," said Carolina.

"All those guys are supposed to have big dongs. Even the ones with glasses. You want to get something to eat?"

"Not with you," she said, "you've gotten too boring."

"Fuck you," I said.

"You already did," she said.

About a week later I saw this guy Sam at the bowling alley. He belonged to a league and maybe I'd once bowled against him, but I couldn't remember. He wasn't the only black guy in the league, but there weren't a lot of them. I mean, they mostly had their own leagues. I wasn't bowling that night. I was just cruising around. I'd been divorced two years and I hit a lot of places. I'd seen Carolina a few more times but the electricity had gone out of it. She'd become a rerun and I knew her moves. And to tell the truth I wasn't igniting her spark any either. I mean, we hadn't joined up to have a conversation, and now we'd done everything else. I hadn't told her I wouldn't see her again, it was just an understanding. And who knows, maybe in six months she would hold a charge and we'd do it some more. It was hard to say what I didn't like about her, but partly it was that she was so direct. She wanted to get laid. When I walked into her house, she would just take hold of me. And here she was married to a black guy who stuck valentines under her pillow. Like he was carving his initials on a tree that was already marked up pretty bad.

I watched him bowl for a while. He was good but no champion. He was friendly to the other guys and they liked him: laughing and drinking beer. He wasn't jivy. He acted more like a white guy than a black guy. I thought of his wife's belly and how somebody else must be shoving it to her right at that moment. He had written *You are always in my thoughts,* and I wondered if he was thinking about her as he was throwing the ball down the alley. He bowled four strikes in a row and his pals were clapping him on the back. The alley was full of rumbles and wood exploding, the echoes of men laughing, the smell of cigarette smoke and chalk. Sam had a big goofy grin, and when he moved he kind of shambled as if his body were too big for him and he was trying to get used to it. His glasses kept sliding down his nose and he shoved them back up with his thumb. He wore khaki pants and a green golfing sweater. I mean, he even dressed like a white guy.

I didn't talk to him that night, but I talked to him another night. I was seeing another woman by then, unmarried, though she'd been around. She liked being with me and she liked that I knew about cars. Her name was Betty. I didn't know if our future would be one week or one month, but I liked spending time with her outside of bed. We were both bowling that night. Stuff like bowling, it's what you do between getting laid.

This guy Sam was using the next lane with three of his white pals. There was no sign of Carolina. I could almost feel how someone else was doing it to her, and it made me remember how slick her belly got. Her husband was grinning, bowling strikes and grinning with those big lips. I bought him a beer. "You're a hotshot," I said. Betty smiled at him, but we went on with our game.

She was just learning to bowl but she had a good eye and I liked helping her. She was having trouble swinging the ball back, then taking a couple of steps forward as she timed her release.

Sam was watching in a friendly way. "Move forward on your right foot," he told her. After a while she figured it out, more or less.

Betty was a secretary and I took her home about ten. "You acted like you knew that colored guy," she said.

"I seen him around," I said.

I stayed until two-thirty. I don't like spending the whole night. It makes women proprietorial. Most women are more into real estate than sex. They want to own you.

A couple of nights later, I saw Sam again at the bowling alley. I was by myself. He was bowling with two other guys and he asked me to join them so we could play teams. We bowled about half a dozen frames and Sam and I won. We were all drinking beer. These were cheerful guys who never worried about what their wives were doing when they weren't home. They all had nicknames: Bobby and Dickie and Sam. Sam had a couple of new fifties and it made me think of the fifty he had tucked into the valentine. He had just earned a big commission and he was celebrating.

"Where's your wife?" I asked.

"Out with the girls," he said.

I didn't say anything about that, though I could have.

We made a hundred bucks bowling strikes that night and I figured we could do it again. I'm pretty good but I'm not a league player. Not because I couldn't be. I just can't stand the bullshit and the T-shirts and the weekend barbecues with the wives. I like the action I can pick up by myself. But Sam was easy to be with and I figured we could make some money together. Also, I was curious about his wife. She was a woman as tough as a shoe sole and he seemed pretty regular, even sweet. Like he hated to win too much off a guy and he wouldn't bowl with suckers. And there was his color. I mean, I'd seen mixed marriages before and there was nothing surprising about it, especially in north Jersey. It had to do with his wife and the kind of life she led; that's what I told myself.

After the other guys left, we had another beer in the bar. I had told him I was a mechanic and he was describing this knocking sound in the right front wheel of his Toyota Camry. It was probably the shocks, but I told him about ball joints and the danger of losing a wheel. The whole thing was a story but it had him worried. "The dealer doesn't like to touch that kind of thing till you're past the warranty," I said. "It costs them too much."

"Would you take a look at it?" he asked. "I'd hate to have anything happen when my wife's driving."

"Sure, I'd be happy to. You got kids?"

"We're putting it off for a while. Carolina says she's not ready."

That's right, I thought, before she makes those black babies she's got to fuck every hotshot north of Camden. I couldn't believe he was so naive about his own wife. Couldn't he smell the other guys? "You two must be pretty tight," I said.

"I don't know where I'd be without her," he told me.

He asked me the usual get-acquainted questions: where'd I'd grown up, who I'd gone to school with, my marriage.

"I found she was fucking other guys," I said. "It drove me crazy." It was a lie. As far as I could see, Jenny hated sex, although now she's married again and has a kid. "I could smell these guys on her. Sometimes there'd still be cigarette smoke in the bedroom."

"Jesus," said Sam. "What'd you do about it?"

"I showed up one night when I told her I'd be out of town. She was with two guys. She was giving it to both of them. I had a shotgun. If I could have found the shells, I would have finished them off good. So I just clubbed them and kicked her out without her clothes. They all drove off naked."

"Didn't you feel bad?"

"Not as bad as I would of felt if I'd done nothing."

We went on to talk about other things. He never mentioned being a Negro. Like it didn't occur to him or he'd forgotten about it. He'd grown up in Teaneck just a few towns over from me. Both his parents were teachers. Middle class, he called them. Of course they were black, just like him. I didn't have any plans yet. I didn't even know I was thinking of anything, except for that valentine under the pillow. Sam was a guy who was always surprised by things. You'd tell him how a car manufacturer had cheated the dealer and he'd be surprised. You'd tell him how a dealer would charge for a piece of work he'd never done and he'd open his mouth and say, "I can't believe it." It wasn't that he was dumb. He just believed stuff, all sorts of stuff that he shouldn't. Newspapers, stuff on television—he figured they were telling the truth. I went over to Betty's when I left him. It was late and she wasn't happy to see me, but I didn't care. I gave it to her anyway. I gave it to her good.

The next day Sam brought his Toyota into the shop. It was his shocks, like I say, and we changed them and gave him a good price. I didn't see him when he picked up the car. A couple of nights later Sam came into the bowling alley with Carolina. He waved and she pretended not to recognize me. She looked pretty good in a red turtleneck and all that black hair. I was bowling with some other guys and didn't go over. I didn't want to seem pushy. One of the guys, Pete, gave Carolina a long look.

"Is she with that black guy?" he said.

"They're married," I told him.

"What a waste," he said.

"She'll give it to you, if you want it."

"No," he said.

"Believe me," I said. "I been there." Pete was like me, no better than he should have been. He's a year or two older than me, maybe thirty-six or thirty-seven, and he's got a little Alfa Romeo that I work on sometimes.

We talked about Carolina a little and I started getting an idea. "Follow her when she goes to the can," I said. "When she comes out, introduce yourself. Tell her that Joey thought the two of you could be friends."

"What about her husband?"

"He doesn't know shit."

"A black guy," he said. "I wonder if he's got a big dong."

Anyway, a little later Carolina goes off to the can and Pete trails after her. When he came back I asked what happened.

"She gave me a look," Pete said.

So I gave Pete her telephone number. When Carolina bowled, her plaid skirt rode up on her legs, and when she released the ball her breasts bounced against her turtleneck. Her black hair was all crazy and she kept tossing it back and laughing. She knew Pete was watching, and she knew I was watching as well. I sent them over a couple of beers and Sam waved to me again. He had a smile like a kid's. He kept pushing his glasses back up his nose and grinning.

That was a Friday night. The next Tuesday, Sam and I had an agreement to bowl a couple of guys from Orange. They thought they were hot and I wasn't sure we could take them. These guys had been after me to bowl for a while. One of them was a fat old guy with a potbelly. I wanted to beat him so bad it was like a taste in my mouth. All I needed was a partner I could count on. Sam wasn't perfect but he was steady. You couldn't rattle him. If we beat them, we stood to make a thousand bucks. These guys were tense at first; they hadn't figured me to show up with a black guy. But Sam made them relax. There was nothing threatening about him. Like it made these guys feel liberal to bowl with us. Sam could bowl and he could talk about sports and who looked good. It was spring training and there was a lot of talk about how Roger Clemens would do with the Yankees. We beat these guys and got our grand. I gave Sam his half in the bar.

"I've never played for so much," he said. "Maybe a hundred, no more than that."

We were drinking Gentleman Jack straight up to celebrate. "Me neither," I said, "but these guys wanted to do it. I feel sort of bad letting myself get talked into it." That was a lie. I'll play for anything that's going. "But I used to like to make fifty bucks and put a new bill under my wife's pillow. It'd surprise her."

"I sometimes do that," said Sam. His skin wasn't black like night. It was a kind of medium brown. He had some white blood in him someplace.

"Then it turned out that the guys she was with took the money," I said. "She'd lend it to them. Some of them were the very guys I'd bowled against and beaten."

"Jesus," said Sam.

"You never know, right? She had these shows she liked on TV. She said she wanted to stay home and see these shows or maybe go out with the girls. Just because we were married, I thought she was telling the truth. She must of fucked thirty, forty guys."

"Jesus," said Sam. His face was open, like a guy who thinks you're going to toss him a ball, and his lips were pink and wet looking.

"I mean, what's your wife doing right now?" I asked. "Do you know? Does a guy ever know?"

"Carolina's fine," said Sam. "She likes to spend time by herself. I have no trouble with that."

He said this so nicely and his smile was so kind that I could see why some women would like him, why they'd want to have sex with him.

"But how do you know?" I said. "How do you ever know?"

We met a few more times and played some other guys. We won all but once. Two guys from Ocean City took us for a grand. It had to go that way sooner or later. Sam was good about losing the money. Some guys keep talking about it, like it's a rag they can't stop chewing. Sam shrugged it off. It was easier for him than for me. The next day I heard from Pete. He was sticking it to Carolina every chance he got. She was still electric for him.

"What do you talk about?" I asked.

"We don't talk. We just fuck."

"An all-protein diet," I told him.

When I saw Sam, I'd talk about my ex-wife and the story I'd made up. I hated to think of him being messed over by Carolina. Nothing could touch her. Like she held all the cards—her and that black hair. Right now she was seeing Pete and soon she'd be seeing someone else while her husband bowled and slipped fifties under her pillow.

"You never know," I told him. "You never know what they're doing. My wife had the sweetest face. She'd tell me shit and I'd believe it was vanilla ice cream."

"I know what's going on," said Sam. "Everything's okay at home. We still have sex a lot."

"Same with my wife. But she was like a bunny. You should show up some night when she's not expecting you."

"I don't have to do that," said Sam. "I already know."

"Does it make a difference?" I asked. "I mean the racial thing? You're a black guy. That's how she sees you, right? It's got to be an issue."

"She doesn't see me as any color," he said. "I'm her husband."

"As long as you're happy," I said.

But the idea was like a little hole and I kept digging at it. I mean, the world he believed in didn't exist. "Test it," I'd tell him. "You've got to be sure." That's not to say we didn't talk about anything else. We talked about lots of stuff: sports and how people try to cheat you, good restaurants. But with Carolina, I told myself I was doing him a favor.

Then, after a couple of weeks, he finally came around. I mean, it was his idea, not mine. He was the one who brought it up.

"I told Carolina I had to go away for a couple of days," he said. We were in the bar of the bowling alley. Sam had taken off his glasses and was fiddling with them, like they were bent in some way. "I'll pack my bag and leave, then come back tomorrow night. Just to be sure." He talked without looking up from the table. We could hear the pins crashing and the machines setting them up again.

"It's best that way," I said. "It's best to know."

"But what does it get you?"

At first I didn't hear what he said, and when he repeated it I didn't understand his question. "You mean what's it get you to be made a fool of?"

Without his glasses, his eyes looked smaller. "That's not what I mean," he said.

We didn't bowl that night. He said he didn't feel like it. He had two beers, then left. "I told Carolina I'd be back by ten," he said.

Later I called Pete. I couldn't afford to have Sam show up at his house and not find any action. Pete said, "Carolina already called me. What's your interest in this?"

"I want to know when you're free to bowl. You been busy a lot lately."

"That's okay. We're getting to the end of our tether."

We agreed to meet the night after next and put a hundred on it. I guessed he was getting tired of Carolina just like I had. "All-meat diet too much for you?" I asked.

"I been down that road a lot," Pete said.

It was Pete who told me what happened. We met at eight o'clock in the bar of the bowling alley. Pete had a mark on his cheek, and I waited for him to tell me how he got it. He's a tall guy, taller than me, and he plays a lot of golf.

"Did he really say he was going out of town?" he asked.

"That's what he told me Monday night."

"What a jerk," Pete said.

Pete had showed up at Carolina's around nine o'clock the previous night. Since Sam was supposed to be out of town, Pete had parked in the driveway. He had been eager and they hadn't even gone into the bedroom. He started fucking her right on the living room rug. I remembered that rug, a light-colored shag carpet. I'd once done the same thing. I wanted to hear more about what they had done and if she grabbed him like she used to grab me, but he just moved on.

"All of a sudden her husband bursts in from the garage," said Pete. "He's screaming at her. I jump up, like one moment I'm giving it to her and the next I'm on my feet. He swings at me and hits me right here on the cheek. I don't care he's her husband. Nobody hits me, especially a black guy. So we go a couple of rounds. Like I'm naked except for my socks and my wristwatch. I bust his glasses. I hit him five or six times. He's no fighter, I can tell you that much. I bust his lip and he's bleeding all over his shirt. Carolina's standing over by the TV to give us room—naked, just like me. Some women like the fighting, but she didn't have any expression at all. So finally he's sitting on the floor fiddling with his glasses. He's weeping and fiddling with his broken glasses. Carolina's got her arms crossed. She says to me, 'Take me with you. I'm not staying here.' Hey, I don't want her at my place but I figure I can give her a lift somewheres. Her husband gets all upset. He wants her to stay. He tells her he can't stand her leaving. Can you imagine it? I mean, she's the one who's been getting poked and by more guys than me, right? But she doesn't like it. She says, 'I hate spies.' He keeps apologizing. 'I don't care what you've done,' he says. She's been getting dressed and grabbing some of her stuff. 'Fuck you,' she tells him. I've gotten dressed as well. 'Maybe you should stay with him for a while,' I say. 'Just to calm him down.' 'Fuck you too,' she tells me. This guy, her husband, keeps begging her not to leave. He doesn't act like a black guy; he doesn't act like a white guy. He acts like a jerk. He's not tough at all. She doesn't say a word to him, and when I give her a lift she doesn't say a word to me neither. When I pull out of her driveway, he's standing in the doorway like she might change her mind, but she doesn't even look at him. I watch him in the rear-view mirror until I can't see him anymore. Anyway, I give her a lift to a friend's place, a woman."

Sam didn't come back to the bowling alley. I called him one night to see if I could get his side of the story, but he said he didn't feel like bowling. He didn't tell me anything else. I don't think he suspected me. I see him now and then, like at the supermarket or just driving around. I seen her too, though not to be intimate. She's usually with different guys, even black guys. She must have an apartment somewhere, but I can't imagine sticking it to her right now. I think about Sam and how he kept asking her to stay even though he'd found her with Pete. His wife naked and Pete naked, too. Except for his socks, like he said. How could Sam do that? He should of shot her instead of wanting her back. Like he's got no self-respect. And maybe Sam and Carolina shouldn't of gotten married in the first place. White, black, the problems are there from the start. It's always a gamble. When I see Sam, he doesn't look so good. He doesn't smile, maybe he nods. What does he know about men and women and the things they do to each other—a guy like that, a guy who believes what he reads in the papers? Who doesn't know shit about cars? But at least he knew about Carolina, right?

KANSAS

The boy hitchhiking on the back-country Kansas road was nineteen years old. He had been dropped there late in the morning by a farmer in a Model T Ford who had turned off to the north. Then he waited for three hours. It was July and there were no clouds. The wheat fields were flat and went straight to the horizon. The boy had two plums and he ate them. He wore a gray cap and he could feel the sun right through it. A blue Plymouth coupe went by with a man and a woman. They were laughing. The woman had blond hair and it was all loose and blew from the window. They didn't even see the boy. The strands of straw-colored hair seemed to be waving to him. Half an hour later a farmer stopped in a Ford pickup covered with a layer of dust. The boy clambered into the front seat. The farmer took off again without glancing at him. A forty-five revolver lay next to the farmer's buttocks on the seat. Seeing it, the boy felt something electric go off inside him. The revolver was old and there were rust spots on the barrel. Black electrician's tape was wrapped around the handle.

"You seen a woman and a man go by here in a Plymouth coupe?" asked the farmer. He pronounced it *koo-pay*.

The boy said he had.

"How long ago?"

"About thirty minutes."

The farmer had light blue eyes and there was stubble on his chin. Perhaps he was forty, but to the boy he looked old. His skin was leather-colored from the sun. The farmer pressed his foot to the floor and the pickup roared. It was a dirt road and the boy had to hold his hands against the dashboard to keep from being bounced around. It was hot and both windows were open. There was grit in the boy's eyes and on his tongue. He kept glancing sideways at the revolver.

"They friends of yours?" asked the boy.

The farmer didn't look at him. "That's my wife," he said. "I'm going to put a bullet in her head." He put a hand to the revolver to make sure it was still there. "The man, too," he added.

The boy didn't say anything. He was hitchhiking back to summer school from Oklahoma. He was the middle of three boys and the only one who had left home. He had already spent a year at the University of Oklahoma and was spending the summer at Lawrence. And there were other places, farther places. The boy played the piano. He intended to go to those farther places.

"What did they do?" the boy asked at last.

"You just guess," said the farmer.

The pickup was going about fifty miles per hour. The boy was afraid of seeing the dust cloud from the Plymouth up ahead but there was only straight road. Then he was afraid that the Plymouth might have pulled off someplace. He touched his tongue to his upper lip but it was just one dry thing against another. Getting into the pickup, the boy had had a clear idea of the direction of his life. He meant to go to New York City at the end of summer. He meant to play the piano in Carnegie Hall. The farmer and his forty-five seemed to stand between him and that future. They formed a wall that the boy was afraid to climb over.

"Do you have to kill them?" the boy asked. He didn't want to talk but he felt unable to remain silent.

The farmer had a red boil on the side of his neck, and he kept touching it with two fingers. "When you have something wicked, what do you do?" asked the farmer.

The boy wanted to say he didn't know, or he wanted to say he would go to the police, but the farmer would have no patience with those answers. And the boy also wanted to say he would forgive the wickedness, but he was afraid of that answer as well. He was afraid of making the farmer angry and so he only shrugged.

"You stomp it out," said the farmer. "That's what you do: you stomp it out."

The boy stared straight ahead, searching for the dust cloud and hoping not to see it. The hot air seemed to bend in front of them. The boy was so frightened of seeing the dust cloud that he was sure he saw it: a little puff of gray getting closer. The pickup went straight down the middle of the road. There was no other traffic. Even if there had been other cars, the boy felt certain that the farmer wouldn't have moved out of the way. The wheat on either side of the road was coated with layers of dust, making it a reddish color, the color of dried blood.

"What about the police?" asked the boy.

"It's my wife," said the farmer. "It's my problem."

The boy never did see the dust cloud. They reached Lawrence and the boy got out as soon as he could. His shirt was stuck to his back and he kept rubbing his palms on his dungarees. He thanked the farmer but the man didn't look at him, he just kept staring straight ahead.

"Don't tell the police," said the farmer. His hand rested lightly on the forty-five beside him on the seat.

"No," said the boy. "I promise." He slammed shut the dusty door of the pickup.

The boy didn't tell the police. For several days he didn't tell anyone at all. He looked at the newspapers twice a day for news of a killing but he didn't find anything. More than the farmer's gun, he had been frightened by the strength of the farmer's resolve. It had been like a chunk of stone, and compared to it the boy had felt as soft as a piece of white bread. The boy never knew what happened. Perhaps nothing had happened.

The summer wound to its conclusion. The boy went to New York. He never did play in Carnegie Hall. His piano playing never got good enough. The war came and went. He wasn't a boy any longer. He was a married man with two sons. The family moved to Michigan. The man was a teacher, then a minister. His own parents died. He told his sons the story about the farmer in the pickup. "What do you think happened?" they asked. Nobody knew. Perhaps the farmer caught up with them; perhaps he didn't. The man's sons went off to college and began their own lives. The man and his wife moved to New Hampshire. They grew old. Sixty years went by between that summer in Kansas and the present. The man entered his last illness. He stayed home but he couldn't get out of bed. His wife gave him shots of morphine. He began to have dreams even when he was awake. The visiting nurse was always chipper. "Feeling better today?" she would ask. He tried to be polite, but he had no illusions. He went from one shot a day to two and then three. The doctor said, "Give him as many as he needs." His wife started to ask about the danger of addiction; then she said nothing.

The man hardly knew when he was asleep or awake. He hardly knew if one day had passed or many. He had oxygen. He didn't eat. The space between his eyes and the bedroom wall was always occupied with people of his invention, people of his past. He would lift his hand to wave them away, only to find his hand still lying motionless on the counterpane. Even music distracted him now. Always he was listening for something in the distance.

The boy was standing by the side of a dirt road. A Ford pickup stopped beside him and he got in. The farmer lifted a forty-five revolver. "I'm going to shoot my wife in the head."

"No," said the boy, "don't do it!"

The farmer drove fast. He had a red boil on the side of his neck, and he kept touching it with two fingers. They found the Plymouth coupe pulled off into a hollow. There were shade trees and a brook. The farmer jammed down the brakes and the pickup slid sideways across the dirt. The man and woman were in the front seat of the Plymouth. Their clothes were half off. They jumped out of the car. The woman had big red breasts. The farmer jumped out with his forty-five. "No!" shouted the boy. The farmer shot the man in the head. His whole head exploded and he fell down in the dust. His head was just a broken thing on the ground. The woman covered her face and tried to cover her breasts. The farmer shot her as well. Bits of dust floated on the surface of her blood. "The last for me," said the farmer. He put the barrel of the gun in his mouth. "No, no!" cried the boy.

The boy was standing by the side of a dirt road. A Ford pickup stopped beside him and he got in. "I'm going to shoot my wife," said the farmer. He had a big revolver on the seat beside him.

"You can't," said the boy.

They talked all the way to Lawrence. The farmer was crying.

"I've always been good to her," he said. He had a red boil on the side of his neck, and he kept touching it.

"Give the gun to the police," said the boy.

"I'm afraid," said the farmer.

"You needn't be," said the boy. "The police won't hurt you."

They drove to the police station. The boy told the desk sergeant what had happened. The sergeant shook his head. He took the revolver away from the farmer. "We'll get her back, sir," he said. "Wife stealing's not permitted around here."

"I could have got in real trouble," said the farmer.

The boy was standing by the side of a dirt road. A pickup stopped beside him and he got in. The farmer said, "I'm going to kill my wife."

The boy was too frightened to say anything. He kept looking at the forty-five revolver. He was sure he would be shot himself. He regretted not staying in Oklahoma, where he had friends and family. He couldn't imagine why he had moved away. The farmer drove straight to Lawrence. The boy was bounced all over the cab of the pickup, but he didn't say anything. He was afraid something would happen to his hands and he wouldn't be able to play the piano. It seemed to him that playing the piano was the only important thing in the entire world. The farmer had a red boil on the side of his neck, and he kept touching it.

When they got to Lawrence, the boy jumped out of the pickup and ran. He saw a policeman and told him what had happened. An hour later he was getting a hamburger at a White Tower restaurant. He heard shooting. He hurried out and saw the farmer's dusty pickup. There were police cars with their lights flashing. The boy pushed through the crowd. The farmer was hanging half out of the door of his pickup truck. There was blood all over the front of his workshirt. The forty-five revolver lay on the pavement. The policemen were clapping each other on the back. They had big grins. The boy began cracking his knuckles. They made snapping noises.

The boy was standing by the side of a dirt road. A pickup stopped beside him and he got in. The farmer pointed a forty-five revolver at his head. "Get in here," he said. They drove toward Lawrence. "I'm going to shoot my wife for wickedness," said the farmer.

"No," said the boy, "you must forgive her."

"I'm going to kill her," said the farmer, "and her fancy man besides."

The boy said, "You can't take the law into your own hands."

The farmer raised his forty-five revolver. "They're as good as dead." He had a red boil on the side of his neck.

The boy was a college student. It was the Depression. He wanted to go to New York and become a classical pianist. He had already been accepted by Juilliard. "Justice does not belong to you," said the boy.

"Wickedness must be punished," said the farmer.

They argued all the way to Lawrence. The boy stayed with the farmer. He could have jumped out of the pickup but he didn't. The boy kept trying to convince him that he was wrong. The farmer drove to the train station.

The farmer's wife was in the waiting room with the man who had been driving the Plymouth coupe. She was very pretty with blond hair and milky pink skin. She screamed when she saw the farmer. Her companion put his arms around her to protect her.

The boy hurried to stand between the woman and her husband. "Think of what you are doing," he said. "Think how you are throwing your life away." The first bullet struck him in the shoulder and whipped him around. He could see the woman open her mouth in a startled O of surprise. The second bullet caught him in the small of his back.

The man's family was with him in New Hampshire when he died: his wife and his two sons, neither of them young anymore. It was early evening in October at the very height of the color. Even after sundown the maples seemed bright. The older son watched his father breathing. He kept twisting and trying to kick his feet. His face was very thin; his body was hardly more than a ridge dividing the middle of the sheet. He didn't talk anymore. He didn't want anyone to touch him. He seemed to be focusing his attention. He took a breath and they waited. He exhaled slowly. They continued to wait. He didn't breathe again. They waited several minutes. Then his wife removed the oxygen tubes from his nose, doing it quickly, as if afraid of doing something wrong.

The older son went back into the bedroom with the two men from the funeral home. They had a collapsible stretcher, which they put next to the bed. They unrolled a dark blue body bag. They shifted the dead man onto the stretcher and wrestled him into the body bag, one at his feet, one at his head. The son stood in the doorway. The men from the funeral home muttered directions to each other. They were breathing heavily and their hair was mussed. At last they got him into the body bag. The son watched closely as the zipper was drawn up and across his father's face. It was a large silver zipper and the son watched it being pulled across his father's forehead. All the days after that he kept seeing its glittering progression, a picture repeating itself in his mind.

SOME CHANGES COMING

When life got too stressful for Ralph Benedetti, he went out to the backyard and shot some red squirrels. He had an old single-shot twenty-two that his daddy had given him back in 1956. His daddy was dead now: twenty years. He had dropped off his tractor and the wagon rolled right over him. The doctor guessed it had been heatstroke, but it just as easily could have been carelessness. Ralph had been in college at the time, getting a degree in business administration. He had gone back to school after a spell in the army. It was in the army that he had learned to shoot with any accuracy. Sighting down the barrel at a red squirrel perched on a branch of the old butternut, Ralph would think, There's the enemy. Then he would pop him and the squirrel would spin in wild cartwheels through the air.

The squirrels had gotten into the house. They stored their seeds in old shoes that no one had worn for a while or in bureau drawers that no one opened from one year to the next. At night Ralph would wake up beside Joanie and hear the squirrels in the ceiling or in the walls, just running and running. He tried to imagine their lives. They never seemed to rest. He imagined one of them gnawing through a wire and the whole house going up. He would lie in bed unable to sleep, wondering what he would save first: clothes, books, papers. For Pete's sake, thought Ralph, his son, Lemuel, was sick in the head, his wife was worried all the time, the bookstore was just about bankrupt, and he had to fuss about a red squirrel gnawing through a wire. Sometimes Ralph was out in the backyard with the twenty-two even before the sun had cracked the edge of the horizon; that's how eager he was.

Lemuel had piled up his Ford Pinto four months before, killing Bobby Watkins, his best friend. Lemuel's girlfriend, Sally Powers, was in the back seat and had her jaw busted and suffered a concussion. Lemuel walked away without a scratch.

Bobby Watkins got his neck broke. They'd all drunk a few beers but nothing serious. Lemuel had been showing off on a gravel road and went into a spin. When the Pinto slammed sideways into the tree, it couldn't have been going more than twenty miles an hour. They had been out in the country. Lemuel ran two miles before he found a house with a phone. But even if help had come within two seconds, it wouldn't have helped Bobby Watkins. He was dead so quick he didn't even have time to shut his eyes.

Lemuel dropped out of the community college. Bobby's death was like a wall that had been set across his life. He couldn't get around it, couldn't climb over it, couldn't bust through it. He sat in the basement rec room on the old sofa and watched TV. It didn't matter if the machine was on or off. After work Ralph Benedetti would go downstairs to check on his son. The TV would show people laughing and having the best time of their lives, and Lemuel would be weeping. Ralph didn't know what to say to him. He didn't know how to say *Snap out of it* or *Try to forget about it*. Ralph would look at him from the doorway. Lemuel had killed his best friend, and Ralph didn't know how to help him.

Lemuel didn't even want to see Sally Powers anymore. For a long time her jaw had been wired shut and she had to talk through her teeth and eat nothing but soup and fortified fluids. She tried to talk to Lemuel but her teeth being clamped shut made her sound sullen or angry. She had some bruises too and they turned an ugly yellow. Lemuel would look at her and weep and shake his head. After a while Sally stopped coming. Every couple of days, however, she would drop by the bookstore and ask Ralph how Lemuel was getting along. "The same," he would say, and shrug.

"He's got to shake out of it," Sally would say.

"I know, I know," said Ralph. Always she bought a paperback romance, even though she didn't read, because she knew the store was doing poorly.

Even Bobby Watkins's parents couldn't help. They came to the house several times. Joanie would give them small glasses of cream sherry. Lemuel would stand in front of them with tears streaming down his cheeks. "I don't want you to forgive me," he would say. "It's unforgivable."

Bobby Watkins's father was a retired fire chief. The death of his son nearly turned him bald overnight. But still he would say, "Anyone can make a mistake."

"No," said Lemuel, "it's worse than a mistake. It's the worst thing there is."

Joanie hovered nearby. She was a big dark-haired woman with an on-again off-again relationship with Weight Watchers. Lemuel was their only child. He would suffer and she would suffer as well. She was like the echo of his suffering. Many times when

Lemuel was weeping in the basement, Joanie would be weeping in the kitchen or bedroom or garage. Ralph would come home from the Book Factory and find the whole house full of tears. He would look at his wife and son, he would think how his bookstore was sinking deeper into debt, and he would say to himself, I should be crying as well. I should let the tears just sweep over me. Instead he got the twenty-two and a handful of shells and popped some squirrels off their branches, watched them make cartwheels through the air.

The accident had occurred in November. By the end of March, Ralph had reached the end of his tether. Every week Lemuel saw a therapist, and every week he attended two meetings of a grief support group. Even Joanie was attending a support group. The psychiatrist and the members of the support groups all said, Express your feelings. As if Lemuel's tears made up an exact quantity, and the more he wept the sooner he would use them up. It seemed to Ralph that life would be better if Lemuel and Joanie *stopped* expressing their feelings.

"You just want to sweep everything under the carpet," said Joanie. "That's always your way."

"I just want his life to get moving again," said Ralph. He was fifty-two and had married late. He didn't think anybody had time to waste.

"It wasn't your best friend that got killed," said Joanie. "Put yourself in his shoes."

Ralph felt he had been as sympathetic as anyone could be, but now five months had gone by and nothing had helped. He had tried to buy Lemuel things: sweaters and books and a personal stereo system, but Lemuel never left the house. He hardly left the basement. Joanie brought him his meals on a tray. Ralph could hear him chewing and blubbering, chewing and blubbering. It made him angry. Jesus, I'm hard-hearted, he'd think. Then he would go get his rifle—maybe he'd clean it, maybe he would just go back outside.

They lived in Easton right on the Pennsylvania border. Ralph and Joanie had a ranch house at the edge of town. The woods stretched off behind his house, and sometimes there would be deer around the bird feeder. When Ralph first opened the bookstore ten years earlier, he had given out free bumper stickers: READ A BOOK—THE MIND YOU SAVE MAY BE YOUR OWN. READ A BOOK—GIVE YOURSELF SOMEONE TO TALK TO. READ A BOOK—EXERCISE YOUR EYES. Ralph made up the slogans himself. He thought the bumper stickers would be a big hit but he never saw them on any cars. Eventually he plastered them on the side of his garage. When the deer came down to the bird feeder, they seemed to stare at the bumper stickers as if here, for the first time, Ralph had found disciples.

Once a day Ralph went down to the rec room to sit with his son. Lemuel was twenty. He was tall and thin and had long reddish-brown hair that was almost the same color as the deer. He had long red hands that he kept twisting like rags in his lap. There was often a drip of snot on the tip of his long nose and a pile of Kleenex on the linoleum between his untied basketball shoes. He wore T-shirts from rock concerts and jeans with the knees cut out. "You got to snap out of it, son," said Ralph.

"Why? Give me a good reason." Lemuel would be looking down at the crumpled Kleenex on the floor.

"Life goes on."

"Not Bobby's life."

"Your life goes on, my life goes on, your mother's life goes on. You want a sandwich?"

"I don't want anything."

"You think Bobby would want you to do this to yourself?"

Lemuel's face grew red but he still didn't look at his father.

"You think I like being like this? You think I'm doing it on purpose? It's right there in my head, every second. It won't go away. Jesus, Dad, if you could have seen how he lay there with his eyes open. He looked like he was thinking!"

"I know," said Ralph, "I know," and he would put his arms around his son and did not know what else to do. I don't know shit, he would think. Holding Lemuel, it seemed to Ralph he could remember every other time he'd held him, going back to when he had held him just five seconds after Lemuel pushed himself out of Joanie's belly. He wished holding his son would fix things, but it only made him sad.

Ralph had a best friend by the name of Jack who was his own age. Jack was a lawyer, an assistant D.A. About once a week he and Ralph would meet for a beer. Jack always spoke with great precision. Listening to him talk was like watching someone paper a room: the sections of information were carefully measured and put into place just like sections of wallpaper. "It is essential to make Lemuel think of something else," said Jack. "Think of his mind as a big screen. You have to put something on that screen other than Bobby Watkins."

They were sitting in the bar of the Holiday Inn. It was the beginning of April, but the bar had no windows so outside it could just as easily have been January in Siberia. Jack had a pipe that he liked to suck on as slowly as possible. It was for him a tangible metaphor for intricate thought.

"But how do I go about it?" asked Ralph. "I talk to him every day. Nothing I tell him makes any difference."

"First of all, you have to get him out of that house. Even in the rec room there must be specific memories of Bobby. It's not as if Lemuel wants to do this. He's as tired as you are of the whole subject, but he doesn't know how to stop."

"What should I do?"

"Take him on a trip. Get him out of Easton."

"But where?"

"It hardly matters: Disneyland, New York City, Washington, Cape Cod—any of those places or others."

"What about the bookstore?"

"Screw the bookstore. It's almost dead anyway."

As it turned out, Joanie said she would run the bookstore and she got Sally Powers to help. Lemuel didn't want to go anywhere but his father said he didn't have any choice. Ralph packed Lemuel's clothes and threw their suitcases in the back of the Dodge Caravan. He imagined he would have to carry Lemuel to the car as well. Lemuel was twenty pounds lighter than Ralph and he felt he could use a fireman's carry. He stood in front of Lemuel in the basement rec room, doing deep-breathing exercises and getting ready to toss his son over his shoulder.

"Okay, okay," said Lemuel, getting to his feet. "I'll walk."

As they backed out of the driveway, Ralph imagined the red squirrels heaving little sighs of relief.

"So where we going?" asked Lemuel.

But until Ralph reached the on-ramp of Interstate 78, he had no idea. Would it be east or west, California or Maine? He turned east. "You'll see," he said.

The countryside was getting green. It had rained earlier that morning and the pavement was still wet. Ralph cracked his window open and listened to the hiss of the tires. There were a lot of trucks heading toward New York City. Forsythia was blooming along the side of the road and in the backyards of the houses they passed. Lemuel stared straight ahead. He was wearing the earphones of his yellow Sports Walkman and at times Ralph could hear a *tchee-tchee* sound. Although Ralph knew it was music, he felt it was Lemuel's grief being fed directly into his ears, as if the Walkman had a tape loop that repeated the news of Bobby

Watkins's death. When they had almost reached New York, Ralph turned south on 95. He decided that Lemuel needed to see the ocean. Perhaps his mind would be soothed by the waves' regulation.

He drove to Chincoteague on the Virginia–Maryland border. He had been there ten years earlier with Joanie. They had eaten crab and strolled along the beach. They had bought the book *Misty of Chincoteague* for Lemuel and a T-shirt with a lighthouse on it. This time Ralph found a motel called the Seatag Lodge right on the water, actually the Assateague Channel. There were ducks that quacked at them and a lone Canada goose. Lemuel stared out at the water as if he saw Bobby Watkins floating beneath the surface. He leaned over with his elbows on the railing and wouldn't talk unless he was spoken to. Ralph was tired of being hearty. He bought a six-pack of Bud and cracked open two beers, handing one to Lemuel as they sat on the porch. Ralph thought how six months earlier he had been trying to keep beer away from his son, how he never brought any into the house. He thought of his plans and expectations at any given moment. He thought how he imagined his life as proceeding along a straight line while it just corkscrewed and corkscrewed.

"Tonight," he told Lemuel, "we're going to eat a shitload of crabs." He began to worry that Lemuel might be upset at bringing death to so many living creatures. Then he told his mind to shut up. "Give me a break," he told himself. There were herons out on the water, and across the channel he could see ponies galloping through marsh grass. Ralph finished his beer and opened another. About twenty ducks had gathered beneath the balcony and quacked up at them. Ralph wondered about their lives; then he thought, I'm tired of worrying about other people's problems.

The bar where they went to eat crabs was across the road from the motel and had a country-western band. No one asked

Lemuel for his I.D. The crabs were covered with pepper and were served with a little wooden mallet. They both got into breaking them open, of learning how to hit them squarely. It was a good kind of violence. A blond singer with hair sticking out a foot from her head sang a song called "Last Night the Bottle Let Me Down." Ralph was glad for the chance to be free of the bookstore. Nobody read anymore anyway. So what if it went bust? He could work for the city or go back to teaching school or become a real estate agent. Jack would help him with the details. What was past was past.

"How're you feeling?" he asked Lemuel.

"I'm okay."

"What about these crabs, aren't they something?"

"I guess so."

"Couldn't you eat them all night long?"

"Sure, all night long." Lemuel's reddish-brown hair hung down over his forehead so Ralph couldn't see his eyes.

They drank more beer. The bar was a long room with tables along the sides and a small dance floor near the band. At a few tables several women were seated together. They kept glancing around while trying not to be caught glancing around. Only two couples were dancing, but Ralph could tell that other people were getting ready. He decided that if he ate any more crabs, he would bust. He had already polished off a dozen. Ralph looked at the women sitting by themselves, then watched a man in a cowboy shirt go ask one of them to dance. The woman smiled and rose to her feet. It occurred to Ralph that he might be able to introduce Lemuel to some young woman. It would be a distraction for him.

"You like dancing?" he asked his son.

"It's all right."

"You dance much in school?"

"Sometimes."

"This country music sure makes me want to move my feet."

Lemuel didn't answer. He was looking across the room at nothing in particular. Ralph felt he could move his son's chair to the left or right and Lemuel would go on staring at the new scene without being aware of the change. Lemuel's indifference annoyed him, considering all the trouble he had gone to, and at the same time Ralph felt guilty at being annoyed. He finished his beer and stood up.

"I'm going to see about dancing," he said. "Don't go away."

He had spotted two women, probably a mother and daughter, sitting at a table near the bar. They were drinking mixed drinks with little colorful paper parasols and weren't eating. The older one was probably in her forties but in good shape. Still, she was younger than Ralph. Both women had black hair and wore country dresses with flounces and petticoats. They kept putting their heads together and giggling.

When Ralph asked the older woman to dance, he saw her look up at him with just a hint of disappointment. He was older than she liked, and heavier, and balder.

"Let's go," said Ralph, trying to give his friendliest smile. "I've come all the way from Easton to have a good time."

Her name was Rhoda and they found the similarity of their names a coincidence. When Ralph put his hand in the small of her back, he could feel it was damp with sweat. She wore big black pointed shoes and Ralph was afraid he might step on them. They reminded him of German U-boats. Rhoda's hair was brushed out away from her head and kept tickling his nose. She was a big woman, thick without being fat.

"How come you came all the way down here," asked Rhoda, "when you could of gone to Atlantic City?"

"I'm with my son," said Ralph. "I'm trying to get him over

a depression." He felt he had to plead his case as carefully as possible. He wondered what words his friend Jack the lawyer would choose. Jack would do it as precisely as laying stones for a garden wall.

"What's wrong with him?" asked Rhoda.

"His best friend was killed in a car wreck five months ago. My son was driving."

Rhoda stopped dancing. "What a shame," she said. Her face was sympathetic. Little wrinkles appeared on her forehead, cracking her face powder.

"He can't get it out of his mind," said Ralph. "That's why we came here."

"Is that him sitting over there?" asked Rhoda. "The boy in the Santana T-shirt?"

"That's him," said Ralph.

"He's handsome."

"He's a good dancer," said Ralph, who had never seen his son dance in his life. "You think you and your daughter would come sit with us for a while?"

Rhoda stopped dancing again. "That's not my daughter. We both work at the deli."

"First I thought you were sisters," said Ralph, "you look so much alike."

They started dancing again. "You try too hard," said Rhoda.

"I'm just nervous," said Ralph.

Rhoda talked to her friend, whose name was Inga. After an intense whispered conversation, the two women walked over to Ralph's table. They wore high heels that made them totter. They giggled together. Looking at Inga more closely, Ralph saw that she was older than he had thought. Perhaps she was thirty, perhaps thirty-five. She wore bright red lipstick that covered an area a little larger than her mouth. She sat down beside Lemuel and put her arm across his shoulders. "I hear you like to dance," she said.

Lemuel looked at her but didn't speak. He glanced at his father. Ralph was smiling and nodding. He wished he could crawl under the table or fly someplace miles away. He drank some beer, then pretended to study the glass.

"Sure, I'll dance," Lemuel said tonelessly.

Lemuel danced with Inga and Ralph danced again with Rhoda. She held on to him and Ralph could feel her breasts rubbing against his chest. It occurred to him that not only could Lemuel get laid but he might get laid as well. He decided after another dance or two he would invite them back to the motel. Ralph had rented an efficiency apartment with a living room and kitchenette, so such an invitation wouldn't seem too improper. He had a bottle of tequila and he could make margaritas. Ralph had never been unfaithful to Joanie except once at a book convention nine years earlier, but he felt his whole life was changing. He wondered if he had a wild streak.

"Your boy seems sad," said Rhoda. Her breath had a sweet smell like bubble gum.

"He's been taking it hard."

"I lost my first husband in a car wreck," said Rhoda. "Dang fool fell asleep at the wheel and went into the bay. Took all day to pry him out, and by then the eels had gotten his eyes."

Ralph tried to maneuver his feet around Rhoda's big black shoes. "At least you got married again," he said.

"Been married five times," she said. "Right now I'm between men."

All four got back to the table at the same time. Inga was pushing her hands through her black hair, tossing it and tossing it. She moved her chair closer to Lemuel. She rested a hand on his shoulder as she looked out across the room. Lemuel glanced at her, then carefully lifted her hand from his shoulder and set it on the table as if it were a heavy glove. He pushed back his chair and stood up. "Excuse me," he said, and walked away. Ralph assumed he had gone to the men's room. He asked the two women what they wanted to drink. They both wanted Black Russians. Inga began talking about a yellow Lab puppy she had seen that afternoon and how she'd been unable to keep her hands off it. Rhoda said how she'd always liked a dog. Five minutes passed. The drinks came and Ralph had another beer. Inga was looking around the bar at other men. The woman singer with the blond hair was singing, "Jack Daniel's, if you please. . . ." Several more minutes went by.

"Excuse me," said Ralph. "I think I'll go check on my son."

Lemuel wasn't in the men's room. He was no place in the bar. Ralph asked the hostess if she had seen him.

"The tall boy? He left fifteen minutes ago."

Ralph went back to the table. Inga was dancing with a man with a black beard. Rhoda was buffing her nails.

"I'm sorry," said Ralph, "but Lemuel's feeling badly. He had to go back to the motel. I got to go too."

Rhoda squeezed his fingers. "Just when we were getting acquainted," she said.

"I feel bad about it," said Ralph. Actually, he felt relieved. If he had had sex with Rhoda, he knew it would have been all over his face when he saw Joanie. His infidelity would be like a flashing sign.

"Grief's a terrible thing," said Rhoda.

Ralph went back across the road.

Lemuel was leaning over the balcony tossing crackers to the ducks that were quacking up at him. He turned when he heard his father behind him. He angrily threw the rest of the crackers down toward the water. "How could you do that? How could you set me up with that old bag? Don't you have any self-respect at all?"

"I'm just trying to help," said Ralph, putting his hands in his pockets.

"By getting laid? What about Mom? You're even worse than I thought you were!" Lemuel walked back into his room and slammed the door so hard the window shook.

The ducks began quacking again. Ralph could see the insides of their mouths, the ridges under their bills. He imagined what their words might be if their quacking could be translated: harsh and critical, but no worse than the words that Ralph was using against himself. A half-moon was up over the water. It had a reddish cast. Ralph thought of his son lying fully dressed on his bed and staring at the ceiling. He thought how his son kept imagining the accident. Lemuel had told him so often about how Bobby Watkins had looked that Ralph felt he could see the dead boy himself, half hanging out of the Ford Pinto with his eyes wide open and his neck bent around. Ralph felt angry at Bobby Watkins for refusing to go away. He pounded the soft part of his fist against the railing. The ducks quacked and he ignored them.

The next morning Lemuel got up early to go running. He didn't saying anything about the two women, Inga and Rhoda, but he didn't say anything else either.

"How'd you sleep?" asked Ralph. He had already made coffee. The orange juice was already poured. He himself had slept badly.

"All right."

"There's something about sea air, don't you think?"

Lemuel didn't answer. He began to put on his running shoes.

"You mind if I come along?" asked Ralph. "There're some trails over by the seashore. We can run there."

"You're not a runner," said Lemuel glancing up.

"I exercise now and then," said Ralph, patting his belly. "Anyway, there're some changes coming."

"I sort of want to be by myself," said Lemuel.

"I won't hinder you any," said Ralph. "You just run and I'll jog along behind. I want to see your stride. I haven't seen you run since high school."

Ralph could tell that Lemuel didn't like it but he didn't say anything else. Ralph put on an undershirt, plaid Bermuda shorts, and blue sneakers—canvas boat shoes, actually. His undershirt was too tight. Lemuel looked at the way he was dressed. "Mr. Marathon," he said.

Ralph grinned. He was glad that Lemuel had made a joke even if it was at his expense, even if it was meant to hurt him.

They drove across the bridge to Assateague Island and the national wildlife refuge. There always seemed to be ponies in the distance, never close up. At one point Ralph had to stop to let a family of raccoons cross the road.

"Will you look at that," he said.

Lemuel didn't say anything. In the marsh water along the side of the road were herons and egrets. On the ponds were hundreds of Canada geese. Ralph thought he had never seen so many different kinds of birds in one place.

"What's your favorite kind of bird?" he asked his son.

"Fried chicken."

At least it was joke number two.

He parked near the trails leading into the marsh. There were no other cars. Green signs gave the names of the trails with the distances measured in both miles and kilometers. Lemuel began to do stretching exercises and push-ups. Ralph tried to copy him but he felt clumsy. Instead, he did some jumping jacks. Ralph hadn't jogged in over three years, and even then it hadn't been much. A cool breeze was coming off the water and he shivered.

"I guess we'll get warm pretty quick," he said.

Lemuel set off down the path. Ralph lumbered after him. With each step he could feel his body protesting. His shinbones seemed to slam into his knees; his thighbones seemed to slam into his hips. Even his ribs ached. He tried to come down on his heels but came down on the flat of his foot instead. His feet went *slap-slap* on the black macadam. The bones of his ankles ground together. Lemuel was already twenty-five yards ahead. Bushes and reeds rose up on either side; the ocean was off to the right beyond the dunes. The path curved between several ponds and a stream. The ducks were just getting settled again when Ralph hurried by after his son. They would flurry away across the water. The path curved again. Lemuel was no longer even in sight. Ralph tried to run faster. His breath was like a sharp thing in his throat. Trickles of sweat ran into his eyes and stung. The inside of his thighs rubbed together and the fabric of his undershirt chafed his nipples. Even his hands felt heavy. When the heart attack came, Ralph didn't even know what it was.

He had shooting pains in his chest and down both arms. He stopped running; then he found himself lying on the path. There was no noise at all except for birdcalls and, in the distance, the sound of the surf. Above him a single cloud shaped like a bicycle floated across the blue sky. There were gulls. He turned his head to look for Lemuel but he was nowhere in sight. He tried to rub his chest. He felt like he was burning and he couldn't get his breath. In falling, he had skinned both knees. They hurt but he couldn't imagine where the pain was coming from. It was as if pain were a room he had entered and the door had been locked behind him. A heron walked across the path as stately as an undertaker.

Ralph shut his eyes. There was the sound of footsteps running. Ralph opened his eyes. Lemuel was coming back.

"Oh, shit," said Lemuel. "Oh, shit."

He knelt down by his father.

"I don't know what's wrong," said Ralph. His voice was no more than a whisper.

"Did you twist your ankle?"

"No, nothing like that."

"Can you get up?"

"I can't even move."

Lemuel carried him to the car. Ralph felt strange in his son's arms and was afraid Lemuel would drop him. His head hung in the crook of Lemuel's elbow and he looked backward and upside down into the marsh. Ducks and geese were standing on their heads. Lemuel put him in the back seat of the Caravan and drove to the hospital. Two orderlies came running out of Emergency with a stretcher. Ralph felt glad he wasn't someplace like New York City where he would have been made to wait.

Lemuel wasn't allowed to visit him until that afternoon. By then the doctor had talked to them both about the heart attack. Ralph was hooked up to half a dozen machines. Several hummed, and sometimes in his heavily medicated state he imagined he was part of an air conditioner or heating unit. The doctor spoke about the possibility of a bypass operation. Ralph would have to be transferred to Baltimore or Washington. Joanie had been called and was driving down. Ralph kept wanting to say, It's not that serious; everybody keep calm. But the nurses looked at him gravely and it made him scared.

Lemuel came in around three. Ralph was struck by how bad he looked, as if somebody big had slapped him several times.

"I'm sorry," he kept saying. "I'm sorry."

"Hey," Ralph whispered, "it's not your fault."

"I made you run fast. I was trying to get away."

"I ran," said Ralph. He didn't want to talk a whole lot. "I ran all by myself. You didn't make me do it."

Lemuel knelt by the bed. Ralph wanted to tell him to get up because he couldn't see him. He wanted to look at his son's face. Then he felt his forehead against his stomach. Ralph reached out and touched Lemuel's hair. He thought of its reddish-brown color. He stroked it.

"It's okay," he said. "You wouldn't let us get laid so I did this instead. It was my own big idea." Ralph started to laugh, then didn't. He kept stroking Lemuel's hair and staring forward out the window. It had gotten cloudy, but maybe it was fog. Fog rolling in from the ocean. He could hear a bell tolling from a buoy and now and then a foghorn. Seagulls flew across the window, flapping hard as if they had someplace important to get to. A nurse pushed a cart down the hall and Ralph could hear the glassware clinking together. It was a noise almost like music.

OUT ON THE WATER

Bobby called his wife La Rosa Luminosa, but that was before.

They were married in Chicago but moved to Benton Harbor, where Bobby worked for Zenith. Bobby said Harriet didn't have to get a job. She could work on her novel. Instead, she had two children and wrote a weekly column for the Benton Harbor paper called Harriet's Hints. Even into her thirties she had very white skin with a tinge of pink and fine blond hair that flew all over her head. La Rosa Luminosa: the luminous rose.

Her children, a son and daughter, inherited her hair: nearly white and unmanageable. The doctors had a name for it: Bent Hair Syndrome. It was a more important word than *messy*. "It's like an angel's hair," Bobby would say. "It shows their blessedness."

Nothing in Bobby's life seemed as wonderful as his marriage to Harriet. She was the garden it was his duty to tend. He had first seen her in a journalism class at the University of Illinois at Chicago Circle. He had followed her back to her apartment and sat outside till she noticed him. She had another boyfriend at the time but he couldn't compete. One night Bobby slept outside her door and she found him in the morning, cheerful and eager to serve her. She personally didn't know what the fuss was about. She had never thought of herself as blessed. She wanted to be a reporter and see the seamy side of life.

Her columns helped women cope with their kitchens, their housekeeping chores, their gardens. One week it was dripping faucets, the next it was Japanese beetles. She wrote the column because the managing editor wouldn't let her cover fires and homicides and abused children. Now and then she would do an article on the activities of the Benton Harbor Women's Guild or the Flower Society. Harriet was a small woman, petite. Both of her children had been C-sections. When Bobby looked at her belly, his throat would constrict. The white line of the bikini cut— this is what he had done to her. He saw it as her only flaw. Harriet liked her scar: its hard ridge of puckered skin.

When Harriet was thirty-two, Bobby bought her a dog, a Doberman by the name of Diablo, a two-year-old watchdog with a strong sense of purpose. Diablo didn't play with the children. Toss a ball and Diablo wouldn't even look at it. If he could have stood around with his arms crossed, he would have done it. He growled in his sleep.

A Mexican family had moved into the neighborhood. They were cheerful and middle class but the father had a gold tooth and Bobby didn't like that. He didn't say he had bought Diablo because of the Mexican family, but he spoke of changes. The mail was delivered through a slot in the front door, and every day Diablo tore it up. When guests came over or the children's friends, Diablo would have to be shut in the basement. One could hear him making warning noises through the floor and grinding his teeth. No visitor stayed for long. Harriet asked Bobby to get rid of Diablo but he refused. "You're my treasure," he said. "I'm terrified of something happening."

The children had a cat named Mousy, and Diablo killed the cat. He broke Mousy's neck with a single swipe of his jaws. Diablo had black ears that pointed forward. Like a salute, Bobby thought. Diablo was the kind of dog that would have wanted a tattoo. He always had an agenda.

"I want you to get rid of the dog," Harriet said one night. It was spring and they sat on the patio in their shirtsleeves. From inside came the sound of the television. The children didn't seem to play as much. Diablo hated sudden movements.

"He's your protection," said Bobby. He admired Diablo. If he had been a dog, he would have wanted to be like the Doberman. Diablo sat by Bobby's chair but he didn't like to be patted. He found it distracting.

"I don't need protection," she said.

"The city's changing."

"Things always change."

"I couldn't live if anything happened to you," said Bobby.

Harriet started to speak, then remained silent. Her clothes felt too tight, although she was exactly the same weight as on the day she had married eleven years earlier: one hundred and five pounds. She had once written a column called "How to Make Your Dog Your Friend." What a sham it had been. It was her duty as a journalist to tell the truth. When she tried to give Diablo tasty treats, he refused. He was the only dog she had ever known that wouldn't eat between meals.

Two days later Bobby found Diablo dead in the basement.

"Stress," Harriet said.

The vet said Diablo had been poisoned.

"I bet somebody threw something over the fence," said Bobby. "A poisoned rabbit."

"I don't want another watchdog," said Harriet.

Bobby bought a rust-colored cocker spaniel by the name of Rags. He barked a lot and peed on the rug. Bobby also bought a nine-millimeter pistol and learned how to shoot. Then he taught Harriet to shoot as well. They would take the pistol to the indoor firing range down by the lake and shoot at paper targets of marauders and housebreakers.

"Aim for the whites of their eyes," said Bobby.

Harriet liked how the pistol would kick in her hands when she pulled the trigger. Bobby bought her a little twenty-two pistol with a pearl handle. "A lady's gun," he said. Harriet preferred the nine-millimeter. The lady's gun was no fun at all.

Harriet wrote a Household Hints column on change. "At times a new wind blows into your life. At times you wake up in the morning and feel like a different person. Your family isn't sure if they know you anymore. These changes are perfectly normal, no matter what anybody says."

Bobby put a bigger chain-link fence around the backyard. Sometimes he took down the license plate numbers of cars that drove slowly past the house. "La Rosa Luminosa," he said to Harriet, "how I cherish you."

"My pantyhose feel too tight," said Harriet.

When Harriet bought a motorcycle, Bobby believed he would go crazy. It was a small motorcycle, a Honda 250. It was painted bright red like a fire engine.

"You'll kill yourself," said Bobby.

"Don't be silly," she answered.

Whenever she drove it, Bobby followed in the big Ford Fairlane station wagon, flashing the headlights so people would stay out of her way. She rode it to the newspaper, about ten blocks from their house. People stopped when they drove past. It was like a parade. Even with a helmet, strands of her blond hair would fly around her face—that's how out of control it was.

Bobby had bad dreams about the motorcycle. He would moan for half the night and suddenly jerk awake. He had seen state police driver education films and knew what could happen. There had been pictures of people flung up into the telephone wires and dangling in the semi-dark. Bobby would lie on his back and watch the little red lights on the smoke alarms flicker. Bobby had more smoke alarms than Buckingham Palace. He could feel Harriet sleeping beside him. He would wonder where she went in her dreams and if she looked out for herself. He wished he could follow her into her head. It distressed him to be excluded.

In the mornings he would say to her, "Won't you please get rid of that motorcycle?"

"I like it," Harriet would say. She made oatmeal for everybody. Bobby wouldn't let eggs into the house anymore.

The children liked the motorcycle as well. They begged for rides. Hank was ten. He would sit on the motorcycle in the garage and go, *"Room, room!"*

"Get off of that!" Bobby would shout. "You could fall!"

Little Betty, who was five, would polish the two side mirrors and stare at her reflection. "I look prettier here," she would say. She would beep the horn and smile like an angel.

They had a ranch house in a nice subdivision. Bobby bought security cameras. From the monitors mounted on the kitchen wall, he could see every inch of his property. More monitors were in the basement hobby room, where he worked on his stamp collection and butterfly collection. He had a monarch butterfly in a Lucite half-sphere. The butterfly had its wings outstretched and seemed to be flying, but it wasn't going anyplace. Bobby hired a portrait artist and paid ten thousand dollars to have portraits painted of Harriet and the children. He hung the portraits in the hall so they were the first thing anyone saw when they entered the house. Sometimes Bobby would have Harriet stand next to her portrait and compare them. He put glass over the portraits to keep them safe.

Bobby began to have stomach pains. He put off going to the doctor, thinking the pain would go away, but it didn't. When Bobby finally made an appointment, the doctor told him he was getting an ulcer. He thought of his body changing: the cells that replaced themselves every seven years. Nothing was dependable.

One day in the fall when Bobby was returning from work his foot slipped from the brake to the accelerator as he was entering the garage. The oversized Ford Fairlane leapt forward and crushed the little red motorcycle against the rear wall. Harriet heard the noise and came running. She looked at the bent frame of the Honda 250 as Bobby stood scratching his head. She didn't accuse him of doing it on purpose. She knew he believed it was an accident. "I guess that takes care of that bad business," said Bobby.

That evening at dinner, she asked him about his job. He was an engineer and worked on portable computers. "They may sell the whole thing to the French," he said. "Jesus, what have the French ever done?" As a kid, Bobby had built Heathkits: radios and stereos. Transistors and circuit boards had killed all that. Sometimes he would still read the old instruction manuals before he went to sleep. The steps were so clear! As long as you could solder, there was nothing you couldn't do. The whole world lay open before you.

"Do you think you're working too hard?" asked Harriet.

"I'm just struggling to keep up," he said. They were having pot roast with potatoes and carrots and onions. The children pushed the onions to the sides of their plates. Harriet's hair surrounded her face like a halo. The children's hair made little halos. Bobby couldn't believe how lucky he was. "Chew your food carefully," he told the children.

"Maybe you should change your job," said Harriet.

Bobby couldn't imagine it. "Zenith is part of my life."

"Then let's go on a vacation. Let's go to Mexico."

Bobby considered how one Mexican family moving into the neighborhood had upset him. What would be the effect of a whole country of Mexicans? "I don't know," he said. "I don't think so."

"We could go to Disneyland," said Hank.

Bobby had an immediate image of his son tumbling out of a roller coaster. "I don't think so," he said. "Anyway, it's fall. It's the wrong season for a vacation."

"There's Columbus Day weekend," said Harriet. "We could go to Chicago. The kids have never been to the Art Institute or the Natural History Museum."

"Dinosaurs," said Hank, in the tone of voice that he might have said "Holy men."

Everything in Bobby's nature rebelled against a trip to Chicago. Although he had spent six years there as a student, he had left ten years before. The paper was always full of terrible things happening in Chicago. It seemed to Bobby that places like Chicago were necessary because they drew the terrible things of the world to them. If it weren't for the Chicagos and Detroits and Toledos, the terrible things would spread out across the whole country and make trouble for everybody else. Such places were collectors of badness in the way that hospitals were collectors of the sick and damaged. It would be sheer lunacy to go there.

Harriet and the children kept asking. Bobby was torn between his desire to please his family and his desire to protect them. At last he made a reservation at a hotel right on Michigan Avenue.

They would drive down on Friday after school. Bobby wouldn't take his family up to Old Town, and they would stay out of the Loop except for the daylight hours.

They were late leaving Benton Harbor, but because of the time change it still seemed early when they crossed into Illinois. "Chi town, that's my town," sang Harriet. Piloting the Ford Fairlane through rush-hour traffic on Lake Shore Drive, Bobby kept the doors locked and both hands on the wheel. He was careful not to make eye contact with other drivers. He parked in the hotel's underground garage, and when he reached the lobby he was breathing hard. The kids kept wanting to run off in separate directions. *Explore* was the word they used. For Bobby it was a word as dangerous as *cocaine*. A bellhop carried their bags to a nonsmoking suite on the twelfth floor. Bobby made him show them the fire exits, then tipped him five dollars. He wanted the bellhop to respect him but not find him slavish. The bellhop didn't appear to notice.

Harriet helped Bobby unpack. "You brought your pistol?" She was surprised to see it at the bottom of his overnight case.

Bobby removed the nine-millimeter and put it in a drawer by the bed. "You can never be too careful," he said.

They saw a movie on the Disney channel and had dinner in their suite. The kids had a room overlooking the lake, and Bobby made sure the window did not open. Harriet ordered a bottle of champagne. After the kids had gone to bed, she popped the cork and said, "I want to be wild." They made love. Her hair kept whipping across his face. Bobby felt nervous and kept his eye on the door the whole time. After she fell asleep, he relaxed. He had a glass of champagne and wandered around the suite. He went to the kids' window and looked out at the lake. There was an orange glow from Michigan Avenue and the surrounding buildings. The honking of cars was a distant tintinnabulation. Far out on the lake a light was twinkling. Bobby thought how lonely it must be out in the darkness away from one's family and loved ones. He imagined sailing alone under the stars in a small boat and being filled with longing and confusion.

Saturday they went to the Art Institute and the Natural History Museum. The children kept saying how big everything was. Harriet loved the Impressionist paintings: the breasts of the Renoir women and their gauzy fabrics. It seemed they walked for miles. In the evening they saw *Guys and Dolls* and the kids fell asleep before intermission. The singing was not like rap singing. Afterward they took the kids back to the hotel and put them to bed. An elderly woman employed by the hotel came up to the room to baby-sit. She had pink cheeks, and her white hair was collected in a bun on the top of her head. Her name was Mrs. MacDonald. Bobby and Harriet had a late dinner at a steak house on Wabash where they had gone several times during their engagement. It was drizzling, and they wore matching tan raincoats. Bobby didn't like the side street and kept urging Harriet to hurry. She wore high heels and walked as fast as she could. She loved how the buildings disappeared above her in the fog. She kept stopping to look up and her hair glistened with tiny beads of water.

They had turf and surf and a bottle of Châteauneuf-du-Pape. The headwaiter was the same man who had been there twelve years before. That made Bobby very happy. Bobby asked the man if he remembered them and he said he thought he remembered Harriet's blond hair. Briefly, Bobby imagined revisiting all their old haunts and finding the same people doing the same things. He imagined living the same minute over and over. He imagined reliving his wedding day again and again. For dessert they had baked Alaska and two Rémys. It was after one o'clock when they left. Bobby wanted to take a cab but Harriet insisted on walking.

It was only four blocks. She wanted to clear her head and feel the cool drizzle against her face.

"A cab will be here right away," said Bobby. But Harriet was already crossing Wabash, and Bobby had to run to catch up with her.

It was when they were walking up Madison that it happened. A man came out of an alleyway. Seeing him, Bobby thought it was something that had happened already; he had been so certain of danger that the man's appearance wasn't even surprising. A large black man staggered between the curb and the building. "Hey!" he shouted. A streetlight was out. The man stood between them and Michigan Avenue. There were no cars.

"Get back," said Bobby, and he pushed Harriet behind him.

"Hey, man, I want you," said the black man.

"He's drunk," said Harriet.

"It's a trick," said Bobby. He put his hand in his pocket.

"Hey, man, I need something," said the black man. His face was almost invisible. Only his teeth showed.

"Go back where you came from!" shouted Bobby. "Leave us alone!"

The black man swayed back and forth. He was about ten feet away. "Hey!" he shouted again. He began fumbling for something under his coat. He took a couple of steps toward Bobby.

Bobby drew the nine-millimeter pistol and fired three times. The black man cried out and fell to the sidewalk. The gunshots reverberated up into the darkness.

"Oh, no," said Harriet.

"Don't get near him," said Bobby. "It's not safe."

They stood in the drizzle as the black man twisted on the sidewalk, moaning and clutching at himself. Bobby held the pistol with both hands and looked up and down the street. He heard Harriet sobbing behind him. After a while the police came.

The sergeant's name was Lucas. He took away Bobby's pistol. "You shoot some drunken panhandler because he wants a quarter? You fuckin' crazy?"

They were in a precinct station. Harriet sat in a chair with her face in her hands.

"He was reaching for something," said Bobby. "He had a gun."

"He had fuckin' nothing," said Lucas. "He had a fuckin' card saying he was a vet."

"Will he die?" asked Harriet.

"He's got a hole in his leg. He won't walk good anymore. He has a hard enough time being a crazy drunken vet, and then some out-of-towner has to go and shoot him."

"We can give him some money," said Bobby.

"It's too fuckin' late," said Lucas.

They drove back to Benton Harbor on Sunday. The kids kept asking what had happened but neither Bobby nor Harriet wanted to talk about it. Bobby would have to go back to Chicago, but it was unlikely that charges would be pressed.

"If I was the fuckin' judge," Lucas had said, "I'd handcuff you to that old bum for the rest of your life."

Bobby kept trying to talk to Harriet but she wouldn't look at him. "La Rosa Luminosa," he said. But she looked out the window at the fruit trees and felt glad that winter was coming on. Bobby kept reimagining the bum digging into one of his pockets and staggering toward him. He tried to find a reason for what he had done. Hadn't the man made a threatening gesture? There were lots of reasons for what he had done, but none that he liked. He thought of his marriage and graduate school, of taking the job with Zenith and buying the house in Benton Harbor. He had arranged the furniture and put up his mailbox. He had thought of the life he had planned for the two of them as stretching ahead and how it was different from the life he had now and how he would never have imagined shooting a defenseless person.

When they got home, Harriet went to bed. Bobby sat in front of the TV and watched football, but he wasn't paying attention. He stared at the men in their tight uniforms crashing into each other. Now and then one of the players would be carried off the field on a stretcher. The children were in the backyard with Rags. Sometimes Bobby heard one of them shout. It didn't occur to him that Hank had fallen from the apple tree or that Betty had twisted her ankle. Often Bobby found the ads on TV consoling. They presented a world of exact value. But this Sunday afternoon he paid no attention. In his hand he kept feeling the kick of the pistol. He wondered where the other two bullets had gone. He thought of the blood that must still be on the sidewalk.

On Tuesday morning Harriet went to the beauty parlor and had her hair cut short. Then she had it dyed black. She also had four more earrings put into her right ear. When Bobby saw her that evening, he couldn't speak. Just a croaking noise, no more than that. He felt his voice had been torn from his throat.

"Neat, Mom," said Hank. "Punk."

Bobby went downstairs to his butterfly collection and wept. The hobby room had gray cinder-block walls and a green rug like Astroturf. He looked at his monarch butterfly in its little Lucite dome. He thought how Snow White had been placed in a glass coffin by the seven dwarfs and how she had remained beautiful and unchanging. When the prince had showed up on his horse to wake her, why didn't the dwarfs chase him away? Bobby began to think of himself as a dwarf, even smaller than Betty. But he wasn't the kind of dwarf who whistled while he worked. He was a dwarf who dug deep in the mountain and suffered and hoarded his gold. He wondered what the bum's name had been and why he hadn't asked at the time. Wednesday morning he called Sergeant Lucas in Chicago.

"Philpotts," Lucas said. "His name's Benny Philpotts."

Bobby was astonished that he had shot someone with such a silly name. It was like shooting a child.

"How's he doing?" asked Bobby.

"He's depressed," said Lucas. "Who wouldn't be?"

"Can't he get job training?" asked Bobby. "Or go back to school?"

"Mister," said Lucas, "it's just not that kind of world."

Every time Bobby saw Harriet's hair, he felt a pain in his side. Her black hair was like a sign of mourning for the life they no longer had. And she wasn't friendly to him. She was barely civil. She wrote a column on metamorphosis and transfiguration. "Many women feel a need to change their lives. Their homes become their prisons. They feel as if they can't breathe." She bought new clothes, sexier dresses.

When Harriet began her affair with the city editor, she made no secret of it. She told Bobby they had gone to a motel. "I can either move out or you can move out or we can both stay here and get used to it."

He told her he didn't want her to move out and he didn't want to move out either. They had the children to consider.

"You can fit a bed into your hobby room," she told him.

The editor's name was Frank Slovak. He addressed people as "guy" and "bub." He had nicotine stains between his index and middle fingers. He wore a torn London Fog raincoat and a fedora hat. Twice a week he took Harriet dancing. Sometimes they went to the movies and Harriet didn't get home until dawn.

Bobby would wait for her to come home. He would lie in his narrow bed in the hobby room. On the wall were his butterflies. He could see them glitter in the crack of light from the hall. He imagined they were moving their wings and he imagined putting more pins into them.

Frank Slovak would pick Harriet up at the house in his red Ford Mustang. The first few times Bobby would answer the door. "Hey, guy!" Slovak would say, with a big grin.

Bobby stopped answering the door. Sometimes when Slovak showed up, Bobby would be in the backyard tossing a football with Hank, who was now eleven. Hank would throw the ball. Bobby would catch it and hug it to his chest. He would run his fingers over the stitching. He would look at how the sky was all gray toward the lake. The doorbell would be ringing. Bobby would think of the water of Lake Michigan and how cold it must be. He thought of being out on the water, of being tossed up and down in a small boat. He thought of the waves constantly arriving, always new and always the same. He could almost see it—no sign of the shore, the gray line of the horizon, the day getting darker. He thought of the loneliness out there.

Hank would grow impatient. "You got to throw the ball back, Dad," he would call. "You can't just hang on to it."

WITH FRANZ AND JANE

Janet had seen herself as happily married, but in September Fred fell in love with a woman who sat across the aisle on the shuttle flying down to New York. They had started talking about golf, then moved on to contemporary poetry. When Fred returned to Boston two days later, Janet's marriage was over.

"Anyone can fall in love," Fred told her. He had a charming smile, which made him look about twelve. It was the first thing that had attracted her to him seven years earlier. "It's like being hit by lightning," he said. "Nobody can be blamed."

Within two days he was gone, taking his rolltop desk but leaving her with the twins.

Janet was teaching two composition classes at Boston University, an adjunct position in the English department with no benefits, no credibility, no future. As she sat in her office the day after Fred's departure, she searched her memory for important literary texts to serve as illustrative icons to guide her through her present predicament. No one used the word "book" anymore.

"Things fall apart," she told her ten o'clock class. "The center will not hold; mere anarchy is loosed upon the world."

There was some discussion. "What's 'anarchy,' Mrs. Flynn?" asked one student.

Anarchy, she wanted to say, is what's always waiting around the corner. Instead, she said "Lawlessness"; then she told them how anarchy had originally meant the lack of a ruler, which could also mean self-governance and increased civic responsibility. She shifted smoothly into Bakunin and his contribution to democratic thought. What she liked about teaching was how it took the world's random phenomena and imposed order and design. In the classroom, there was no confusion. In the classroom, one's husband of six years did not run away with a woman he had met on the shuttle. Self-governance, Janet asked herself. Is this what I have to look forward to?

"Her name's Meg," Fred had told her. "I look into her eyes and go into an emotional swan dive. My knees get all wobbly. Haven't you always liked green eyes?"

The twins were two and a half. They were not identical but almost: blond, sturdy, and flat-footed. They were rudimentary intellectuals and had fallen in love with the word "no." They had strict ideas as to how the world should be ordered. Yet when the unexpected happened, like chunks of plaster falling from the ceiling, they accepted it philosophically as part of a grander design. The disappearance of their daddy was mysterious and sad but made sense in some way they were struggling to grasp.

"The world is big," said Harry.

"Bigger than our block," said Matt.

Their father had fallen into this world. It was an explanation with which Janet couldn't quarrel. She thought of those houses perched on California hillsides that always seemed to be tumbling down a slope to become toothpicks in a ravine. Wasn't that the natural order of things? Surely, the people who bought those houses had an idea of permanence that bordered on the psychotic.

Janet stopped reading Jane Austen—the subject of her Ph.D. dissertation—and began reading Kafka. The fact that Gregor Samsa awoke to find himself transformed into a gigantic insect was almost reassuring. Hey, he was lucky. It could have been worse.

"Kafka is telling us not to make plans," she told her two o'clock class.

She and Fred had rented the top half of a house in Cambridgeport, a section of Cambridge that jutted out into the Charles like a fat peninsula. Boston University lay just across the river, and she often rode her bike to work. For some years the area had been in the process of gentrification. But it was like a hair transplant: one constantly doubted it would take. Often at night she would hear young men quarreling in the street and once there had been gunshots. The mysterious forces that led to these quarrels were the same forces that introduced Fred to Meg on the 9 A.M. shuttle. Maybe the enemy was a form of social entropy.

"Kafka is telling us that beyond our world of illusion is a world of hard truths," she told her two o'clock class.

"Isn't that awfully pessimistic, Mrs. Flynn?" asked a student.

Janet didn't see it as pessimistic, only as useful wisdom, like the fact that moss grew on the north side of trees and knowing what green plants one could eat in the woods. It was survival lore. "It's best to learn these things when young," she said. "The way to protect yourself from being turned into a beetle is to be prepared for it." She herself was twenty-six, and she felt this information had come too late.

Her parents lived in Castine on a hill overlooking Penobscot Bay. "Down East," her father liked to say. On the telephone, her mother kept asking, "Had everything been all right at home? Have the twins been crying a lot? Have you been reading too much? He must have had some reason."

Her father offered a thousand dollars to help with the rent. "Is he paying child support?"

"He didn't even leave a forwarding address," said Janet.

The twins would look up at her from the kitchen floor. Their expressions seemed to be saying, How strange! Fred had taught them to call him "the big guy" and they kept repeating, "Where's the big guy?" They said it all day long and it became like a birdcall.

It was early October and there were still hot days. Janet would take the twins to Harvard Square, sit on a bench, and let them eat ice cream. They didn't eat it so much as participate with it. She watched the hundreds of people hurrying to hundreds of specific destinations. They've got a shock coming, thought Janet. In graduate school she had had a friend who carried a small wooden block in her purse just to knock on when she needed it. Janet bought a science magazine at Nini's with an article about comets whipping around the earth. It was only a matter of time before one hit Boston. The blue sky was just a distraction to keep one from seeing what was always there.

"Kafka is telling us that free will is a phantasm," she told her class. "Anything can happen at any moment. Never sit with your back to the door."

"Have you thought of seeing a therapist?" asked her friend Shirley, with whom she shared an office at B.U. "You need to reknit yourself."

Maybe that's it, thought Janet. I have a run in my soul.

But sitting at home at night, when the twins were in bed and with a stack of papers in her lap, she would think how she missed Fred, missed being held by him, and it was hard to imagine life going right again. His arms had felt so permanent. And she believed that if it hadn't been for the twins and their need of her, she would have gone spinning off into space.

The danger of being whisked into the sky was one she began to worry about. Increasingly, as she rode her bike across the B.U. Bridge above the Charles, she felt as exposed as a cockroach on an empty plate. She would hunker down over her handlebars and will herself to stay on the ground. She thought heavy thoughts. Although she was only five feet six and slender, she filled her mind with images of enormous beasts: elephants and hippos, even dinosaurs. It was a ten-minute ride by bike. A bus would take half an hour and the T could take forty-five minutes. Even so, she wasn't sure she had the courage to keep riding across the bridge. She imagined herself sucked into the air like a feather caught in an updraft. She had always felt small; now she felt smaller.

Janet began to seek out stories of strange disappearances and spontaneous combustion. She was positive many terrible things happened to people that never made it into the papers. She paid more attention to the tabloids in supermarket checkout lanes, which described people who fell asleep for twenty years or aliens who used powerful lasers to scoop up people from city streets like a vacuum cleaner sucks dust kitties from under the bed. She felt surrounded by dangers that had never worried her before, and she felt lucky to have survived for so long despite her ignorance. Looking at the sky, she imagined a rip in the fabric. She felt pursued by that rip, a jagged slit in the air, as if at any moment there existed this sudden unexpected exit and some sinister something was always tugging her toward it.

Fred wrote and asked her to send him his clothes. "We're in Montana. You wouldn't believe the sunsets. I feel my life is just beginning."

Janet took Fred's clothes, even his leather jacket, and dumped them in the Salvation Army drop box in the parking lot at Star Market. She also put in his shoes, his umbrella, and the beret he had bought during their honeymoon in France. She wished she could take all the memories of being together, the times they made love or when they had simply talked, or when the twins had been born, or when they first met at a party at Columbia and he had said how he loved her yellow hair—she wished she could shove these memories into the drop box as well, and she stood in the parking lot and wept with her head resting against the red metal. Cars slowed and shoppers with bags of groceries looked at her curiously. Then she got back in her rusty Honda Civic and drove home. At four o'clock she picked up the twins at day care and tried to be patient and loving, but all she really wanted to do was get in bed, pull the covers up to her eyebrows, and wake up in another life.

Even though she saw herself as a feminist, she realized how much she had depended on Fred to take care of the bills, to see that the car was running properly, and to carry out the garbage. They had been married after her sophomore year in college. He had been a graduate student in Columbia's MFA program. Writing a novel had stretched ahead of him just like the Antarctic had stretched ahead of Captain Scott. For six years he had done preparatory work, gathering notes and writing a number of practice chapters, while Janet worked on her Ph.D. The novel concerned the philosophical necessity of being spiritually challenged. It was set on the streets of New York. The main character was a young doctor named Willard who joins the ranks of the homeless in order to experience totemic isolation. Fred talked about

Willard so often he was like a member of the family, an invisible sibling to the twins.

Not only did Janet miss Fred, she missed Willard as well. She had come to think of him as living inside the rolltop desk. Now that desk was in Montana on the back of Meg's pickup truck. Now Janet was carrying out the trash by herself and trying to figure out the telephone bill and the electric bill and whether the car needed an oil change. In the *Boston Phoenix*, Janet saw ads for feminist car mechanic courses and she thought seriously about enrolling. She didn't mind making some of the decisions in her life, but she hated making them all.

One Saturday morning in the middle of October, Janet took the twins to Harvard Square. She had no particular errands but she couldn't face a Saturday morning in the apartment with the lively chatter of cartoon shows, nor did she feel strong enough for any other project such as coloring or playing horse. It was a bright sunny morning with a crisp breeze. She decided that in the afternoon they would drive out to Lexington and buy apples and perhaps a pumpkin. Occasionally, she looked at the sky, hoping to see ragged Vs of geese flying south.

They took the bus to the Square. The twins sat by the window and pointed at things. They had eerie communication skills and could exchange information with no words passing between them. She wondered if they could ever be lonely or if being a twin meant a constant loneliness that was beyond her comprehension: the loneliness of being always a fragment.

In front of the shops along Holyoke half a dozen street musicians were playing their separate and conflicting musics: guitars, keyboards, and saxophones, pop music and classical. Standing between two of them produced cacophony, but standing in front of one it was hard to hear the others. A young man with a guitar and half a dozen harmonicas sang old labor songs in front of a clothing store.

> *Homeless, homeless are we,*
> *Just as homeless as homeless can be.*
> *We don't get nothing for our labor,*
> *So homeless, homeless are we.*

It was a song with many verses. Before him on the sidewalk lay an open guitar case with coins and dollar bills. The twins tried to take the coins but Janet stopped them. Her reasoning made no sense to them but they smiled at her with kindly indulgence. They watched the singer. He had red hair in a ponytail and a bright red-and-blue plaid shirt. He looked about Janet's age, perhaps younger. The twins liked the simplicity of the labor songs and bounced gently on their toes. Janet kept glancing around, almost without knowing what she was looking for. Even though Fred was in Montana, she kept expecting to see him. She knew this was preposterous, but she kept looking for his face to appear from the mass of people and make everything good again. It made her dislike herself.

The musician suddenly shouted, "Hey!" Then he rushed past her, still holding his guitar. Turning, Janet saw that Harry had stepped off the curb. There was a lot of traffic and Harry stood a foot off the curb staring at the sky. Cars began honking. The musician snatched up Harry and returned him to the sidewalk. Janet's mind had wandered; she had stopped paying attention. And in that moment her son could have been killed.

Janet knelt beside Harry and squeezed him tight. She began to sob. Although Harry was unhurt, the burst of emotion from his mother made him cry as well. Then Matt embraced them and soon all three were crying. Through her tears Janet saw the color-fully patched knees of the musician's jeans upright beside her. She couldn't stop crying. She knew she wasn't just crying for Harry but for the whole situation beginning with the departure of her husband and how that departure and her grief had let her forget her duty to her children and she hadn't even noticed when one of them strayed into the street.

The musician stood next to her, looking concerned. "Hey," he said softly, "it's all right. Nothing touched him."

Janet was embarrassed by her tears but she had no control over them. She even wondered how long they would continue. An hour, two hours? She imagined the steady flow of salty water making a lake at her feet. It would be something at which she might excel. Passersby gave them a wide berth, leaving them as a little island of sadness in the middle of the sidewalk.

"Come on," said the musician. "I'll get us some cappuccinos." He packed away his guitar and harmonicas and led them past the Coop to a Starbucks over on Church Street. "Maybe the kids could have juice. They like scones?"

Janet let herself be directed. She didn't want to make any decisions. She held the twins' small hands and squeezed them too tightly without thinking.

"My name's Antelope," said the musician, as he held open the front door of the coffee shop. "Of course, I wasn't baptized Antelope, but I've been Antelope since high school and so I think of myself as Antelope in all my conversations with myself."

Janet nudged the twins along ahead of her. She stopped crying. "What was your name before it was Antelope?"

"My parents called me Tommy Epstein. I mean, their name was Epstein and they called me Tommy. But from the very beginning, I didn't feel like a Tommy Epstein. It wasn't me somehow.

Once I hit on the name of Antelope, I knew that was the right name. I'd tried some others before that, like Zebra and Raccoon, but Antelope felt like an exact fit. I don't particularly believe in the reincarnation stuff, so I couldn't say I was an antelope in a previous life. I'm not saying it's false, but I'm not saying it's true. Sometimes I do singing gigs at colleges and they make me have two names for the check, so in those places I'm A. Antelope. I try to get my mom to call me Antelope, but she just calls me Tommy. My dad's too pissed to call me anything at all."

During this, Antelope steered them to a table by the window, leaned his guitar against the wall, helped the twins remove their jackets, then headed for the counter. Janet had plain black coffee. The twins had mango fruit drinks and crumb cake. The shop was crowded and people kept dropping things. Matt got his crumb cake in his hair. Janet told Antelope their names. "I kept my maiden name, Flynn," she said. "My husband's name is Pepper, Fred Pepper."

"My name's not Matthew," said Matt. "It's Matt."

"Fred ran off with a woman he met on the shuttle," said Janet. "We're still very upset about it."

"The big guy's gone," said Harry.

Janet didn't intend to tell Antelope everything that had happened, yet the subject rose around her as the only one worth talking about. At that very minute Fred could be holding Meg's hand, or worse. "He's a writer," said Janet, "or he wants to be. He took his rolltop desk and old Remington typewriter. He scorns computers. I guess he's lucky that the woman he ran off with has a pickup truck." She found herself choking up again and she sipped her coffee; then she wiped bits of mango pulp from Harry's forehead.

"Relationships, man," said Antelope, "how can you figure

them?" He was twenty-three and from Seattle. He'd been moving across the country, supporting himself with his singing. Sometimes he'd take a bus, sometimes he'd hitchhike. He'd met hundreds of wonderful people and felt humanity had a deep well of benevolent feelings that had hardly been tapped yet.

"People love to feel," he said. "They love to be happy. Music is like a door into their deep isolated centers."

Matt crawled into Antelope's lap and was looking drowsy. Harry was walking around the coffee shop to see what other people were eating.

"We were going to drive out to Lexington and get some apples," said Janet. "Would you like to come?"

"Where would we be without apples?" said Antelope. "Johnny Appleseed was like an itinerant musician. Instead of songs, he planted seeds."

They took a bus back to the house. Janet made peanut butter and cheddar cheese sandwiches. Antelope didn't eat meat. "It would be like eating my brothers and sisters." He played horse with Matt and Harry. He looked at Fred's books. "Did he really read all these books?" he asked.

"Most of them are going into the Salvation Army drop box as soon as I can pack them up," said Janet.

"Did your ex ever publish anything?" asked Antelope.

Janet thought, My ex, is he really my ex? She imagined a black X painted across Fred's photograph, an X across his face in each of her memories. It made her sad. It was like driving out of a town but not yet arriving at a new one. Fred had become something disappearing in her rearview mirror, while ahead was nothing but desolate landscape.

"He had some stories in small magazines," she said.

She put the sandwiches into a brown paper bag. They would buy cider and apples and have a picnic. She got a blanket, napkins, cups, and extra sweaters for the twins. Antelope helped carry everything down to her Honda. He left his guitar on the couch but took one of his harmonicas.

Janet drove out of Cambridge on Route 2. "Would you like to stop at Walden?"

"Thoreau's my main man," said Antelope. He had been playing "Jingle Bells" on the harmonica for Matt and Harry.

They parked in the lot between two Volvo station wagons. A park policeman directed traffic. More than a hundred people were visible walking around the edge of the pond. Matt wanted to go swimming and Janet had to tell him it was too cold. Harry threw a pinecone into the water.

"Think of living out here one hundred and fifty years ago," said Antelope. "There were probably bears."

"His mother brought him milk and cookies every day," said Janet. She was struck by the crowd of people wearing clothes from L. L. Bean and Eddie Bauer. She thought of them as seeking out scraps of spirituality like children searching for eggs on an Easter egg hunt. Was this how they kept from being frightened? When they got back to the car, she saw that her left front tire was flat.

"Oh, no," she said. "Now what?"

"No problem," said Antelope. He removed the jack and squatted down on the muddy ground. Janet had never changed a tire. She assumed one had to take the car to a garage. She even wondered if the tire was safe when attached by an unlicensed mechanic. "This spare isn't good for much," said Antelope, "but it'll get us to Lexington and back." He washed his hands in the pond and wiped them on his jeans. "It's like baptizing my hands in Thoreau's water," he said. "It makes them tingle."

They found a farm that sold apples and cider. There were

picnic tables but most were occupied by the same kinds of people whom Janet had seen at Walden Pond: couples with a deep sense of correctness in their dress, behavior, and automobile choices. They looked on-track and their marriages would last forever: lives without cancer or heartbreak. Janet drove on to a picnic area by the side of the road. Antelope carried the bags to the table. Janet poured cider into cups.

"Where are all the buildings?" asked Matt. He distrusted the countryside and its openness. Janet worried he might have genetically acquired her fear of being sucked into the sky.

They had lunch and Antelope talked about his travels. "I'd like to settle down in Oregon with a small farm, and other times I think about living in Maine and fishing. Or maybe I'll go back to school." He had dropped out of the University of Washington after his sophomore year. "Being an anthropology major was too much, but I could dig living with a tribe of headhunters and learning how they operate." The twins collected pinecones and made squeaking noises on Antelope's harmonica. "My parents split up when I was a kid," he said. "They both remarried. It's like having two places and no place at the same time."

It was dark when they got back to Cambridge. The twins had fallen asleep in the back seat and Janet and Antelope carried them upstairs. Janet thought that without him she would have had to wake the twins, since she could only carry one at a time and she wouldn't have wanted to leave one alone in the car. She thought, The world is designed for couples. People weren't meant to be by themselves.

She put the twins in bed and gave Antelope a beer. When she joined him, she said, "I'd never thought about the possibility of my marriage coming to an end."

Antelope was playing some sad tune on his guitar.

"And if there was no permanence in my marriage," said Janet, "there was no permanence anywhere. Everything became scary."

"I'd spend the summer and holidays with my dad," said Antelope, "and the rest of the year with my mom. After a while, that was just the way things were—until I changed my name, of course. Changing my name was like getting my own divorce."

She gave him dinner, pasta with pesto, and he played songs for her. Later in the evening he told her he wanted to make love to her, but she didn't want to. "I'm not ready yet," she said. But actually she found nothing sexual about him. He seemed contemporary with the twins. He was young and his face looked unused. She remembered how he had changed the tire and she liked that. But she still didn't want to have sex with him.

"Do you mind if I crash on your couch?" he said. "My stuff's in Somerville and I'm just passing through."

He went to bed and she read for a while. She tried to read Jane Austen—*Emma*—but Austen's orderly world felt wrong to her. It didn't account for enough. At this rate she would have to change the thesis topic. She imagined writing on Kafka or Céline. She missed Jane Austen but didn't see how to get back to her. At last she looked in on the twins, brushed her teeth, and went to bed. As she got comfortable, she heard Antelope snoring softly from the living room.

Very late she was roused by screaming. At first she thought it was the twins and she was halfway to their room before she was really awake. "No, no!" came a voice. Then she realized it was Antelope. She hurried to the couch and half tripped over his guitar case. "No, no!" he cried.

Janet knelt beside him and touched her hand to his cheek. His face was wet with sweat and his hair was stuck to his forehead. The light from the streetlight through the window made his face look orange. When she touched him, his eyes flicked open. "Shit," he said, "oh, shit." He was shaking and she put her arms around him.

"They almost got me," he said.

"Who?"

"I don't know, these men." He continued to shiver and she held him. He was thin and she felt his ribs and the bones in his shoulders. The twins were making rustling noises and she went to check on them. When she came back, Antelope was sitting on the edge of the couch with his head in his hands. She smoothed his hair for a minute; then she took his hand and led him to her bed.

They didn't make love but she held him until he went back to sleep. She heard no sounds from the street. She liked the feel of him but she knew it wasn't Antelope in particular but the idea of a human being in general that comforted her. She slept a little, then woke at daybreak. Antelope's back was to her in a way that almost let her imagine he was Fred. But Fred was gone. He was no more. Janet wondered if she wanted Antelope to stay with her, but she only had to begin the question to realize that she didn't.

As Janet recalled her day with Antelope, her mind drifted toward her aging Honda. She decided to take the automotive course she had seen advertised in the *Phoenix*. It seemed like a constructive gesture, a movement in a direction away from imagined victimhood. Then she again saw Harry wandering into the street. How could she be so caught up in her grief as to forget her children? Fred was gone, and later she would take the rest of his things to the Salvation Army drop box. Perhaps Antelope would help her.

In her imagination she looked for the tear in the fabric, the slit in the stage set of the world. It was smaller now. Franz Kafka on one side, Jane Austen on the other: older siblings to keep her from playing in traffic. Antelope made a moaning sound and Janet patted his back. She would make applesauce in the morning. She would buy a book on car repair. A street cleaner whooshed by outside. In the backyard the morning's first crow announced the dawn with its raucous three-caw greeting.

DEVIL'S ISLAND

When Caspar Boudreau parked his little Toyota in the garage and shut off the engine, he heard laughter from inside his house. It was Thursday afternoon and Joyce was entertaining her bridge group. He listened. The laughter reminded him of turkeys gobbling together. Caspar imagined their eight heads lined up on the walkway as he went from one to another with his little hatchet: chop, chop, chop. Caspar Boudreau ran his tongue across his small teeth; then he opened the trunk of the Toyota to fetch the groceries.

Holding four bags, he kicked at the kitchen door but no one came. Caspar set down the bags and unlocked the door. The laughter grew louder. Perhaps one of the women had heard news that her husband had died and they were planning how to spend the insurance money. Caspar carried the bags into the kitchen, put them on the counter, and stuck his head into the dining room, where the women were playing cards at two tables.

Joyce must have seen him, but she was dealing and didn't look up. A cigarette was stuck in the corner of her mouth and her left eye was squinched shut against the smoke. "You get my eye shadow?"

"I got everything on the list," said Caspar.

"I'll take a Diet Coke if you have any," said Harriet Newcomb, who lived right across Bailey Street. She didn't look at him either.

"Right away," said Caspar.

There were other requests. Caspar ducked back in the kitchen to put away the groceries. Mostly it was snacks and soft drinks. He heard cards being shuffled, women commenting on their poor hands and the general unfairness of it all. Caspar himself didn't play cards. He had once lost ten dollars playing poker at college in Buffalo twenty-five years earlier and had never played again. At times he thought he might take up chess if he had someone to play with.

He got a tray from the cupboard and set eight glasses on it. He added a bucket of ice and opened two big bottles of Diet Coke and Diet Sprite. Then he opened bags of taco chips and popcorn. He scooped chili dip into several bowls. He sliced the Monterey Jack and arranged the slices. He fanned out thirty Triscuits in a perfect circle on a blue plate. Standing back, he imagined putting a dollop of rat poison in every glass, then adding sugar to conceal the taste. He carried the tray into the dining room.

"Isn't he an angel," someone said.

Caspar offered the tray to each woman. In age they ranged from thirty-five to fifty-five, with Joyce exactly in the middle. They were oversized women with big pores and musky smells and thick earlobes hung with inexpensive gold. They played cards every Thursday afternoon. Caspar thought of them in terms of acreage, which was what he called them in private: the Acreage. He worked nights at the newspaper as a copy editor and so he was often in the house to help out.

"No peanuts?" asked Joyce. She wore a tent-shaped turquoise dress, and her bronze-colored hair was piled high on her head.

"You said not to get any after all," said Caspar.

"I thought you might have changed your mind," said Joyce. She giggled at Lucy Cargrove, her constant bridge partner.

As soon as he could get away, Caspar slipped down to his workroom in the basement. He was a small man, nearly bald on top, who wore white shirts and ties even on the days when he didn't have to be at the paper. In his shirt pocket was a case with four ballpoint pens: red, black, blue, and green. The fronts of his shirts and cuffs were always dotted with specks of ink. He sat down at the table of his workroom, flicked on the overhead light, and put on his green plastic visor, making the top half of the room appear to be underwater. Then he got to work.

Caspar made models of prisons and prison scenes and had been doing it for twenty years: Sing Sing, Alcatraz, San Quentin. The individual scenes included Al Capone in his prison cell, the four Lincoln conspirators being hanged in the yard of Washington's Old Penitentiary, the deaths of the Rosenbergs in the electric chair. On the two shelf-lined walls of his workroom the prisons looked like miniature cities: Leavenworth, Joliet, Jackson. The top shelf had picture books showing prisons from all over the world. Sometimes Caspar gave his prisons away as gifts, but he hated giving a prison to anyone who wasn't appreciative, and not many were.

At the moment Caspar was finishing a model of Devil's Island. There were miniature stone houses surrounded by a high wall. Tiny prisoners in striped suits carried bushels of bananas into a warehouse. Here was the cell where Dreyfus had been kept, and here was Papillon looking from a barred window. Because of his job at the newspaper, Caspar was used to being awake all night and on his off nights he often sat up with a little Scotch and imagined the sufferings of the little people he had made.

Caspar Boudreau had two daughters who still lived at home. Janie was twenty, Elsie was twenty-two. Caspar thought of them as the sergeants. His older daughter was engaged, the younger was in beauty school. He had assumed that Elsie would be moving out next June after the wedding, but recently Joyce had said that Elsie and Bob might have to stay with them until they got settled. Bob worked for Xerox but had been laid off. At the moment he was living off workman's comp and waiting for the right thing to come along. Joyce had said the kids could turn the basement into an apartment. Caspar hadn't made any complaint, even though if he didn't speak up Joyce would see it as settled. There was no place upstairs for him to have a workroom, what with the sewing room and the den. Often Caspar slept in the den when he came home from work because Joyce didn't like being disturbed. But he couldn't work there. As a result he had begun to think of a little studio apartment downtown, perhaps a pied-à-terre, because his solitude was precious to him.

Caspar settled down to his model of Devil's Island. He had read about the spiders and snakes but they were too small to replicate, so he had had to satisfy himself with tiny models of vicious guard dogs. At the moment he was working on the prison graveyard with its rows of white crosses. From upstairs he heard women laughing. Even though they weren't right above him, it seemed they were all stamping their feet, and he imagined them doing a rhinoceros dance. The Acreage is having fun, Caspar thought to himself. He imagined sawing the floor in a circle and having the women crash down into the basement, where he might arrange sharpened stakes or vats of boiling oil. He couldn't decide which. Sometimes the sergeants joined the Acreage to play a few rounds or to spell a woman who had to pee. If Elsie and Bob got the basement, Caspar would be upstairs with the rest of them. There was a great cackling of laughter and stamping of feet. Caspar put his hands over his ears. Perhaps the Acreage was prying the toenails off neighborhood children. He had never heard them so loud before.

Later Caspar learned what the commotion had been about. Joyce told him at dinner. "We've decided to go down to Allegheny State Park next weekend. There're cabins. We'll play cards all night long and cook pancakes for breakfast. Doesn't it sound great? The trees will just be turning." Joyce and the sergeants stared at him blandly. All three had bronze-colored hair, although Joyce's hair color now came from a bottle and the beehive shape was constructed by a fellow named Raul Bobo.

"Won't it be cold?" asked Caspar. He did not particularly like the out-of-doors.

"They have woodstoves. Don't be such a wet blanket. Do you plan to eat your broccoli or just poke at it?"

"Daddy likes to divide his food into little piles," said Janie, chuckling.

"He eats all of one thing before he eats another," said Elsie. "First the chicken, then the rice, then the vegetables."

Caspar didn't mind Joyce and the Acreage going down to Allegheny and taking the sergeants with them. It meant they wouldn't be playing bridge on Thursday and it meant he would have the house to himself over the weekend. But he made sure to look disappointed. He was afraid that if he looked pleased they wouldn't go.

The only person who was upset about the trip to Allegheny

was Bob Lewiston, Elsie's fiancé. "A bunch of women going into the woods? Give me a break!"

He was a hunter who had studied survival training and subscribed to magazines that appealed to mercenary soldiers and paint-ball enthusiasts. He had shaggy brown hair and a shaggy mustache. He was over six feet, and when he stood, he was always hunched over as if ready to leap in any direction. He was twenty-five.

"The cabins have stoves," said Caspar.

"They got black bears down there," said Bob. "They don't like to be riled up in the fall. And it will be bow-hunting season. How'd you like your wife to get an arrow through her gut?"

Caspar thought about it. "It will never happen," he said.

It was Saturday afternoon during the halftime of the Michigan–Ohio State game and Bob was taking a break from the TV to visit Caspar in his workroom. Bob liked the fact that Caspar was a copy editor at the paper. He would say, "Commas are a complete mystery to me. I'm an idea man, not a word man." Bob stood in the doorway. He wore jeans and a Buffalo Bills T-shirt. His face looked like a loaf of unsliced bread standing on end: a loaf of bread with a mustache. "I sure don't like Elsie going down there next weekend. Those bow hunters can be wild men. Howling and throwing moons at the ladies. You want your wife to see some bow hunter's fat white bottom?"

"I hadn't thought about it," said Caspar. He realized his sympathy lay with the bow hunters. He saw the Acreage as disturbing the solitude of the forest.

The week was spent making lists and buying food. Whenever Caspar came upstairs, Joyce or Elsie or Janie was talking about the trip to somebody on the telephone. All three were big women. They wore hard-soled shoes and they walked on their heels, which made the house shake. As they rushed from closet to closet, packing their clothes, the house creaked and the windows rattled.

The women left Saturday morning while Caspar was still asleep. Generally, he got home from the paper between five and six and slept till noon. When he woke up the house was strangely quiet. No vacuum cleaner, no cupboards slamming, no heavy footsteps. At first he couldn't think what was wrong; then he realized they were gone. He got up and walked naked through the house, which he never did when they were home. The cat looked at him and crawled under the couch. Caspar flicked on the public radio station. A pianist was playing a Chopin étude.

Caspar stood in front of Elsie's full-length mirror and did a little dance. He liked being alone in the house. He put his two pink hands on the top of his bald head and turned in a little circle. His penis flopped lazily. He touched his round belly and squeezed it, making half a basketball shape. He trotted his little feet up and down on the shag carpet. When the doorbell rang, he scampered as fast as he could for his bathrobe.

It was Bob. "Well, they're gone." Bob sighed. He went to the refrigerator and got a beer. Caspar began making coffee. He didn't understand why Bob had come over. "They're not there yet," said Bob, "but they're on the road. I hope Elsie's not driving. You know those deer caution signs? She drives right by them. Never looks." He took off his leather jacket and hung it on the back of a kitchen chair.

"I don't know who was driving," said Caspar. "They took two cars." He imagined both cars—vans, actually—upside down in a ditch with the tires spinning.

"They don't even have any weapons," said Bob. "No survival gear, no strike-anywhere matches."

Caspar sipped his coffee. He wondered how long Bob intended to stay. "They'll be all right."

"It's not over till it's over," said Bob. "Mind if I see the game on your tube? Mine's on the fritz."

"I guess it's okay," said Caspar, regretting his words. He didn't watch football himself. It didn't hold his attention: young men leaping on each other.

"Can I see if there's anything else on the radio?" said Bob. "That stuff reminds me of a funeral. It'd be just my luck if Elsie got killed."

Bob remained in the house until midnight. He saw several football games and wandered about aimlessly. Twice he called out for pizza. He took a shower. In the evening he rented a Jackie Chan movie. He laughed and drank beer. Caspar worked on his model of Devil's Island. He put half a razor blade into the guillotine and added an executioner with a black hood.

"Doesn't that stuff fuck up your eyes?" asked Bob. He ducked into the workroom about every fifteen minutes to make sure Caspar was still in the house. "I'd sure hate to have my eyes go on me."

When he left, he said, "I'll stop by for breakfast. Maybe we can call out for waffles."

"You don't need to," said Caspar.

"I worry about you by yourself, old buddy. What if there was a break-in?" Bob held his hands out palms upward to suggest anything could happen.

After Bob left, Caspar poured himself some Johnnie Walker Red, a bigger glass than usual. He thought about Bob as a son-in-law. Caspar was forty-five. His own father was eighty-five and lived in St. Pete, where he played golf every day. Caspar guessed that Bob might remain in his life for fifty more years. He imagined Bob driving across Rochester to his apartment. There were murderers out there, sadists who liked to hurt people just for the fun of it, drunk drivers weaving from one side of the road to the other. Caspar imagined Bob breezing through them and arriving home without a scratch. He sighed. He considered the concept of fairness and how it was something that only happened in other people's lives.

Caspar went to bed at three. He lay in the middle of the king-sized bed and thought of the place he'd rent downtown: a large, airy living room–bedroom combination with a kitchenette. Being at the paper, he could get first crack at the classifieds. It wouldn't be a permanent move, just a quiet retreat.

Bob showed up the next morning at nine. He said he felt restless in his apartment by himself, unable to concentrate. There were noises in the back alley. The people downstairs had a barking dog. His loaf-of-bread face looked anxious. Bob and Elsie always spent weekends together. He watched a Buffalo Bills game and roamed the house. He brought the comics section of the Sunday paper into Caspar's workroom to show him what Garfield was up to. In the afternoon Caspar went out for a walk even though he never went for walks.

"You want me to come with you?" asked Bob.

"I'll be right back."

Caspar walked for two hours. When he returned hungry and exhausted, Bob looked at him with disappointment. "I thought you were coming right back," he said.

"I got lost," said Caspar. It wasn't exactly a lie. It was a warm Sunday in late September. In the blueness of the sky, Caspar had seen the shark-infested waters around Devil's Island. The prisoners who tried to escape to French Guiana by swimming were quickly devoured. Caspar considered making several dozen little sharks and lost track of the time. Besides, what did he have to come home to? Another pizza with Bob?

The Acreage pulled into the driveway at eight o'clock: two Astro vans full of cheerful women. Joyce had called from a gas station two hours earlier, and Caspar made lasagna, a green salad, and garlic bread.

"We had the best time of our lives," said Joyce.

"I laughed until I thought my stomach would burst," said Elsie to her fiancé. "You should have been there."

"I had to keep your dad company," said Bob.

There was a confusion of stories: a raccoon that had gotten into the garbage, a skunk that half paralyzed Molly Jacobs on her way to the toilet, a group of college students from Brockport who had been drinking beer, a cot that mysteriously collapsed in the night, dumping chubby Peggy Fisher on the floor, a deer that had clumped up onto the porch. They had played bridge till three in the morning. Caspar opened two bottles of Chianti and set out the wineglasses. From the dining room came happy talk.

Bob stuck his head through the kitchen door. "Jesus, they're talking of doing it again. Can you beat it?"

And this was the general idea. They had had such a fabulous time they wanted to do it again in two weeks. It would be the second weekend in October and there might not be another opportunity, what with winter approaching. They would take better food and warmer blankets. Still, there were husbands to placate, children to cajole.

"Oh, Caspar won't mind," said Joyce. "He'll just play the whole time with his prisons." When Joyce opened her mouth to laugh, Caspar imagined popping a dead toad inside it. Her bronze-colored hair shook with merriment.

"I think it's a terrible idea," Bob told Elsie. "You were lucky this time, but who knows what might happen next time?"

Elsie patted his cheek. She was a chubby girl with big feet. "I love it when you worry about me," she said.

That night when everyone was asleep Caspar worked on his model of Devil's Island: the stone huts with thatched roofs, the white barracks, tall guard towers. He kept thinking that, while on the outside all appeared calm, inside men were having their manhood challenged with shining knives. They lived in terror. Using a magnifying glass and a small brush, Caspar painted a single face staring from a window. The face was too tiny to make it very intricate. Caspar stared at the man, who he imagined was staring out at the shark-infested sea. What crime had he committed to deserve being sent to Devil's Island? Was he a murderer, a rapist, or even worse?

Caspar sipped his Scotch. If the Acreage drove to Allegheny in two weeks, he would most likely spend the whole time with Bob. And wouldn't there be other trips despite what they said? At least when Joyce and the sergeants were at home they left him alone. Caspar decided he didn't like them going away, but he didn't know what to do about it. If he said he didn't want Bob to come over, the sergeants would get angry. Could he afford to make an enemy of Bob if he was going to be around for half a century? Caspar felt he had to start looking into apartments right away.

The plans to go again to Allegheny grew over the next week. Four extra women decided to come along. Caspar's daughters ran from one room to another, taking things from the closets: Girl Scout songbooks, marshmallow roasting forks. Caspar tried to ignore the disruption. At night he read copy, corrected punctuation, made sure the right words appeared in the right order and no unfortunate puns occurred: no crackdowns on prostitutes or muffs on debutantes. The reporters translated the world into language, and Caspar made that language exact. He made a garden of it. It was not exciting work, but it was good work.

Bob showed up in Caspar's workroom Friday evening. "I can't stand this," he said. "All next weekend will be shot."

Caspar was making a miniature flogging post to set before the governor's bungalow. "You had other plans?" Perhaps Bob had meant to take Elsie to a dance, though they never went anyplace, as if Caspar's house were his future son-in-law's Shangri-La.

"No. She's going to be gone. They'll all be gone. And what are we going to do?" Bob pushed his hands through his hair.

"I have my work," said Caspar.

"Kids' models? Come on, Caspar, tell Joyce you don't like it."

Caspar knew that if he complained, Joyce would cover him with a Niagara of righteous indignation. She hated the least quibble. When he found his pied-à-terre, he would give strict orders to the doorman as to who was welcome. Already he had been checking the classified ads, making phone calls, talking to real estate agents. Still, Caspar didn't want Joyce to go to Allegheny either, if only because it meant being stuck with Bob. "They'll be back."

"Sure," said Bob. "By then I'll have calluses on my butt from sitting. And this isn't going to be the end. There're weekends all year long. Every month has at least four. That's a whole shitload of weekends, Caspar. We got to do something."

"Like what?"

"We need a plan." Bob ducked out of the workroom. He never stayed long, only long enough to disrupt Caspar's thoughts.

The next Thursday, Joyce and the sergeants laid out their camping gear on the living room floor. They were going to take more batteries, a radio. Caspar made four loaves of bread to send along. The Acreage meant to leave earlier, come back later. They were going to take wine and chocolate. Caspar imagined bears feasting on their bodies, crows picking over their bones.

That evening when Bob hurried into Caspar's darkroom his loaf-of-bread face was shiny with optimism. "I got a plan. After this they'll never do it again."

"What is it?"

"I'll tell you after they're gone. I don't really trust you."

Caspar got back from the paper at six-thirty Saturday morning and the Acreage left at seven: fourteen women in two vans. Bob was ringing the doorbell by ten.

"I didn't get to sleep until seven-thirty," said Caspar. His eyes felt sandy.

Bob got a beer from the fridge. "You get plenty of sleep. Look at me, I stayed awake all night worrying. With my blood pressure I don't have the life expectancy of other men my age. It's a constant weight on my brain." He began to look through the cupboards for something to eat.

Caspar prepared coffee. He thought of the top of Bob's head exploding and his brain going *splat* against the ceiling.

"What we're going to do," said Bob, "is drive down there."

"To Allegheny?"

"We'll leave about eight tonight, sneak up to their cabin around two in the morning, and scare the bejesus out of them. They'll never go down there again."

"I'm not going anywhere," said Caspar.

"Sure you are. You want them gone every weekend?"

"I don't know," said Caspar. He disliked going out of town. Then he thought of spending the weekends with Bob.

"You're just afraid of being caught. They'll never see us. I got animal calls. Pumas and wolves. Very realistic. Believe me, the rangers will have to peel them off the walls."

"I don't know," said Caspar again. He imagined Joyce catching him and yelling at him. He imagined the sergeants yelling at him and all the heavyset women of the Acreage. He imagined a Himalaya of verbal abuse being dumped on his head.

"It's all set," said Bob. "I'll swing by later and we can hash out the details."

Caspar sipped his coffee as Bob's Dodge backed out of the driveway. It had a bad muffler and rumbled. How could they sneak up on anybody with a bad muffler? And clothes, thought Caspar, I don't have the right clothes. All he had were white shirts and thin Italian shoes that showed off his small feet. Caspar went down to the workroom. He knew Bob would be back in an hour, then go away, then return an hour after that. Later stretched an afternoon of college football, and at every time-out Bob would check in to say a few words. Caspar was still searching the classifieds for apartments and making calls, but nothing seemed suitable. Either the neighborhood was wrong or the apartments too expensive. But maybe he could borrow the money; maybe his father would lend it to him.

Caspar put on his green eyeshade, turned on the light, and bent down over his model of Devil's Island. It was his biggest model, three feet by four feet, and nearly completed. There were isolation chambers, punishment blocks, and interrogation rooms. Hundreds of miniature people suffered in hundreds of different ways. The doorbell began to ring. Caspar tried to ignore it. The bell kept ringing. He put his fingers in his ears, then gave it up.

While Bob drove he kept his right arm on the back of the seat and sat half turned toward Caspar. His left hand rested lightly on the top of the wheel. Between his legs was a can of Budweiser. He didn't wear a seat belt. Caspar did. He would have worn several, had it been possible. Caspar faced straight ahead with his feet firmly on the floor, imagining how to brace his hands against the dash if there was trouble. It was dark. The Dodge's bad muffler roared and there was a smell of exhaust fumes. Caspar had his window cracked open but it gave him a chill in his ear.

"Elsie told me which cabin they were in," said Bob. "We'll

park on the road and sneak up on them. I been down there during hunting season. You ever use one of these babies?" He held up a small wooden tube with a mouthpiece on one end.

"Never," said Caspar.

Bob put it to his lips and blew it forcefully. The scream of a great cat filled the car. Every hair on the back of Caspar's neck shot to attention. "You got to blow it as hard as you can," said Bob. "You got to put a lot of force into it."

"What will we do when they come running out of the cabin?"

"You kidding?" asked Bob. "They're going to be piled in a ter-rified heap. Movement's the last thing they're going to be capable of. Here's another, just turn the crank." He gave Caspar some-thing that looked like an antique coffee grinder. Caspar turned the crank. A wolf howl blossomed in his lap. It grew, peaked, shuddered at its highest point of ululation, and died away. Caspar couldn't help being impressed. He imagined Joyce lying in her sleeping bag hearing this right outside the window. He didn't think she would have time to unzip the bag. Probably she'd just burst right through the feathers. He saw her clinging to the ceil-ing like a cat.

"Are these things legal?" asked Caspar.

"Sure. Hunters use them all the time."

They entered the park. There was a series of forking roads. The park was about sixty miles long and twenty wide, and the women were camped up at the north end. Trees arched over the road and their orange leaves shone in the headlights. It was shortly after one o'clock. Bob kept yawning, but Caspar was used to being awake at this time. The top light was on. Bob studied a map while steering with his knees. "Here it is," he said.

They drove ten minutes. Then Bob pulled onto the grass. "It's up about half a mile. We don't want them to hear the car."

"What if we get separated?" said Caspar. Bob had a big flashlight. Caspar had a small one in his back pocket.

"We'll make our racket, then run back to the car," said Bob. "Then we drive back to Rochester. A piece of cake."

Caspar didn't like how dark it was. There weren't even any stars. He wore a black sweater and a dark wool jacket. Bob had lent him a watch cap to cover his bald head. Bob himself had blackened his face with charcoal and wore a camouflage jacket and camouflage pants. He wore hiking boots. Caspar's shoes were his regular shoes, but an old pair: Italian leather with thin soles. He could feel every pebble right through them. They walked along the side of the road. Now and then Bob would flick on his light. The wind in the leaves made a whishing sound. When Bob stopped, Caspar bumped into him.

"It's along here somewhere," said Bob.

They found a turnoff and then spotted the two parked Astro vans. Caspar thought of his wife sleeping snugly in her sleeping bag. He thought of the sergeants side by side. When they had been young girls, they often slept holding hands. He thought how he had used to look in on them at night and straighten their blankets. Then they had reached puberty and everything had changed.

"It's the cabin on the right," whispered Bob.

They left the road and began moving through the fallen leaves. There were roots and big stones. Caspar stumbled, then caught himself. Bob took his arm. "Just ten more yards. We'll get up under their windows. But be quiet."

Caspar crept up to the cabin. From one window came the flicker of a candle. He leaned with his back against the rough logs. Bob whispered in his ear, "I'll go around to the other side. When I start, you start too."

Caspar felt like a speck in the dark. The only sound came from the wind through the leaves. Then he heard someone snoring and wondered if it was Joyce. He tightened his hold on the wolf call and got ready to turn the crank.

Suddenly he heard the scream of a giant cat. It was so loud and terrifying that Caspar at first couldn't imagine that it came from a whistle. Briefly, he felt in peril. Then he began to turn the crank. A wolf howl rose up into the trees. One could almost hear the teeth in it, the dark bristling fur. Cries of slaughter and death filled the darkness around the cabin. If the wolf howl was like a great murderous space, the scream of the cat was a knife blade cutting across it.

Caspar was so caught up in turning the crank he hardly paid attention to the noises from inside the cabin. Feet hitting the floor and loud voices, someone falling, a chair being overturned. Then he realized they were men's voices. He had a moment of confusion before he understood. It was the wrong cabin. These were hunters, men with guns. Caspar ran.

Behind him a screen door slammed open and boots clomped onto the porch. Caspar stumbled on a root but kept running. Branches slapped across his face. He had no idea of the direction. There were lights and rough voices. The door kept slamming. Then came a gunshot, then another.

"What the fuck, what the fuck?" shouted a man's voice.

"Over there!" The beams of powerful flashlights crisscrossed the dark.

"It must be a whole pack!" shouted another.

Caspar kept pushing through the branches, keeping his head low. He had lost his hat. He threw away his wolf call. There was another gunshot.

"There's one!" came a voice, farther behind him.

"It's a man!"

"Grab him, the sumbitch!"

Caspar imagined Bob lying on his back with a bullet hole in his forehead. It didn't seem so fantastic. Caspar didn't even slow down. He was running downhill with his hands stretched in front of him, pushing himself from tree to tree. His heart felt lodged behind his teeth. He reached for the small flashlight in his back pocket but it was gone.

Caspar had no idea how long he ran or how far. When he stopped, he heard no noise but the wind. He was surrounded by trees, though he could see nothing. He sat down on the ground with his back to a tree and breathed heavily. There were no stars, but even if he could see the Big Dipper or Orion he wouldn't have known what to do with them. He had once gone camping when he was in third grade and caught poison ivy. He never went again. He put his hands to his face and rubbed his eyes. He wondered if he would die here. He couldn't even see his hands.

Caspar sat leaning against the tree for half an hour; then a crashing noise far to his left frightened him and he hurried off in the other direction. He held up his arms to protect his face from the branches, but he already had a scratch on his chin, as well as a bruise on his knee. And his soft-soled shoes were no help at all. It was like being barefoot. He climbed a hill and went down the other side. There were no lights anywhere. He walked for an hour, then another. By the tiny light on his wristwatch he could see it was four o'clock. He was cold and his body hurt. He thought how people must look forward to death if their bodies hurt a great deal. Then it began to rain.

Around four-thirty, Caspar bumped into a cliff face. His clothes were wet through. He felt his way along the rock, until he came upon a little indentation, not a cave but at least a shelter. He thought of the black bears in the forest and how this might be one of their hiding places. But he didn't care anymore. If he were eaten, his troubles would at least be over. He ducked down against the wall, pressing his back against the rock.

Caspar Boudreau waited for daylight. He was too cold to sleep. He sat with his knees drawn up and his arms around them. He regretted the foolishness that had led him to drive down to Allegheny with Bob. Then he thought of Bob and Elsie moving into the basement. He thought of the expense of renting a studio apartment and all of Joyce's objections. Even if his father lent him the money he knew he would never make the move. He thought of his world—the space in which he lived—getting smaller and smaller. And would he ever be able to do anything about it? Yet surely tonight he had tried to teach Joyce a lesson. Even if he had failed, it had been a step in the right direction. Then why should he feel so guilty? For years he had fantasized about leaving his wife, but he stayed on and on. He wished his brain had a switch so he could flick it off. It was clear to Casper that he wouldn't leave Joyce. He wouldn't get an apartment, a little pied-à-terre. He wouldn't protest about Bob and Elsie moving into the basement. The life he had was the life to which he had sentenced himself. The sound of the rain kept Caspar from hearing any other sounds, but he was too tired to feel anything but miserable. His fears had vanished—the bears, the wolves, the hunters—and he wished he could summon them back again. They had kept him from thinking about the future.

It began to grow light: a gray morning with a cold drizzle. Wet yellow leaves drooped from the maples. Caspar got to his feet and followed the cliff face down a hill. If he could find a stream, then he could follow it until it reached a bigger stream. Several times he stumbled; his pants were torn. After three hours he found a road. He turned toward what he hoped was north. He imagined walking all the way back to Rochester.

For an hour no cars passed. Then an old Ford drove by

Caspar made no attempt to stop it. He felt too defeated to make a gesture in his own behalf. When the Astro van drew up beside him shortly after one o'clock, Caspar glanced at it without surprise. Indeed, he almost felt relief. Peggy Fisher was driving. Joyce slid open the side door and stared at him. Caspar looked down at his wet and torn pants, his ruined shoes. His hands and face were smeared with dirt.

"You get in here right now," said Joyce. "You're a bad boy, a very bad boy." Her bronze-colored hair shook with impatience.

Caspar moved toward her, dragging his feet just a little. Even though Joyce looked angry, he knew it wouldn't last. Soon he would be back in his workroom. He would add some vultures perched on the roofs to his model of Devil's Island, perhaps an execution. He imagined the exercise yard with the prisoners marching in a circle. Each would have his right hand on the shoulder of the man in front of him as their feet kicked up small clouds of dust. Caspar could almost feel the rough cotton uniform of the man ahead of him with its alternating black and white stripes, the half-starved convict's bony shoulder and collarbone. It would be a comfort of a sort. Glancing up, Casper would see the sun directly above him, as if the sun were always at its zenith: bronze-colored, shiny, and ferocious.

BLACK ASHES

Nathan called it Burning the Black Forest.

He would step into a kid's dorm room, pull down his jeans, and set fire to his pubic hair with his Zippo. He was a hairy guy. Thick black hair on his head. Thick black hair on his chest and back. Thick black pubic hair. He had a big uncircumcised prick and you could almost see it cringe. There would be a flash of flame; then Nathan would pat it out. That's when there would be the smoke. And the smell, of course. Nathan did it for the smell. He would be in and out of a kid's room before the kid could say, "Hey, what's going on?" Then the kid would be left with a smell that was worse than the smell of burning tires: a dead-thing smell, a dead-thing-mixed-with-rubber smell. And it stayed. Even the next morning you could smell it and you'd think of the kid who had been breathing it all night even with the windows open.

Nathan didn't care who he did it to. His maliciousness was

general, not specific. But he didn't do it to any of the football
players or ex-army guys. No jocks. Nathan was big but he wasn't a
fighter. He would do it to little guys, the guys who read a lot and
liked the privacy of their rooms. Nathan was more interested in
the act itself, but he needed a victim because he needed an audi-
ence. And he was fast. From entrance to exit might take no more
than five seconds. Then you would hear his laugh, a donkey bray
echoing down the hall. Sitting in your dorm room, you knew that
right at that moment a kid was opening his windows and waving
his hand in front of his nose. Some kid had planned a quiet evening and now he had that smell of burning pubic hair like a loud
noise all around him.

The fact that it came from a general maliciousness was typical
of Nathan. One couldn't imagine him aiming himself at something in particular. Nathan was strictly scattershot. He didn't do
well in his classes and he didn't like to read. He found it hard
to focus. When he wasn't working on his car, he would be hanging around telling stories about what he and his friends used to do
in high school in Hyde Park. There was a whole series of pranks.
His favorite was attaching a condom to the exhaust pipe of a
VW Beetle with a rubber band. First, however, he would put a
dab of Vaseline on the tip of the exhaust pipe. When someone
started the car, the condom would fill with hot fumes and slide off
the pipe. Then it would close, bob up into the air, and float toward
the treetops, leaving a small crowd staring after it. Little kids
would point.

Maybe it was the way Nathan told these stories that made
them tiresome. He was so eager to have you laugh that you would
decide not to laugh no matter what. Nathan wanted you on his
side; he wanted complicity. By laughing he felt you were joining
him. You were both pranksters together. But basically you felt he
was just fucked up. And that trick he called Burning the Black

Forest, it didn't win him any friends. You knew him as someone who didn't care about the consequences, who would do anything. It wasn't bravery but a perilous indifference. And he was always after you to light his farts. People thought he had a one-track mind. Even his few friends he would betray, set fire to himself in their rooms, or do something nasty to their toothpaste. Nobody trusted him.

When Nathan got Paula pregnant, I thought it was just another example of his indifference to consequence. It was hard to see what she liked about him. She was smart, a good student and very quiet, while he was always talking loudly about tits. He would tickle her ferociously and sometimes pick her up. He called himself her caveman and would chase after her making gorilla noises. He would lope along and she would run off down the hall laughing. You guessed it was the sex she liked, of being abandoned, of doing it with an animal.

Nathan would sneak into her dorm room, although this was more than thirty years ago and they could have been kicked out of school. That same semester two girls spent the night with three boys in their room and all five were kicked out, even though the college needed their money. These days it's hard to think what the fuss was about. But Nathan spent many nights in Paula's room. They made a tent with blankets on the floor. Margaret was Paula's roommate. She said Nathan would growl and snarl. Paula would say "Shhh" and then giggle, "Shhh" and giggle. After five minutes Margaret would grab her pillow and go sleep someplace else.

Paula managed to graduate even though she was four months pregnant. Nathan dropped out or maybe he was kicked out. He had keys to buildings he shouldn't have had, and the dean of students, who was also head of athletics, wanted to get rid of him. The dean had heard about Burning the Black Forest and it filled him with moral horror. Clean boys didn't do such things. Dropped out or kicked out, Nathan was gone.

When Nathan and Paula got married, we were all surprised. In those days abortion was illegal, and middle-class white kids had little idea how to find someone to perform one. But there was adoption, and we assumed that Paula would give up her kid and go on to graduate school. In the circle of friends we belonged to, either you went to graduate school or you moved to New York and got into publishing. But married to Nathan and saddled with a kid, it was hard to see that Paula would get back to school very soon. When we were nineteen or twenty, the idea of being out of school for five years was impossible to imagine. One's life would be over. People in our group talked about getting two or three Ph.D.s at the University of Chicago. It was bound to take time.

Nathan's father was a doctor, a bone surgeon. The doctor and his wife were very supportive of Paula. One guessed they knew their son was irresponsible, that he had a messed-up sense of cause and effect. Paula's parents lived back east in Connecticut. They didn't come out for the wedding, which was small in any case, just a brief visit to city hall. Afterward about ten of us went to a Greek restaurant in the Loop. Nathan had these chicken drumsticks that he had picked clean. First he put them in his nose, then he put them in his ears. Later he put his napkin on his head and said he wanted to dance, but the waitress wouldn't let him.

A couple of months later, I found out that Paula had left Nathan and moved in with his parents, taking the kid. It was in the fall and the kid was about six weeks old. Nathan had hit Paula, but I'm not sure if that was true or was what everyone assumed. Living with Nathan seemed the same as being hit.

But the story we heard next, and the story I heard from Paula when I saw her, was that Nathan had come to his parents' house and they hadn't let him in. He knocked and rang the bell. It was a Sunday afternoon in December and he knew they were home. After a while he began running around the outside of the house. "He ran like a machine," Paula told me. He ran around and around the house, jumping over hedges and going around the garage. Paula could see him from the windows. He wasn't even trying to look into the house. He stared straight ahead and made a noise like a wounded bull. Literally, he was making cow noises. His own father had to call the police.

Nathan was locked away for about six months. That was before the time of a lot of corrective medication, but the doctors gave him what they had. Downers, mostly. And they gave him shock treatment. Lobotomies were still important back then, but I don't know if that became an issue with Nathan. Anyway, he didn't have one. The point is that none of us would have been surprised if Nathan had been given a lobotomy. There was a character in a Harold Pinter play who had had a lobotomy and all the life had gone right out of him. A real zombie. Seeing the play, it was hard not to think of Nathan as winding up like that.

Paula showed up back at college in late spring just for a visit. She was getting a divorce and planned to go to the University of Chicago in the fall. She showed off her little boy—eight months old and he could stand by himself. Altogether she had only missed a year of school. Some people felt sorry for Nathan. They had seen Paula as the victim; now they saw Nathan as the victim. He was still locked up in the hatch. We didn't really know what shock treatment did to a person, but we knew it wasn't nice. And the people who had it seemed to hate it.

When Nathan got out, he found a job at a sports car garage. He loved taking apart engines. You'd see him around Chicago over the next few years and you'd think he would never burn the

Black Forest again. There was nothing dangerous about him any-more, no malicious glitter. He looked like someone walking on tiptoe, not secretively but to keep from breaking. He had a black beard and was hairier than ever. Sometimes in locker rooms you see guys with hair all over them, even on the cheeks of their asses, guys who have to shave way down past their Adam's apples. Nathan was like that. Working at the garage, Nathan had grease all over his hands and face. You would see Paula at the university that fall, all pretty and prim in light-colored dresses. You would see Nathan, and he looked like he'd crawled out of a furnace. He looked like someone who worked underground.

Nathan wanted to visit Paula and his son but she didn't trust him. She had taken a restraining order out against him, and if he tried to see her he would be sent back to the hatch. Sometimes he would hang around the university, hoping to catch a glimpse of her. He would sit on a bench leaning forward with his elbows on his knees and his head turned sideways as he watched the door of some classroom building. But Nathan was scared of being arrested. He was scared of going back to the hatch and the shock treatment. That was one of the big changes in Nathan—he didn't used to be scared. We would ask Paula about him but she claimed not to know anything. She wanted to forget him, like washing him off a blackboard. One wondered what she was going to tell her kid when he was old enough. And you wondered about Nathan's par-ents, who had taken Paula's side against him.

A mutual acquaintance, Freddy, sometimes saw Nathan in Chicago. Freddy was a fat kid who had got into museum studies and was doing an internship at the Art Institute. Freddy and Nathan used to meet at a restaurant off Wabash. Freddy said that Nathan kept talking about college and their shared experiences. He tried to mythologize them and make them bigger than they were so his own irresponsibility didn't seem so severe. When he talked about Burning the Black Forest he made it sound like a pointed criticism against the foolishly popular and powerful, not against the weak kids who liked to read. Not against Freddy himself, for example.

"He'd tell a story," said Freddy, "and it would take a minute for me to remember that I'd been there, because he'd changed it all around. It wasn't that he was crazy. He just wanted everything to be different. He was rewriting the story, taking out the accidental and inserting intentionality. He was giving it meaning."

I realized that even though I hadn't liked Nathan, I liked his indifference to consequence, how he would act without being afraid of what might happen. But he had been caught. He must have loved Paula and loved his son even if he didn't know how to behave toward them. You can only have that indifference if you truly don't care. You have to be indifferent all the way through. But he had stuck himself out too far and the world had picked him off, like a sniper sighting on a soldier poking his head up over a log.

Nathan stayed at the garage for two years, working on those British sports cars that need lots of attention: Jags and Triumphs, Austin Healys. The Vietnam War was building up, and those of us without college deferments were getting worried. I was in graduate school in chemistry, but I was considering getting married just to protect myself. We knew nothing about Vietnam. In the mid-sixties hardly anyone was protesting. I couldn't imagine Nathan being a soldier but it seemed he might get drafted. He wasn't seeing a psychiatrist anymore, although presumably he could get a letter saying he was mentally unstable. But perhaps he wouldn't want that, especially if he was in the business of revising his history, of making a new story for himself.

It was Freddy who told me Nathan had joined the Peace Corps. I assumed he had done it on impulse, as he did most things, but, according to Freddy, Nathan had been talking about it for months. Nathan was sent to language school for Spanish and eventually wound up in Guatemala. His being a trained mechanic made him useful. Lots of kids my age who went into the Peace Corps with degrees in English or science ended up digging ditches in Africa. Nathan's assignment was to work in a small village in the mountains. The Indians had a bunch of broken-down cars and maybe a truck or two. It was Nathan's idea to form a cooperative, link together several villages, and transport produce down to the city. Freddy said Nathan hoped to make the Indians self-sufficient, maybe start a little school.

Whenever I ran into Freddy, I would hear a little more. He said Nathan was trying to teach a dozen Indian kids to read and write Spanish. Another time he said Nathan was becoming unpopular with the landowners and the military. In his letters to Freddy, Nathan made the work sound romantic and exciting. I felt envious. It seemed Nathan had gotten his life on track while the rest of us were still casting around for something to do or getting locked into routines. As far as I could see, I was getting a Ph.D. just to avoid being sent to Vietnam, and by then I was married as well. I felt I had hardly time to breathe. I'd set the alarm for four in the morning just so I could study. Freddy had a nine-to-five job at the museum and was taking classes at night. We'd meet now and then and complain to each other.

In high school, kids took Spanish because it was thought to be easier than French or German. It was a dumb kids' language. We knew little about South America or even Mexico. No one we knew went there. It was a place for dropouts and beatniks, as if to go there was a sign of defeat. Then, when I was in graduate school, the news was mostly about Russia and Vietnam, not South America. Che Guevara was killed sometime back then. Places like Bolivia and Colombia seemed to have new governments every other week. One had the sense that South America could explode, and there was talk about Cuba's pernicious influence. Nobody particularly believed our own government anymore, but neither did anyone else have a lot of credibility.

When I heard that Nathan had died, I assumed it was a political thing. At first we only knew he was dead and that it was sudden. I imagined soldiers coming into the village and Nathan standing up to them. Maybe he had been protecting a woman and her child. I imagined the soldiers shooting him. You know the kind of stuff you can imagine. A few people said if you went to a place like Guatemala you had to expect trouble, meaning sudden death. It was Freddy who found out the truth. Nathan had stepped on something and got an infection in his foot. Instead of leaving the village and going down to the doctor, he had tried to treat it himself. He kept working on the cars and two or three pickups. His fever had gotten worse. At last he collapsed and was taken down off the mountain. He had died in a hospital in Guatemala City.

Nathan's body was shipped back to Hyde Park. Freddy went to the memorial service. It was a rainy morning in early November. There were a few other people from college and a couple of guys from the garage where Nathan had worked. I was studying for my orals and couldn't go anyplace. And by then my wife was pregnant. Nathan's parents were there but not Paula or the kid, who must have been about four years old. A guy from the Peace Corps talked about Nathan's work in Guatemala. There was nothing heroic about it. Long hours, lots of grease. Sometimes the soldiers shot up the cars out of spite. Nathan had kept working; then he stepped on something nasty. His whole foot swelled up so he couldn't even put a sock on it. He kept saying it would get better. Then he died.

Right now his kid must be in his early thirties. I don't know his name or anything about him. I don't know if he's hairy like Nathan or smooth like his mother. I don't know if he plays crazy jokes. I don't even know where Freddy is anymore or even if he's still alive. He was too fat to live long. These people you used to see every day, friends or acquaintances, after a while they become as distant as any stranger, people you suddenly recall late at night—you remember something they said or something silly that someone once did. For a few moments they completely occupy your mind; then you forget them again.

Nathan's indifference to consequence: first he had it, then it went away, then it came back and killed him. It's shape that makes a person's life interesting. When Nathan ducked into my room, pulled down his pants, and set fire to his pubic hair, he seemed to do it without thought. It was just a crazy idea that had struck him. Then he left and the smell would hang there. You could almost see it as bits of black ash drifted down over my books and papers. I hated to brush them away with my bare hand. Nobody liked him for it. Burning the Black Forest was an absurdity without issue, except to the dean and those jocks who got excited by what they didn't understand. It wasn't a graceful action, but it was done with a kind of grace. It wasn't the action of a guy who feels he must work sixteen hours a day to keep people from yelling at him, a guy who wakes up before the crows to think about mortgage payments, health insurance, life insurance, his kids' college education, and how he's going to pay for his retirement. Does Nathan's son have any of that? Sometimes I hope he's hairy like his father, just a ball of thick black hair. And when Nathan's foot had swollen up to the size of a basketball, what did he think then? I imagine him sitting in his hut with the Indians hovering outside the door. He had a terrible fever and was sweating his guts out. There must have been flies all over the place. Was he afraid? I like to think he didn't care. An ex-wife who hated him, a child he didn't know, his foot as big as a basketball—I like to think that Nathan didn't even feel fear. That's how he stays fixed in my mind: indifferent to consequence. It's something we like to hear that other people can do. I mean, even if we can't manage it ourselves, don't we want to believe it's possible?

For Thomas Lux

DEAD MEN DON'T NEED
SAFE SEX

When the autumn ended, George Lewis packed up the cabin and drove his Ford Explorer back to Plattsburg. There was already snow, about six inches, and the pines wore their white coats. George's boys were in school: ninth and eleventh grade. Even though barely three months had gone by, he felt he hardly knew his sons, or they wouldn't recognize him. And when he thought of his wife, Polly, it was first with surprise and then anger. He thought of her and Bob Phelps. He imagined them having sex. When she and George made love, she would often push at him and say, "Deeper, deeper." He thought of her saying that to Bob Phelps. It made him want to drive his Ford Explorer straight into a tree. And maybe he would have gone ahead and yanked the wheel if he hadn't known it would mess up his IBM Pentium III 700 MHz computer with an 18-inch Sony Trinitron monitor that was strapped down on the passenger's seat right beside him with the seat belt tightly around it.

In September, George had told Polly that he was no longer certain he loved her and he needed time to reassess his feelings. He had taken a sabbatical from teaching and wanted the opportunity to be alone. He wanted to work on his screenplay. He had a camp in the woods, a cabin near Altona, where he meant to spend the fall. His life, it seemed, had reached a fork, and he felt he should consider his options. He wanted to think things over. What was the use of teaching cinema studies at Plattsburg when his ambition was to be a screenwriter? And his marriage, where was it actually going? What were their expectations?

Polly had been furious. She had turned her back and refused to speak. In fact, they hadn't exchanged a word since that day. All their communication was done through the boys. When George had called home a week later, he learned from Timmy, his younger boy, that Polly was going out with Bob Phelps. George had been astonished. He and Polly had been married for twenty years. He couldn't get over the fact that after all that time it had taken her less than a week to start shacking up with somebody else. He had brooded about it all fall, brooded about it when he should have been concentrating on his screenplay.

The screenplay was about two New York City undercover cops who are also gay lovers. The head of a Colombian drug cartel has learned of their homosexuality and means to use the knowledge to get them bounced from the force. The two cops, Paco and Mike, have only two days to catch the drug lord before they are exposed in the *New York Post*. Suddenly the drug lord's mother is hit by a car in Medellín and he rushes back to Colombia to be by her side. Paco and Mike follow him. They plan to neutralize the drug lord in the hospital, so they disguise themselves as young interns. There are further complications, including a mudslide.

The mother is a tough old woman who, after an astonishing recovery, hides her son from the New York cops. Then Paco and Mike find out that the drug lord has a younger brother who is gay, a female impersonator who calls himself Fifi. He sings Janis Joplin songs in a gay bar in Medellín called La Galopé. A ménage à trois develops.

George would work furiously all day, pounding the keys of his IBM computer; then, as he sipped his six o'clock martini, he would stare into the leafless dark and ask, Why am I writing this? By December he had nine hours of material. He had brought in members of Sendero Luminoso, headhunters, soldier ants, and a banana plantation and there was no end in sight.

It was probably the violent nature of his screenplay and the violent nature of his fantasies that led George Lewis to decide that his only intelligent course of action was to kidnap his wife. He reached this conclusion while driving back to Plattsburg. The closer he got to home, the angrier he became. In twenty years of marriage he felt he had amassed many legitimate complaints. His writing had been put on the back burner, and often the flame had gone out. First Polly wanted a home, then their sons had been born, then there was George's teaching. If he hadn't been the film professor, he would have thought less about screenplays, but every day of the week he had to see movies. In eighteen years he had seen *Casablanca* eighty times. Screenplays were always on his mind. And eventually he got the idea of Paco and Mike, the two gay undercover narcotics detectives. It seemed like a winner. It hit all the bases. It pushed the right buttons.

While George brooded about Paco and Mike the seasons had come and gone. Students arrived as freshmen, served their four years among the ivied halls for good or ill, and graduated. Each time George took out the garbage he thought how John Huston probably never had to take out the garbage. When he mowed the lawn, he thought how Clint Eastwood probably never mowed the lawn. Paco and Mike hovered around his head and whispered, "When are you going to give us life?" It seemed to George that the entire world stood as a barrier between him and his screenplay. Teaching, his family, daily chores, the distraction of friends— all formed the wild torrent of a surging river, and on the distant shore he could see Paco and Mike waving to him.

George became resentful. When anyone asked him to do anything—grade a paper, wash a dish, serve on a committee—he saw it as another nail driven into the coffin of his writing career. In the early days he imagined explaining this to Johnny Carson after his movie was successfully produced. Later he saw himself explaining it to Jay Leno. George knew exactly how the future should be. What he didn't know was how to get there. At last he was pushed to the point where he had to act or admit that he wasn't a writer after all. That was when he told Polly he felt confused about their relationship, when he said he wanted to spend a couple of months at his camp working on his screenplay. And he would have succeeded—he was sure of this; a wonderful screenplay would have been written—if only Polly hadn't taken up with Bob Phelps. It kept George from focusing on structural problems. Every time George hammered his head wondering how Paco and Mike were going to get themselves out of their present fix, he would think of Polly gripping Bob Phelps's buttocks and moaning, "Deeper, deeper!"

The script had had several titles. The first was *Boy Crazy*. The second was *Queer Oblivion*. Now it was called *Dead Men Don't Need Safe Sex*. There was a scene somewhere in the third hour when Paco and Mike kidnapped Fifi on the streets of Medellín. They had a van and handcuffs. They put a pillowcase over Fifi's head and tossed him in back. It occurred to George that he could do the same to Polly. Paco and Mike had rented a shack in the

Colombian cotton belt where no one could hear Fifi's cries for help. George too could rent someplace outside of town. In the screenplay Paco and Mike kidnapped Fifi in order to make him come over to their side: queers against straights. Couldn't the same be done with Polly? Of course he would have to make her think that a stranger had kidnapped her, a stranger in the pay of her husband, and this stranger would convince her of her husband's good qualities. Bob Phelps taught math and his glasses were always thumb-smudged. He never read a single book and never went to the movies. He was even a year older than George, for Pete's sake.

When George and Polly had married twenty years ago, the summer after George received his M.F.A. from Cornell, she promised to support his writing. At that time George wrote poetry, but his undergraduate degree had been in film studies. Then, a year later, the job teaching film had opened up at Plattsburg and George was hired. They moved into a nice house in town and George worked on his poems. But as time passed, he wrote fewer poems. He loved his wife and kids, he was happy with his job, his childhood had been okay, people treated him with respect—he had no anxieties, no reason to suffer, no existential dilemmas, and consequently he had little to write about. His poems were happy poems, poems about how nice it was to have a backyard barbecue. And even though George loved writing poems, they kept getting worse.

That was when George began thinking about Hollywood. Film scripts didn't require a deep emotional commitment on the part of the author. You could write them without being in a good mood or a bad mood. You only needed concentration, a certain amount of uninterrupted time, and the right software for your computer. When George and Polly had sex, not only did she say "Deeper," she also sometimes said "Harder." It was amazing how those two words could so completely push aside all the intelligence and snappy language that went into the adventures of Paco and Mike.

George rented a van and a dilapidated mobile home outside of Plattsburg. He bought two pairs of handcuffs and an oversized pillowcase. He bought an over-the-head rubber mask of President Jimmy Carter. He bought a voice distorter that made him sound like Darth Vader with a head cold. He did all this on his first day back in Plattsburg. He called nobody he knew, although he happened to see his neighbor Peggy Ashley in the Grand Union when he was stocking up on several weeks of supplies. George had ducked behind a display rack of Oreo cookies. Peggy waved and said she was "in a rush."

Even though George had no phone at the camp, he had driven into Altona every couple of nights to call his sons. From Willis, who was seventeen, George had learned that Polly drove to Bob Phelps's condo each evening around ten. Sometimes she spent the night, sometimes only a couple of hours. Phelps lived in an old grade school that had been converted into eight condominiums. George found it spooky. The high ceilings, globe lights, marble floors, and dark oak woodwork had reminded him of his own grade school in Kingston. Even the blackboards were still in place. It struck George as especially offensive that Polly and Bob Phelps were having sex in what had been a second-grade classroom, as if they were doing it in front of children.

That night George parked in front of the old school building. He guessed Polly would park in the side lot and walk around to the front door. In this he proved correct. It was mid-December and there was snow on the sidewalk. More snow was piled along the curb. George had an old mattress in the back of the van. He also had chloroform and a chunk of cotton. He wore his over-the-head Jimmy Carter mask and an oversized black raincoat he had purchased at the Salvation Army.

Through the back window George saw Polly park her red Mazda 323 and get out. He hadn't seen her for three months, and in the glow of the streetlight she looked younger. She was a small woman, under five feet four, with shoulder-length black hair. She wore a long green coat and Timberland boots. George crouched in the van by the side door and waited for her to walk by. He held the pillowcase, chloroform, and handcuffs, moving them from hand to hand because he wasn't sure which would be more efficient. Should he gas her with the left hand or the right? After all, when Mike and Paco had kidnapped Fifi, there had been two of them. At no time did it occur to George that he was doing something foolish. Polly was his wife. They had known each other for twenty-four years. He couldn't imagine there was something she wouldn't forgive.

But from the start, nothing worked well. She heard him jumping from the truck and turned. George grabbed her and shoved the chloroform against her face. Instead of gracefully passing out, she began to throw up while making great gagging noises. George yanked the pillowcase over her head but it became soaked with vomit. He tried to push Polly into the back of the truck but slipped on the ice. Then he picked her up while she was gasping for breath and heaved her onto the mattress. Climbing in behind her, George knocked his knee badly against the door. He cuffed her hands behind her back and then stood up too quickly and hit his head on the roof of the van, making a loud booming sound. He scrambled into the driver's seat but couldn't find the keys. He was afraid he might have dropped them in the snow. But no, they were in the ignition. He started the van, spun the wheel, popped the clutch, and the tires spun frantically on the ice. From the back he could hear Polly choking. George shoved the truck into reverse, rocked back, and shoved it into first gear again. It crept forward into the street as the tires whined. By then Polly was shouting for help. George growled at her through his Darth Vader voice distorter, "Shut up or you'll be sorry."

"You son of a bitch!" shouted Polly. "Who the fuck d'you think you are?"

George had never heard Polly talk like this. He thought of Paco and Mike and how kidnapping Fifi off the streets of Medellín had been a piece of cake. Polly continued to scream for help. Her cries reverberated against the metal walls of the van, making them seem not like single words but one long howl. George flicked on the radio. On the college station The Doors sang "L.A. Woman." The sounds joined together to make one clangorous agitation, a riotous porridge. In another minute George was out of town. He expected to see police cars in his rearview mirror, but he saw nothing. The over-the-head Jimmy Carter mask made George's face sweat and the mask stuck to his skin. He was afraid he would inadvertently swallow the voice distorter. His head hurt from bumping it on the roof. His knee hurt from banging it against the door. Polly kept screaming. George kept shouting "Shut up!" with his Darth Vader voice. Jim Morrison's voice rose toward its orgasmic crescendo. George thought to himself, This is madness; this is what madness sounds like. When he pulled into the snowy driveway of the dilapidated mobile home, he felt he had reached the promised land.

In the screenplay of *Dead Men Don't Need Safe Sex*, Paco and Mike have no trouble in transporting Fifi from their van to the living room of their hideout. Indeed, he lay quiescently in their arms. Not so with Polly. She kicked and yelled. The vomit-smeared pillowcase made her slippery. Although there were no neighbors to hear her screams, George imagined small animals waking fearfully in their holes; rabbits and woodchucks clenching their small furry bodies. He carried Polly over his shoulder, and again he couldn't find his keys. He put her down. She began to crawl away through the snow, still shouting. George felt exasperated. Unlocking the door, he went after Polly. She tried to kick him. The difference between Paco and Mike's kidnapping of Fifi and his own kidnapping of Polly was so great that George wondered if his entire screenplay might suffer from a reality problem.

George set Polly on a straight chair in the small living room. She knocked it over and fell to the floor. He again put her on the chair and she again knocked it over. At last he left her on the floor with her hands cuffed behind her and her left foot cuffed to her right hand. She kept coughing and gagging so he removed the pillowcase. Her face was smeared with vomit. George wet a towel and cleaned her face and neck. She glared up at him. George wore gloves, the oversized raincoat, big rubber boots, and the Jimmy Carter mask. Polly stared at him with no trace of fear, only fury. Her green coat was spotted with yellow food chunks.

"You're going to be in a shitload of trouble," said Polly. "They're really going to put your prick through a wringer."

George couldn't recall his wife using such language. Although she sometimes swore, she had never been so obscenely metaphoric. It occurred to George that he should have given her Valium. Maybe it was the chloroform that made her mad.

"It's possible," said George, "that I'll bury you in the backyard." The voice distorter seemed to give him a thick Eastern European accent. He had spoken quickly; now he spoke more slowly. "I can be very cruel."

"Don't give me that shit. How're you going to dig a hole when the ground's frozen? You talk like some fuckin' retard. Who are you anyway?"

George wanted to say "a friend," but he felt Polly would make another crude remark. He took a chair and positioned it about

eight feet away. The Jimmy Carter mask kept slipping so he coul
see out of the left or right eye but not both together. The inside o
the mask was slick with sweat. George rubbed his knee where
Polly had kicked it. "You hurt me," he said.

Polly lay on her belly and her black hair hung in clump
around her face. She moved her tongue over her upper teeth. A
piece of yellow foodstuff was caught in her hair, one of the man
that George had missed with his towel.

"*I* hurt *you*?"

George stopped rubbing his knee. He thought of what Pacc
and Mike had said when they kidnapped Fifi. "You're in a lot o
trouble," he growled. Despite its limitations, the voice distorte
gave his voice a certain authority.

"*I'm* in trouble?" asked Polly contemptuously. "Do you know
how long they'll keep your ass in jail?"

"They'll have to catch me first," said George. That had beer
one of Paco and Mike's lines.

Polly laughed with a complete absence of good humor. "Who
are you?" she said again. "Why're you doing such a stupid thing?

"I'm a friend of your husband's."

"That schmuck. I should have known this was his idea." Poll
twisted on her belly and then turned over on her side. Rolling o
the floor in her green coat, she reminded George of a crippled
caterpillar.

"No, no," said George. "Your husband knows nothing abou
this. I'm acting solely on my own. He doesn't have the least con
nection with this. He's a good guy."

Polly made a spitting noise. "The fool."

George winced. He thought of when he had first seen her tha
September he had entered the M.F.A. program at Cornell and
Polly had just entered the regular M.A. program in English litera

ture. There had been a reception for new students and he had spent an hour talking to her about Wallace Stevens. He had found her so beautiful he could hardly look at her directly. It had taken three weeks for him to build up the nerve to ask her out.

"How can you call him a fool? He's the father of your children."

"Anyone could've done it. When're you going to let me go?"

When Fifi had asked Paco and Mike a similar question, they answered, "When we're good and ready to." George lowered his voice so the voice distorter became all breathy. "When you promise to stop seeing Bob Phelps."

"Pooh," said Polly.

"Don't you realize I could have you killed?" said George.

"Pooh again," said Polly.

"What do you like about this Bob Phelps character?" said George, making his voice sound terrible.

"He's there. He finds me desirable. He talks to me."

"And your husband?" George found it difficult to use his own name. George, how was George?

"He was there only sometimes. And when he was there, he always found something wrong. He always made it clear he'd rather be working on his stupid screenplay."

"What's so stupid about it?"

"Paco and Mike the fag narcotics cops? Give me a break."

"It's a topical idea."

"Jesus, you're as stupid as he is."

George flicked a speck of his wife's vomit off his raincoat. "What about as a lover?" he asked. "Wasn't your husband the better lover?"

"He was a jerk."

"How?" George almost shouted the word.

"He made me feel he was always in a hurry. He never cared about my pleasure and went to sleep as soon as he was done. It made me wonder if he was secretly gay."

"Gay?" asked George, astounded.

"You figure it out. The sex doesn't interest him and all he wants to do is write this drivel about two gay cops. Doesn't it suggest he might be gay?"

"Not at all. I know he liked making love to you. I mean, he told me."

"Yeah? How can you believe him? I never could."

George began to feel desperate. "Wasn't there anything you liked about him?"

Polly looked thoughtful. Several times she started to speak, then shook her head. "He once cooked me a pretty good lasagna," she said at last.

"That's all?"

"Do you know what it's like living with someone who always lets you know he has something better to do? There was always the sigh, the rolling of the eyes, the stooped shoulders and dragging footsteps. Sure, he was nice to our boys, paid the bills, and was moderately polite, but there was never a moment when he didn't make it clear he was making a sacrifice. It wouldn't matter if Bob Phelps was an octogenarian in a wheelchair: he loves being with me."

George and Polly had gotten married the August after they had received their degrees. George had already had six or seven poems published in magazines and a one-year job had turned up at a local community college. Both he and Polly had been certain that their lives—destined to be full of wonder and event—were at last under way. Polly kept a file of where George had submitted poems and whether or not the editors had written a note of encouragement on their rejection slips. Their marriage had been celebrated in a field outside of Ithaca on the western side of Lake Cayuga so they could look down on the lake, which was sprinkled with sailboats. Over one hundred people had come to the wedding, tramping nearly a mile across the fields from where they parked their cars. There had been a small ensemble called the Elizabethan Players who had performed music by Dowland and Purcell. George and Polly had written the wedding ceremony themselves and it had included several of George's poems. Polly had worn a white dress. George remembered how the morning sun had made it blaze.

George put his hands to his over-the-head Jimmy Carter mask, which pressed the clammy sweat drops against his skin. "If you're so happy with Bob Phelps, why were you so mad when your husband left in September?"

"I was mad for a day, no more. Mostly I was mad because he never gave me any warning. He said he was leaving, then he was gone. You see what a shit he was?"

"He had his writing."

"Yeah, Paco and Mike, the gay cops. Move over, Thomas Mann."

"Can't you say anything good about him?" Even through the voice distorter, he detected a whine.

"He never hit me. Maybe it would have been better if he had. He did all the proper middle-class things like paying the bills and driving the boys to Little League. When I started seeing Bob Phelps, he never came back or called to protest. George isn't evil, he's just dull. Sometimes that's worse than evil. I mean, at least evil can be interesting." She gave him an exaggerated wink.

George stared down at his wife. Was this the woman he had hoped to make apologize and move back in with him? He hardly knew her. Yet didn't this show how much she had been brainwashed by that fruitcake Bob Phelps?

"Didn't you have a comfortable life?" asked George.

"Sure. The same way Novocain is comfortable."

"Do you hate him?"

"He's too boring to hate. It's like hating a bad night's sleep."

"Jesus," said George.

"What about you?" asked Polly. "Here you're doing some dumb thing because you think you're helping him out. He doesn't want me back. Only his vanity wants me back. He's happy without me. Believe me, I'd never go back, but if I called him and said, 'Honey, I'm coming home,' his response would be disappointment."

"You almost make me dislike him myself," said George.

"So what're you going to do?"

"I don't know." George started to wonder about Paco and Mike. He had been planning another high-speed chase, then another sex scene, followed by a running gun battle across the roofs of Medellín. Something might have to be cut, but that could be done later. It was even possible that he could sell the whole thing as a series. Then George realized he was sick of Paco and Mike. Two campy gay guys. How in the world did he ever think they were a good idea? "I guess I'm in a fix," he said.

Polly rolled over on her side and tilted her head up toward him. "Look, take me back to Bob Phelps's apartment house and I'll never say a word."

George flicked away another speck of vomit. "I don't know, how could I trust you? What if you went to the cops?"

"And get the whole thing in the papers? My kids would be humiliated. And the gossip, people stopping me on the street and wanting all the pathetic details. If it weren't for that, I'd be glad to see George go to jail. So you see, I'm the best friend you've got."

"You mean it?"

"You're just a poor sucker working for someone who's even

dumber. Why should you spend twenty years in jail when it's George who should go to prison?"

George thought of how for years he had showed Polly his poems. More often than not she would make suggestions—places that might be cut, places that needed more work—and he had come to trust her judgment. Indeed, he had found the poems that passed before her eye often had a better chance of getting published. Now he realized he had also hoped she would read his screenplay. Surely the fact that he had nine hours of material was a bad sign. Why couldn't he bring the story to a close? If they had reached a reconciliation, she might have helped him with Paco and Mike, but there seemed little chance of that now.

Polly was glancing around the trailer. Then she yawned and rubbed her nose on the rug. As he watched her, George realized that he had made no contingency plans for failure. Had that been wise? What was he going to do with her? Somewhat grudgingly George got to his feet, slouching a little. "Maybe I should take you back."

"It's for the best," said Polly.

George lifted her carefully in both arms and carried her to the van. He set her on a dry part of the mattress; then, after a moment's hesitation, he unlocked the handcuffs. Polly smiled up at him—there was irony in her smile, but kindliness as well. George drove back to Plattsburg. Every few seconds he began to think about what he had done; then he made his mind go blank. Better not think about it. He wondered if there were any benign amnesia-creating drugs. Polly was humming in the back. She seemed quite chipper. George pulled up to Bob Phelps's elementary school condominium and ran around to open the side door of the van.

Polly brushed herself off and climbed out. She patted the

cheek of George's over-the-head Jimmy Carter mask. "You ask George to show you his Paco and Mike screenplay. You'll get a big chuckle. You have any idea what he's calling it now?"

"Dead Men Don't Need Safe Sex," said George.

Polly gave a hoot of laughter. "Doesn't that tell you all you need to know?" She made her way through the snow to the front door of the condominium. Every few feet she stopped and laughed a little, then moved on.

George watched her. Is that really all I need to know? he asked himself. At the door she glanced back over her shoulder and raised her hand in a farewell gesture, her fingers curling, straightening, and curling again. Then she was gone. George walked back around the van. He had some whiskey at the mobile home. He hoped it would be enough.

There are times in people's lives when the changes they require are so radical that even the realization itself is a radical change. It seemed to George his only hope was to move to Borneo and become a missionary. And that thought, that sudden soul-cleansing realization, was itself like packing his bags and getting all the necessary shots. Beyond that, George needed a lot of time, a lot of forehead beating, a lot of staring out the window at the rain. Antidepressants, self-help books—just how long can a man look in the mirror and say, "Oh, Jesus?" How many times can he wake up at 4 A.M. and think how he hates who he is? Winter passed. Spring came and went. Summer wound to its conclusion.

In August, Polly was talking to Peggy Ashley on the phone. "I told you about the trick that George pulled last winter? You should have seen him all dressed up in that silly mask. Poor dear, he was so serious! Yes, he gave me the house with no trouble. Alimony, child support, he's doing all he can. He's teaching Wordsworth and Keats this fall. His old loves. He's gone back to writing poetry. I've seen some. A strangely elegiac mood. He hopes to have a book out soon."

And George, the poor beleaguered soul, where was he?

That particular day he was sitting on a hillside above Lake Champlain with his back against the rough bark of an old oak. In the distance he could see sailboats. White clouds scudded across a blue sky. On the grass by his left knee was a copy of Keats's letters, by his right knee was Wordsworth's *The Prelude*. But George thought of neither. He was staring down at a yellow legal pad in his lap and idly running over the rhymes for "catamount." "Learn to count?" "Eternal fount?" "About to mount?" None seemed satisfactory.

George sighed and looked out at the water. A red speedboat was cutting between several sailboats, sending them jostling. Once more he wondered if Polly had recognized him when he had abducted her and once more he decided she had not. His disguise had been too good. He was safe. He had reached a point of crisis and had weathered the storm. The divorce had been unpleasant but he still had his job, and his sons spent most weekends with him at his new place, an old farmhouse attractively rustic with an overgrown orchard and collapsed barns—a Wordsworthian setting.

Occasionally, George thought of Paco and Mike, the gay undercover cops. He missed them, as one misses old friends who have moved to California. George gently chided himself. How foolish to have put them in a screenplay when they were better suited to a sonnet cycle. He imagined a hundred sonnets with two sonnets printed on each page: a substantial collection. But forget about New York City and narcotics and Colombia drug cartels. He was astonished at his sophomoric ambitions. Polly had been right to laugh. It was their souls that were important, their affective impulses. Paco and Mike would become forces of nature, animals out in the wild: a wolf and a panther who, against all odds, triumph over adversity and reach an emotional closeness rarely achieved in the animal kingdom.

George reread the first lines of his sonnet. Perhaps he could solve the problem of a suitable rhyme by changing the line breaks. As he began to write, the sailboats faded from consciousness. His debts, his students, his ex-wife drifted away. He entered the realm where he felt happiest. For a moment, he experienced some anxiety. Was he again crossing that fateful line between the world of fancy and the world of repercussions, the world where *seem* became the finale of *be*? He lifted his pen from the paper. Wasn't that the place where his life tended to go off the rails, where something became true simply because he thought it so? For a moment, George Lewis pondered. On the other hand, he asked himself, wasn't that his peculiar gift? Those mental meringues and linguistic marinades—as an artist wasn't it his duty to keep the kitchen busy? His was the larger calling, to merge his soul not with the quotidian but with the eternal. His business was with causes; as for the effects, let them fall where they may. George brushed aside his fears and once again put pen to paper. He swam within the life-sustaining element of creation.

> *The catamount feeds upon inferior folk,*
> *Hunting in snow where winter is no joke.*
> *But this creature in his woolly underwear*
> *Feels neither toil nor trouble, cold nor care.*

George momentarily looked upward for inspiration—cottony clouds were intermingling their soft white bodies, sun-shot and looped with blue. Honeybees meandered from flower to flower. Then, once more, George Lewis began to write.

SO I GUESS YOU KNOW
WHAT I TOLD HIM

Floyd Beefus was picking a tick off one of the springers when the gas man slipped on a cracked dinner plate on the cellar stairs and went *bump-bump-bump* right to the bottom. "Yow!" shouted the gas man. The springer jumped but Floyd kept gripping him tight between his knees until he had cracked the tick between his forefinger and thumb; then he limped slowly to the cellar door.

The gas man lay in a heap at the bottom. He was a well-fed-looking fellow in a green shirt, green pants, and a little green cap. He was moaning and rubbing his leg.

"You hurt yourself?" called Floyd Beefus.

The gas man stared up the stairs at him with a confused look as if his eyes had gone loose in his head. He was about forty, maybe twenty years younger than Floyd himself. "I think I broke my leg. I need an ambulance. You got a phone?"

"Nope," said Floyd. "No phone." He limped back to the springer and let him into the pen in the backyard before he peed on the rug. The springer had picked up the tick when they had gone out looking for pheasants that morning. Floyd had a small farm outside of Montville about twenty miles from Belfast. It was early September and Floyd had thought the cool weather would have killed the ticks. As he put the springer into his pen, he glanced around at the maples just beginning to turn color under the bright blue sky. Soon it would be hunting season and Floyd might get himself a nice buck. Frieda would appreciate that if she was still with them. After a moment, he went back inside to check on the gas man.

"You want an aspirin or maybe a Coca-Cola?" he called. He understood that the gas man posed a problem, but he wasn't yet sure how to deal with it.

"Jesus, I'm in pain. You got to call a doctor." The gas man had stretched himself out a little with his head on the bottom step. He had a thick red face. Floyd Beefus thought the man looked excitable and it made Floyd suck his teeth.

"I already told you I don't have no phone." Floyd had had a phone but he lost track of the bill and the phone had been temporarily disconnected. Frieda used to take care of all that. Floyd Beefus lowered himself onto the top step and gazed down at the gas man. He guessed he'd have to step over him if he went into the basement to fetch any of his tools.

"Then use a neighbor's phone. This is an emergency!"

"The nearest neighbor's two miles," said Floyd. "That'd be Harriet Malcomb in the mobile unit. 'Course I just call it a trailer. I'd be surprised if she had a phone. She don't even have a car. If you'd done this a week ago, then you would have caught some summer people, but the last of them left on Tuesday: Mike

Prescott, he's a lawyer from Boston. Sometimes he has parties. I'd hate to tell you what goes on."

"Then use my car."

"I can't drive no more on account of the Dewey."

"Dewey?"

"D.W.I."

The gas man was staring at him in a way Floyd Beefus thought bordered on the uncivil. "You sure you don't want that aspirin?" added Floyd. "Or maybe a pillow?"

"I can't just lie here," said the gas man, letting the whine grow in his voice. "I could be bleeding internally!"

Floyd scratched the back of his neck. He saw cobwebs on the stairs that would never have been allowed to settle before his wife got sick. "I don't like to leave Frieda. She's up in bed." He started to say more, then didn't.

"Jesus," said the gas man, "don't you see this is a crisis situation? I'm a supervisor. I can't just lie here in your cellar. I could die here."

"Oh, you won't die," said Floyd. He considered the gas man's excitability. "If you're a supervisor, how come you're reading my meter?"

"We're understaffed. You got to get a doctor!"

Floyd pulled his pocket watch out of the pocket of his dungarees and opened the lid. It was shortly past ten-thirty.

"The visiting nurse should be here in a while. She usually shows up a little after lunchtime. Billy, that's my son, he took the Ford down to Rockland this morning. He said he'd be back by late afternoon. Had to go to a pharmacy down there. I don't see why they don't sell the damn stuff in Belfast. You'd think bedsores'd be the same in both places."

"After lunchtime?" said the gas man.

"Around one, one-thirty. Loretta likes to stop for the blue plate special out at the Ten-Four Diner. And if they have blueberry pie, she generally takes a slice. She's a fat old thing. She'll fix you right up."

"That could be three hours," said the gas man.

"Just about. You want to think again about that aspirin?"

"It upsets my stomach. You have any Tylenol?"

"Nope," said Floyd. " 'Course, Frieda's got her morphine. I could give you a shot if you like. I've become some practiced at it."

The gas man had big blue eyes and Floyd found himself thinking: googly eyes.

"Morphine?"

"The visiting nurse brings it. A month ago Frieda only needed two shots a day. Now she needs four. Loretta, that's the nurse, she said she's seen patients taking six and even eight shots before their time's up. You sure you don't want a little shot? Loretta will be bringing some more."

The gas man shut his eyes. "I don't take morphine. Perhaps you could get me a glass of water. And I'll have some aspirin after all. God, it'd be just my luck to start puking."

The aspirin was above the bathroom sink. Before getting it, Floyd looked in on Frieda. She was sleeping. Her gray hair was spread out on the pillow around her face. Floyd thought of the tumor in her stomach. It didn't sleep; it just got bigger. The bedroom was full of medicines and an oxygen tank. It had a sweet hospital smell. Floyd himself had been sleeping in the spare room for six weeks and he still couldn't get used to it. He got the aspirin and went downstairs for the water. One of the springers was barking but he was just being conversational.

Floyd had to wash out a glass. Since Frieda had been sick, he and Billy had been doing the cooking and cleaning up but it didn't come easy. A pot on the stove was still crusted with spaghetti sauce from two nights earlier.

Floyd descended the cellar stairs, watching out for the stuff that was on the steps: newspapers and empty Ball jars. He sat down above the gas man and handed him the water and bottle of aspirin. "You married?" he asked.

The gas man pried the top off the bottle of aspirin. "I got a wife," he said.

"Kids?"

"Two."

"I been married forty years," said Floyd. "We done it right after Frieda finished high school. I didn't graduate myself. Didn't need it back then."

The gas man didn't say anything. He took two aspirin, then took two more. There was sweat on his forehead. Floyd thought his face looked unhealthy but maybe it was the pain. The gas man drank some water and shut his eyes.

"You like your wife?" asked Floyd.

The gas man opened his eyes. "Sure. I mean, she's my wife."

"How'd you feel if you didn't have her anymore?"

"What do you mean?"

"Well, if she died or went away."

"She wouldn't do that. Go away, I mean." The gas man's voice had an impatient edge.

"But what if she died?"

"I guess I'd be surprised."

"Is that all? Just surprised?"

"Well, she's thirty-eight. There's nothing wrong with her." The man took off his green cap and pushed a hand through his hair. It was dark brown with some gray at the temples.

"A car could hit her," said Floyd. "She could be struck down when crossing the street. It happens all the time."

"She pays attention. She looks both ways."

"It could still happen."

The gas man thought a moment, then got angry. "Can't you see I don't want to talk? I hurt and you won't even get help!"

Floyd pursed his lips. He sat above the gas man and looked down on his bald spot. "I already explained about that." He thought how the gas man's bald spot would get bigger and bigger till it ate up his whole head. "You live around here?" he asked.

"I live in Augusta."

"They got a lot of dangerous streets in Augusta," said Floyd. "I seen them."

The gas man sighed.

"Wouldn't you mind if your wife was hit by a car?"

"Mind, of course I'd mind! Jesus, what are you saying?"

"I'm just trying to get the picture," said Floyd.

"We got two kids, like I say. They're both still in school. Who'd take care of them?"

"My two oldest are grown up," said Floyd. "A daughter in Boston and my older boy in Portland. But they'd be here in a minute if Frieda got took worse. You sleep with your wife?"

"Of course I sleep with my wife. What are you getting at?" The gas man turned his head but it was hard to see Floyd seated behind him. Floyd had his arms folded across his knees and was resting his chin on his wrist.

"Me and Frieda, we can't sleep together no more. At first without her there I could hardly sleep at all. The bed seemed hollow, like it was no more than an empty shoe. She'd move around a lot in the night and she'd cry. She's scared but she won't say anything. I would of stayed right there in the old double bed but the visiting nurse said it would be better if I moved. At first I sat up in a chair with her but I couldn't do that for too many nights. Sleeping in the spare room feels like I done something wrong."

The gas man didn't speak for a moment. Then he said, "Can you get me a pillow for my head?"

Floyd got a pillow upstairs from Billy's room. His knee hurt from walking around the fields that morning and he moved slowly. Frieda was still asleep. He stood a moment in the doorway and watched her breathe. After she exhaled there was a pause that seemed to stretch on and on. Then she would breathe again and Floyd would relax a little. Her skin was the color of old egg cartons. He took the pillow back down to the gas man, who was rubbing his leg below the knee.

"I can feel the bone pressing against the skin," said the gas man. "It's sure to be bleeding inside. I could lose my whole leg." He had pulled up the green pant leg and showed Floyd the red bump in his skin where the bone was pressing.

Floyd put the pillow behind the gas man's head. "I broke my leg falling off the tractor once. I lay in the field for two hours and no harm was done except for the pain. It's not like cancer. The body can take a lot."

"It hurts," said the gas man.

"That's just your body telling you there's something wrong. You want me to haul you upstairs and put you on the couch?"

The gas man considered that. When he thought, he moved his tongue around in his mouth. "I think I better stay right here until the rescue squad shows up."

Floyd wasn't sure he could get the gas man up the stairs in any case. "You pray?" he asked.

"I'm not much for church," said the gas man.

"Me neither, but there's a Bible around somewheres if you need it. Frieda likes to look at it. Right up to last March she'd never been took sick. Never complained, always kept us going with her jokes. You ever been unfaithful to your wife?"

The gas man's head jerked on his pillow.

"Jesus, what kind of question is that?"

"I just wanted to know."

"My affairs are none of your business, absolutely none of your business."

Floyd settled himself more comfortably on the step. He was sorry that the gas man was so unforthcoming. "You know Belfast?"

"I been there."

"You know how it used to have those two chicken processing plants? Penobscot Poultry and the other one. I forget its name. A guy named Mendelsohn run it. Every summer Belfast used to have a poultry festival with rides and activities in the City Park. It used to be something special and high school bands would come from all over. And the Shriners, too."

The gas man didn't speak. He began rubbing his leg again. There was a bend in it that Floyd didn't think looked right.

"There was a woman who worked upstairs at Penobscot. She had a job putting the little piece of paper between the chicken parts and Styrofoam. Her name was Betsy. My, she liked to make trouble. She was never buttoned clear to the neck. About fifteen years ago me and Frieda went to that poultry fair. The kids were young enough to still like it. I was drinking beer. That's always a mistake with me. After dark I got Betsy back on a tree stump. I was just unbuttoning myself when Frieda found me. Jesus, I already had Betsy's shorts off under her dancing skirt."

"Why are you telling me this?" The gas man stretched his neck to get a glimpse of Floyd.

"I was just thinking about it, that's all," said Floyd.

"Don't you see I don't care what you've done?"

"Then what do you want to talk about?" asked Floyd.

"I don't want to talk at all."

Floyd sat for a moment. The gas man had a fat gold wedding ring, then another ring with a blue stone on his right pinkie finger.

He had shiny teeth. Floyd thought it was the kind of mouth that was used to eating a lot, the kind of mouth that enjoyed itself.

"How's your leg?" asked Floyd.

"It hurts."

"That aspirin help any?"

"It makes my stomach queasy."

"You sure you don't want a Coke?"

"I just want to get out of here. You got to take my car."

"I can't leave Frieda," said Floyd. "If she woke up, you couldn't help. Anyway, the moment I got out on the highway, the Dewey'd get me for sure."

Floyd leaned back with his elbows on a step. The cellar was filled with evidence of forty years in this house: broken chairs, old bikes, tools, canning equipment, a dog bed for Bouncer, who had been dead ten years. The cellar had a musty smell. He wondered what he would do with this stuff when Frieda died. The thought of her death was like a pain in his body.

"You ever think," said Floyd, "that a bad thing happens to you because of some bad thing you've done?"

"What do you mean?" asked the gas man suspiciously.

"Well, that time I fell off the tractor and broke my leg was right after I'd been with Betsy at the poultry festival. Even when I fell I had the sense that something was giving me a shove. If I'd had two more seconds I'd of stuck it into her—"

"I don't want to hear about this," said the gas man.

"What I was wondering is, maybe you've been doing something you shouldn't. You always play straight with your wife?"

"This is none of your business."

"You never felt temptation?"

"I only wanted to read your meter," said the gas man. "That's all, just your meter."

"You're a better man than I am. I felt temptation. I felt it every time I went into town. It wasn't that I don't love my wife. I was just exercising myself, so to speak. I'd go into Barbara's Lunch and just breathe hard. Going into houses like you do, you must of felt temptation a whole lot."

"I don't want to talk about it. I'm a supervisor."

"But younger, when you were a plain gas man. Didn't some woman look at you and smile?"

"Why are you saying this?" asked the gas man. He spoke so forcefully that little drops of spit exploded from his lips. He tried to turn but couldn't quite see Floyd sitting behind him.

"You know," said Floyd, "after Frieda caught me behind the beer tent with Betsy McCollough, she'd look at me with such . . . disappointment. I don't mean right at the time. Then she was just angry. But later, at dinner or just walking across the room, she'd look up at me and I could see the wounding in her face. She still loved me and I loved her too. It was thirteen, almost fourteen years later the cancer took hold of her, but I find myself thinking that my time with Betsy had opened the cancer to her. It made a little door for the cancer to enter."

The gas man had his face in his hands. He didn't say anything. The tips of his ears were all red.

"We were married right in Montville," said Floyd. "All our families were there, most of them dead now. We meant to be happy, never thought we'd ever have bad times. Even now, lying in bed, Frieda will look at me with that look of disappointment. Maybe that's too strong a word. She doesn't regret her marriage or regret having met me. It's like she thought I was a certain size and then she found out I was a little smaller. And I can never say she's wrong. I can't make myself bigger. When she was first sick, I used to make her dinners and bring her stuff and she appreciated it, but it never made me as big a person as she used to think I was.

And soon, you know, she'll be gone, and then I won't be able to explain anything or fix anything. All our time will be over."

The gas man didn't say anything.

"What d'you think about that?" asked Floyd.

"I just want a doctor," said the gas man.

"If you're so good," said Floyd, "why won't you talk to me about it?"

"About what?"

"About what I done."

"Because I don't care," said the gas man. "Don't you understand? I don't care."

"Fine gas man you are," said Floyd. He sat a while without speaking. He rubbed his knee and the gas man rubbed his leg.

"I don't mean to hurt your feelings," said the gas man.

"That's okay," said Floyd, "I'm not worth much."

"It's not what you're worth," said the gas man. "My leg's broken. I hurt. I'm preoccupied."

"You think I'm not preoccupied?" said Floyd. "My wife's dying upstairs and I can't do anything about it. I look in her face and I see the memories there. I see how I hurt her and how I said the wrong things and how I got angry and how I wasn't the man she hoped I'd be. I see that in her face and I see she's going to die with that. You think I'm not preoccupied?"

The gas man put his cap back on his head and pulled down the brim. "I don't know what to say. I come into this place. All I want is to read your meter. Why the hell can't you keep that stuff off the stairs? You think it's nice to be a gas man going into strange basements all the time? All I want is to get in and get out. Then I go home, eat dinner, watch some TV, and go to bed. Is that too much to ask? Instead, I slip on a dinner plate and you say I must've deserved it. I must've been cheating on my wife. All I want is to get my leg fixed. I'm sorry your wife's dying. I can't do anything about it. I'm just a gas man."

Floyd leaned back and sighed. He heard one of the springers howling. Frieda had a buzzer that sounded off in the kitchen if she needed anything. Apart from the springer, the house was silent except for the gas man's heavy breathing. Floyd felt dissatisfied somehow, like finishing a big meal and still being hungry. He looked at his watch. It was almost eleven-thirty.

"Old Loretta should be reaching the Ten-Four Diner in another hour," he said. "My, she loves to eat. I've known her even to have two pieces of pie with ice cream. If they got blueberry and if they got rhubarb too, I bet she'll have both."

"What's the latest she's gotten here?"

"Three o'clock."

The gas man groaned. "I hurt. I hurt a lot."

"There's still that morphine," said Floyd.

"No morphine," said the gas man.

"Anything else you want? Maybe a tuna-fish sandwich?"

"You got any whiskey?"

"There might be some White Horse somewheres."

"Maybe a shot of that, maybe a double."

Floyd made his way back upstairs. He was sorry the gas man didn't want a tuna-fish sandwich. He wanted to feed him, to have the gas man think well of him. Looking in on Frieda, he saw she had turned her head but that was all. She said the morphine gave her bright-colored dreams. She dreamt about being a kid or going to school or having children again: rich vigorous dreams. Floyd Beefus envied her for them. When he went to bed he was just grinding and grinding all night long like a tractor motor.

Floyd poured the gas man half a glass of whiskey, then poured himself some as well. He made his way back down the cellar stairs and handed the gas man the bigger glass.

"Here you go," he said.

The gas man gripped it with both hands, took a drink, and coughed. He had fingers like little sausages.

"You like being a supervisor?" asked Floyd.

"Sure."

"What do you like about it?"

"It commands respect."

"You ever fired anybody?"

"Well, sometimes you have to let somebody go."

"You feel bad about that?"

"I feel my duty is to the company and to the trust they put in me." The gas man took another drink.

Floyd couldn't imagine being a gas man or what it would be like going into people's houses. He had been a farmer all his life. "You ever stole anything from them?"

The gas man twisted his head around. The whiskey had brought a little color to his nose. "Of course not!"

"Not even a ballpoint pen or a couple of paper clips?"

"They trust me."

"How long you worked for the company?"

"Almost twenty-three years."

"That's a big chunk of time. You must of done a lot of stuff for them."

"I've had a wide variety of experience." The gas man talked about the sort of things he had done: office work, fieldwork, repairing broken equipment. He finished his whiskey and Floyd gave him another. The gas man took two more aspirins. It was just after twelve o'clock.

"You won't change your mind about that sandwich?"

"I don't like tuna fish," said the gas man. "Maybe some toast with a little butter. Not too brown."

Floyd went back up to the kitchen. The bread had a little mold but he cut it off. He checked the toaster to make sure no mice had gotten electrocuted. Sometimes they crept inside and got caught like lobsters in a trap. Floyd wiped a plate off on his pant leg; then he buttered the toast, using a clean knife. Through the kitchen window he saw four cows moseying in a line across the field. He and Billy had milked all twenty before sunup. Floyd took the toast back down to the gas man.

"How many houses can you go into in a single day as a gas man?" asked Floyd.

"Maybe fifty out in the country, double that in the city." He had his mouth full of toast and he wiped his lips with the back of his hand.

"And nothing strange ever happens?"

"In and out, that's all I want. Sometimes a dog gives you some trouble. I'm like a shadow in people's lives."

"And you've never felt temptation?"

The gas man drank some whiskey. "Absolutely never."

"No women give you the eye?"

"Their lives don't concern me. It's their meters I'm after." The gas man put the empty plate on the step. He was still chewing slowly, getting a few last crumbs, running his tongue along the gap between his teeth and his lower lip. "It's my duty not to get involved."

"But people must talk to you. A woman must give you a friendly look."

"Oh, it's there all right," said the gas man. "I could be bad if I wanted."

"You seen things."

"I seen a lot."

"It must be a burden sometimes."

"My duty's to the gas company, like I say. That's why they made

ne supervisor—because I make the right decisions, or try to.
They appreciate my loyalty."

Floyd leaned forward a little. "What kind of things have
ou seen?"

The gas man drank some more whiskey, then rested the glass
on his thigh. "There was a woman in Augusta, a divorcée, who
had it in mind to make trouble. I seen that."

"Good-looking?"

"A little thick, but good-looking. This was ten years ago."

"What'd she do?"

The gas man took off his cap again and wiped his brow. He set
his cap carefully on the step beside him. "Well, the first time I
went by her house she offered me a cup of coffee. I know that
doesn't sound like much, but it was just the beginning. She asked
f I wanted a cup of coffee and if I wanted to sit down and rest
awhile. She was wearing a bathrobe, a cream-colored bathrobe.
She had thick brown hair past her shoulders and it was nicely
brushed."

"You take the coffee?"

"I always make a point of never taking anything."

"Then what happened?"

"A month later, I went by her house again. She was waiting for
me. She followed me down to the basement when I went to read
her meter. I turned around and she was standing right in front of
me, still in her bathrobe, like she'd been wearing it for the entire
month. I said howdy and she asked if I'd like to rest a little and I
said I had to keep moving. Then she asked if I liked to dance and
I said I didn't, that I hadn't danced since high school. So I walked
around her and left."

"You think she wanted to dance right then?" asked Floyd. He
liked dancing but he hadn't had much occasion in his life. When

he was younger, there had been barn dances during the summer and sometimes he still recalled the mixed smells of perfume and hay.

"I don't know if she wanted to dance," said the gas man. "I didn't think about it. I was in a hurry. When I'm in one place, I'm already thinking about the next."

"She must of been lonely."

"A gas man doesn't socialize. It's like being a priest except you're dealing with gas meters. One time a man asked me for five dollars so he could feed his family. I didn't answer him. I don't even like it when people ask me the time of day or what the weather is like outside. In and out, that's my motto."

"So what happened with the woman?" asked Floyd.

"So the third month I check her meter she doesn't follow me down to the basement. She was still wearing her robe and I thought she'd been drinking a little. She was wearing this red lipstick and she greeted me heartily, like I was an old friend. People have done that before, trying to get around me. I just nodded. I go down in the basement and check her meter. When I start back up the basement stairs, she's standing at the top. She's taken off her bathrobe and she's wearing this pink underwear, pink panties. Her titties are completely bare and she's pushing them up at me. Big pink titties. She was blocking the door so I couldn't get through. 'Take me,' she says, like she thinks she's a cab or something."

"What'd you do?" asked Floyd.

"I asked her to get out of my way, that I was in a hurry. She still didn't move. So I yelled at her. I told her I was a busy man and I didn't have any time to waste. She took her hands away from her titties pretty quick, I can tell you. I said her behavior was awful and she should be ashamed."

"Then what happened?"

"She stepped aside and I left."

"And the next month?"

"The next month she was gone and the house was shut up. I didn't think much of it but a month later I asked one of her neighbors if she'd moved. I don't know why I asked, maybe it was because the woman seemed crazy. Anyway, the neighbor told me the woman was dead. One morning she just hadn't woken up. The neighbor said it was pills. She just took all the pills she could find. It was the neighbor who told me that the woman was a divorcée. She said the husband had gotten the kids and married someone else. I don't know when she died, just sometime during the month."

Floyd finished his whiskey. One of the springers was barking again. Floyd thought that no woman in his entire life had ever looked at him and said, "Take me," not even his wife. "You could of kept her alive," he said.

"What d'you mean?"

"You could of talked to her. She might still be around."

"She wanted sex. She was crazy."

"But you could of talked to her. She probably only wanted a little conversation."

"That's not my job. To me, she was only a person with a gas meter. In and out, like I say."

"What if you'd found her bleeding on the floor?"

"I would have called the cops."

"But the stuff she told you, it was like she was bleeding." Floyd regretted he had given the gas man any of his White Horse.

"It's not my job to deal with bleeding."

"You should of danced with her," said Floyd. "I would of danced with her. I would of danced till my feet fell off."

"We already know about you," said the gas man. "You and that woman behind the beer tent."

Floyd felt angry, but he knew that only a piece of his anger was connected to the gas man. The rest seemed a blanket over every thing else. He didn't like the whole setup: people coming into life and going out of life and none of it by choice. Hearing Frieda's buzzer, he got to his feet, feeling dizzy from the whiskey. He made his way upstairs, holding on to the banister. The gas man kept saying something but Floyd didn't pay any mind.

Frieda's eyes were only half open. "I would like some more water." Her voice was very soft.

Floyd got the water from the kitchen and put in a couple of ice cubes. When he handed it to Frieda, he said, "I got a real character downstairs in the basement."

"Tell him to go away."

"I can't. He's broken his leg."

Frieda nodded solemnly. The morphine and her approaching death made her more accepting of the world's peculiarities. "Then give him something to eat."

"I already did."

"Then just bear with it," she said.

When Floyd looked back down the basement stairs, he saw the gas man was holding his head in his hands. "More aspirin?" He found it hard to be polite.

"Leave me alone."

"Any food? Maybe a blanket?" It was approaching one o'clock. Loretta could be arriving in as little as half an hour.

"I don't want anything from you," said the gas man.

Floyd was about to turn away and fix himself some lunch; then he changed his mind. "That's why you fell," he said. "Because of that woman who wanted to dance. That's the punishment you got, busting your dancing leg. Ten years ago, you said. That punishment's been coming after you for a long time, just creeping along waiting for the right opportunity."

"Shut up!" said the gas man. "Shut up, shut up!"

Floyd told Billy about the gas man that night at dinner. Billy was a thin, heavily freckled youngster in his late teens who wore old dungarees and a gray University of Maine sweatshirt. His mother's illness was like an awful noise in his ears.

"So the rescue squad is carrying this fellow out of the house," said Floyd. "His hands were over his face, but you could tell he was crying. I was standing there holding the dog. The guy sees me. 'Damn you,' he says, 'God damn you to hell!' "

"After you'd been taking care of him and fed him?" asked Billy. They were eating beans and franks at the kitchen table.

"Some people have no sense of how to behave," said Floyd. "Some people would act bad even in front of Saint Peter. 'Damn you,' he kept saying. Well, I wasn't going to take that in front of the rescue squad. A man can be provoked only so far."

"I can't believe you kept your trap shut," said Billy.

"I don't like being messed with." Floyd paused with his fork halfway to his mouth. "So I guess you know what I told him."

"I bet you gave him the very devil."

"That's just the least of it," said Floyd.

FLAWS IN THE LATEX

Denise knew that her marriage was over the night Josh tried to fuck her with a carrot. Even though he had tried to warm the carrot in the microwave, it wasn't enough. They had both been bored for a long time and he had meant it as a joke. Denise had been half asleep and had turned toward him. It had been a surprise. More than a surprise, actually.

After she moved out, Denise got a job at Fay's Drugs near the high school. Boys bought condoms from her. They would avoid her eye as if buying condoms from a machine. She would cough and clear her throat just so they would look at her. Sometimes she made choking noises. The youngest couldn't have been more than twelve. She supposed she was their mothers' age. To one boy she said, "These often have a flaw. It's best to use more than one." The boy thanked her and bought a second box. She liked to think of him drawing on one condom after another until he had created a protective layer as thick as the finger of a leather glove. Afterward, she warned many boys about flaws in the latex. She also warned Father O'Flynn from St. Benedict's and he said, "Aw, go on with you."

Sometimes she saw Josh around town, either walking or driving his dented blue Ford pickup with his carpenter tools jumbled in back. When she left, they had spoken of a trial separation, but she knew she would never return. A line had been crossed that could not be uncrossed. In memory she could still see the carrot clutched in his fist: orange and erect, like the torch held by the Statue of Liberty. And perhaps it truly signified liberty, not Josh's but hers, but at first it didn't feel like liberty. It only felt as if she'd been cut loose, like a boat that didn't want to dock up anymore.

Seeing Denise on the street or in the supermarket, Josh would look sheepish. He would look away, then look back at her with his head lowered and moving from side to side, staring through his bushy black eyebrows and tousled hair. Sometimes he would shrug, the kind of shrug that tries to be philosophical about human nature, as if human nature were at fault and not he. When she was younger, she had found something charming in his apologies, something boyish, as if he were a victim of circumstance. Now she thought, There's the man who fucked me with a carrot.

Denise rented a two-bedroom apartment over the Trustworthy Hardware store in downtown Cortland so her son or daughter could stay with her when they visited. She never saw women going into the hardware, although they must have. The men looked at her speculatively, glances that lasted several seconds longer than was polite. She never looked back. She was still attractive, with a good figure and only a little gray in her auburn hair, but she had no interest in dating. "I'm full up to here," she said to Mildred, who worked the back counter at Fay's, and she drew a finger across her eyebrows.

And to a blushing fifteen-year-old boy, who had whispered his condom request, she said, "These can tear like a wet tissue. I hope you know what you're doing." And she nodded solemnly when he dug into his pocket to see if he could afford another box.

Sometimes in the early evening Josh came and stood on the sidewalk beneath her window. He would sway slightly and she would understand he'd had a few drinks. By then it was April and she had moved out at the end of February. It was a rainy spring and often Josh would stand under a black umbrella and the umbrella would sway back and forth. He had gotten a dog, a dachshund puppy, and the dog would sit beside him. Josh would stare up at her window and the puppy would stare up as well. Several times she thought of dropping things on him—a plant or a chair—but she was afraid of hitting the puppy. She understood that he had gotten the dog not because he liked dogs but to appear endearing.

Sometimes Josh would whistle, sometimes he would sing "Here Come the Clowns," because he thought she liked it, but she hadn't liked any of his music except for the "Lieutenant Kije Suite." He sang it slowly with his hands folded across his heart while holding the puppy's leash. He was proud of his singing voice and the fact that he had been president of his high school glee club for three years running. Across the doors of his truck was printed JOSH LINDSTROM: THE SINGING CARPENTER and his address and phone number.

The men in the hardware store would come out and look at him. Denise couldn't see them directly but she could see their reflections in the windows of Bob's Men's Clothing across the treet. It made the men look like ghosts: maybe half a dozen hosts listening to her husband—already she thought of him as her x-husband—sing "Here Come the Clowns." They were farmers, or the most part, with big hands and lumpy bodies dressed in lue overalls. When Josh finished, several of them would clap, but sually they just stared.

Then, in the window across the street, she would see Josh alking to them and pointing up at her apartment. He probably lready knew some of them from softball and Scouts and deer unting in the fall. Denise was positive Josh didn't tell them about he carrot. "And that was only one thing from a whole list of hings," she said out loud to her empty apartment. The times vhen Josh hadn't come home for dinner, when he had been lrunk, when he had been rude, the affair with the woman from Buffalo—but her grievances depressed her and she would sit lown on the couch and put her head in her hands. "Why do I other?" she asked herself. Then she thought, How can I get out of this?

Her children were worried, but both seemed to think the eparation was something she had done personally against them. 'oung Josh was a freshman at Albany. "You were just waiting for ne to get out of the house," he said. "My grades are going to take dive." He wanted to major in business, but right now his frater-ity was taking all his attention.

Sally worked in Rochester for Eastman Kodak. "If you moved ere, you could rent an apartment in my building, but maybe not n my floor." She was seeing a young man in a managerial position nd had begun to fantasize a future with him.

Denise didn't tell her about the carrot. She felt her daughter hould look into the future with as much hope as possible. Why dd such a burden to her own child?

"He's always concerned about how it was for me," her daughter said one night on the phone, talking about her young man. "I haven't told him about you and Dad. He says he comes from a traditional family. It would help a lot if you and Dad patched things up."

"It's too late for that."

"Isn't Regret adorable?" said Sally.

"Regret?" Denise wondered if one of them had slipped a synapse or two.

"That's what he named the puppy."

In the back of the newspaper were listings for local support groups, everything from fat people to child beaters. Some were in Ithaca, some in Syracuse. There was one for abused women, and Denise imagined herself sitting in a circle with a dozen women with black-and-blue marks on their arms and faces, telling them her husband had fucked her with a carrot. She imagined how their lack of response would be like a room in which the air hadn't been changed for a long time. Maybe they would roll their eyes and look down at the floor. Denise imagined the silence continuing until the chairwoman or whoever said, "Is there anyone else with something to say?"

Then she considered seeing a therapist and going that route, and it was by thinking of these possibilities that she came to realize the degree of her humiliation, and it wasn't the carrot she didn't wish to talk about but her humiliation. Added to that was the question of how she contributed to the collapse of her marriage. Certainly Josh had his flaws, but what were hers? And she imagined the other abused women—women with serious injuries, not comical ones—asking about her role in the relationship: had she been good in bed and cooked his favorite foods? Standing alone in her apartment, Denise would say out loud, "But none of that makes any difference!" And she realized there was nobody she could tell about what had happened, nobody but Josh himself, and he was like a dead man to her.

When she went on her ten-minute break at the drugstore, she often talked to Larry the pharmacist. Denise was trying not to smoke. It seemed all the single women she knew smoked, as if they had left their men and bought a pack of Salems. "I could give you a patch," Larry told her. He was very religious and was losing his hair in a way that made people look at it—pieces here and there. Whenever they talked, Denise found herself yawning. Larry spoke with great deliberation and paused before the important words of his sentence, as if the words were very heavy. Into that pause Denise inserted a yawn, quickly covering her mouth and apologizing.

"A patch," she said.

"They help you quit . . . smoking."

"What do they do?"

"They kill the desire for . . . nicotine by giving your body just a taste of it. A hair of the . . . dog, so to speak."

Larry was her age, just forty, with five sons whom he had named after the Disciples, working his way through the Disciples alphabetically.

Sometimes Denise imagined having sex with him, not because she desired him but from a mixture of loneliness and curiosity. It was on those days when she felt she had a story she could never tell and the men from the hardware store had stared at her longer than usual. She would imagine having sex with Larry right on top of his pharmacist's counter. She imagined having to struggle with her pantyhose. It was not something she actively thought; rather, the images swept over her. And sometimes when she gave an absolute stranger his change, just the brief touch of his hand was comforting. She even felt this way with children, even with the boys who came to buy condoms. She wondered if this was why single women bought cats or small dogs and talked to them lovingly.

"Do you ever feel you are going to explode?" she once asked Mildred when they were working at adjoining registers.

"Mr. Hendricks doesn't like that kind of talk," Mildred warned. "He wants us to be upbeat." Mr. Hendricks was the store manager, a heavyset man who always wore a white shirt. He used verbs like "network" and "brainstorm." Denise thought he was fifty but he might have been older.

Denise felt it was wrong to expect her to be upbeat when she wanted to scream. And that day she told a sixteen-year-old boy, "I've known men to wear six of these things and still get the girl pregnant. There can be microscopic holes in the latex."

Sometimes she saw Mr. Hendricks watching her. She assumed he was assessing how well she did her job, but one afternoon Mildred said, "He likes girls' bottoms." And Denise tried to determine whether Mr. Hendricks's eyes were focused above her shoulders or below. He had the dark watery eyes of one of the larger grass-eating animals in the zoo, unhappy animals with long confinements. On his desk was a photograph of his wife, a woman named Flo who had exactly his figure, as if by eating together twice a day for thirty years they had acquired the same meat-loaf shape. They had no children.

In her apartment at night Denise read or watched TV. Sometimes she would visit a friend, but she felt uncomfortable with people who had known her when she and Josh were a couple. She could see the question marks in their eyes, their silent inquiries about her own responsibility for the breakup. Sometimes she would have a salad at Friendly's or go to a movie. About once a week Mildred came over to talk about her boyfriend Frank, who was often on the road. "He loves me but I just don't feel like settling down," she would say. Mildred was thirty-five. She had very tight orange curls. Denise felt if she pulled one away from Mildred's head and let it snap back, the curl would go *boing*.

Mildred was there one evening when Josh appeared beneath the window with his puppy. At first he just stood swaying slightly; then he began to sing "Here Come the Clowns." It was dark but Josh stood near the streetlight. Denise and Mildred watched him, standing back so he wouldn't see them.

"He wants you to forgive him," said Mildred.

"No," said Denise, "he wants to show me he's forgivable." She thought how Josh tried to appear winsome and boyish. She wanted to tell Mildred there was really nothing winsome about him, that the winsomeness existed so people wouldn't know how angry he felt, because if people knew about the anger, somebody might hit him.

"He's a coward," said Denise. "He sings that song because he's a coward."

"He loves you," said Mildred.

"No," said Denise, "he wants to show me that he's lovable."

"What did he do?" asked Mildred, lowering her voice.

"I'm not ready to talk about it," said Denise. And it occurred to her that by being lovable, Josh would convince everybody he wasn't at fault, that he wasn't the one with the hard heart. The night he had fucked her with the carrot, he had kissed her. She had been surprised and couldn't remember when he had kissed her last. Certainly not that week or the week before. It was only later that she realized he had been setting her up for his trick with the carrot. He had washed it and peeled it as if he thought that making the carrot cleaner somehow made it better.

Denise felt that people had funny ideas about cleanliness and funny ways to talk about it. At the drugstore Mr. Hendricks

referred to condoms as "sanitary supplies," and at first Denise had
no idea what he was talking about.

"Our sales of sanitary supplies have more than tripled," he
said. When Mr. Hendricks was happy, he went up and down on
his toes.

Denise's face assumed a pleased expression but one that also
indicated she bore no sense of responsibility for this happy event.
"People like to be clean," she said. She thought he was talking
about soap and brushes.

Mr. Hendricks looked her in the face for what seemed the first
time. "Thank you for your input," he said.

Later Mildred told her, "He means rubbers."

Denise felt more surprised than embarrassed. After all, she
wasn't the one who had been speaking unclearly. That afternoon,
the delivery truck unloaded a large cardboard crate of Trojans and
she saw Mr. Hendricks pat the top of it approvingly.

Larry the pharmacist didn't like the condoms and didn't like
how they were displayed in what he considered his part of the
store. "The best protection is . . . abstinence," he liked to say.

And Mildred answered, "Look who's talking. And you with five
sons. When are you going to get yourself some nice girls?"

Larry blushed easily and Denise wondered if his frequent
blushing was connected to how his hair was falling out in funny
patches. As a child she had heard that masturbation caused hair to
grow on a boy's palms. The boys who bought the condoms all had
shiny palms. She knew of course it was a joke—hair on the palms
and warts—those jokes that are embarrassing the first time and
funny the second when you are no longer the victim. But if sexual
self-abuse could make hair grow, then perhaps abstinence could
make it fall out.

Denise unpacked the crate of condoms and put them on a

shelf in the stockroom. She liked the stockroom because she could be alone there and didn't have to pay attention to what her face was doing. You never had to look upbeat in the stockroom. But that particular day, Mr. Hendricks came into the stockroom about five minutes later. He seemed pleased to see her.

"Those are moving nicely," he said, nodding toward the condoms. He kept raising his eyebrows, and his face was shiny. It was a round face, shaped more like a knee than a face, and his nose was just a nubbin.

Denise said nothing. She thought of smiling but that, too, seemed inappropriate.

"Are you happy here, Denise?"

For the briefest of moments Denise thought he was referring to the stockroom itself; then when she understood she responded too strongly. "Oh, yes, Mr. Hendricks, I'm very grateful." She grew embarrassed and returned to putting the small boxes on the shelves. She worried that Mr. Hendricks would think her simpleminded.

"I like a good worker," he said. And he went up and down on his toes.

He watched her for a while and Denise could feel him behind her, but when she at last turned around Mr. Hendricks had gone.

Denise tried to make her life move forward but it seemed the details of each day conspired to make it slide back. She and Josh had been married twenty-two years and she felt she had been married to a stranger. When he had kissed her that night, she had turned to him almost joyously, a welcome surprise before the unwelcome one. There had been other practical jokes—the time he had hidden her underwear, the rubber dog messes and dribble glasses—but nothing like the carrot. The silence to which she felt herself condemned was like a cage. Yet to tell people would be worse. When Josh sang beneath her window and then chatted with the farmers, Denise felt envious. Their joking and neighborliness. Some of them knelt down to pat the puppy, curled up on the sidewalk at his feet, and she imagined Josh explaining why he had named it Regret. She thought of introducing the subject of the carrot to Mildred: "Have you ever had a man take an object like a vegetable—" There was no way Mildred wouldn't think that Denise hadn't brought it on herself. She wondered if she should leave Cortland, go to Rochester after all. She thought how people were constantly being retooled for other professions. Denise decided she needed to be retooled as well, but there was no job she could imagine wanting.

To a fourteen-year-old boy, Denise said, "The condom companies send their worst condoms to third-world countries. That's what's caused the population explosion. Don't you understand that central New York is like a third-world country? Even a sock would work better."

In no time the crate of Trojans was nearly gone. Mr. Hendricks would stand before the condom display with his arms folded across his white shirt and his lips pursed into a satisfied smile. He would bob up and down in time with his happy thoughts. Although nothing was actually said, Denise came to be in charge of the display, dusting it and making sure there were no shortages. From a Valentine's Day display, she appropriated a red heart-shaped balloon on a stick. She had seen how several boys spent ten minutes searching the aisles just because they were too embarrassed to ask where the condoms were located. Now, even though the condom display was at the back of the store, its location was obvious because of the balloon.

A new crate of condoms arrived at the drugstore. It was a Friday afternoon in late April. Denise directed the deliveryman to the stockroom, opened the crate, and began replenishing the storage shelves. That evening she meant to go to a movie. She didn't care what was playing; she only wanted to get out of her apartment. But she hated it when people she knew saw her at the movies by herself and felt sorry for her, so she always arrived at the theater a few minutes after the movie began. She heard a footstep and turned to see Mr. Hendricks standing nearby.

"You have my A-plus, one-hundred-percent appreciation, Denise." Mr. Hendricks's knee-shaped face was red as if his collar were too tight. To his shirt pocket was pinned a black plastic name tag with MR. HENDRICKS in white lettering and under it the words I CARE.

"I'm glad, Mr. Hendricks."

"And you're happy here?"

"Very happy, Mr. Hendricks." Denise felt Mr. Hendricks looked strained, as if he were trying to lift something heavy.

"If there is anything I can do to make you happier . . ." His voice trailed off.

Denise smiled, shaking her head; then she turned and bent over the crate of condoms. Mr. Hendricks's attention embarrassed her. As she took hold of the crate, she felt a sharp pain on her bottom. At first, she couldn't imagine what it was. Then she realized Mr. Hendricks had pinched her. She straightened up immediately.

"Mr. Hendricks!"

Seeing her anger, the anticipation in his eyes changed to alarm. He jumped back.

"I'm terribly sorry."

"What in the world are you doing?"

"Please, it was a mistake. I don't know what came over me."

Mr. Hendricks's fear was such that Denise's own anger began to diminish.

"How in the world could you do such a thing?"

"It was a mistake. I let bad thoughts carry me away. Please don't tell anyone." He stared at his pudgy white hand as if the hand were the culprit, a rascal unrelated to him.

"You should be ashamed of yourself," said Denise. She wondered if Mr. Hendricks had taken her success with the condoms as proof of promiscuity, as if the high school boys bought the condoms because of her advocacy of sex and not because of the fear she instilled in them. Even Mr. Hendricks's questions about her happiness had been a secret probing. From a few false assumptions he had built a teetery structure of cause and effect. Mr. Hendricks patted his forehead with a white handkerchief as if he had spilled something there.

"I can't tell you how much I regret this," he said.

It occurred to Denise that she enjoyed the power she held over him. Because of his foolishness, she had become the one in charge. But she disliked that awareness and in that moment she decided not to file a complaint. Maybe she'd encouraged him unconsciously or maybe by being alive we constantly give encouragement to each other. But she didn't mean to spend her life tiptoeing around. She couldn't live in ways contrary to her nature as long as she felt she had done nothing wrong.

Mr. Hendricks refolded his handkerchief and returned it to his hip pocket. He glanced at her nervously, then looked away. She asked herself what he had imagined they would do back here, only a few yards from Larry and Mildred. And she wondered what confusions and shortcomings in his life had led to such foolishness.

"I won't tell anyone," said Denise, "but never touch me again."

"No, never," said Mr. Hendricks, shoving his hands in his pockets. "I don't know what got into me." Mixed with his embarrassment, Denise also saw relief. He took a deep breath and shook his head, more at himself and his failings than as an apology to her. He raised his eyebrows and pursed his lips. She knew he felt safe now.

When Denise walked home after work she kept thinking about Mr. Hendricks's face and her pleasure at seeing his fear. Although it was a small pleasure, she felt unhappy with it. The pleasure made her wonder about her own capacity for meanness. And it made her again question her own responsibility for the failure of her marriage and if she could ever understand that responsibility. What was understanding but an opinion that might or might not be true? A person said *I understand*, and it meant that person felt comfortable with a certain interpretation of events, but as for actual understanding: maybe he did or maybe he didn't.

The evening was warm and couples were window-shopping and eating ice cream. A toddler on a tricycle zigzagged along the sidewalk. As a result, Denise didn't notice Josh until he was standing directly in front of her. He wore a white shirt and a tie, and his black hair was still wet from when he had recently combed it. Josh never wore ties and Denise realized he had put on this one to convince her of the seriousness of his intentions. He tried to reach for her hand, but she stepped back. The dachshund puppy sat at his feet, scratching at its red leather collar.

"I love you, Denise," he said.

The way his eyelashes fluttered, the way he held his jaw— Denise knew he was lying. And she understood that it was more important for Josh to be believed than to tell the truth. His words existed not to convey his feelings but to conceal them.

"I never want to live with you again," she said. And she knew she was lying as well, but it didn't matter. It was a healthy deception and after enough time passed it would become true. Josh stared at her and his face reddened. His face reminded her of Mr. Hendricks. Josh, too, seemed anxious. He, too, seemed about to admit his mistake. But suddenly Denise didn't care what he had done and or what she had done to help cause it. She was tired of worrying about her imperfections. In her mind she pushed Josh back over the line she had crossed and would never cross again. Already he was far away, someone from her past rather than her present. Denise walked around him without glancing at him. She heard the puppy bark but she didn't turn to look. Regret, what a stupid name. It, too, was part of the lie. She continued along to her apartment over the Trustworthy Hardware. Three farmers stood in front, leaning against the display window and chewing slowly. They stared at her but Denise ignored them. She didn't even feel angry with them.

As she climbed the stairs to her apartment, she realized she had forgiven Josh, just as she had forgiven Mr. Hendricks. No, she hadn't forgiven them, she had pardoned them: a subtle but distinct difference. She had come to terms with their actions. The pardoning made her feel better but it didn't fix anything. It would make neither man treat her well. She knew Mr. Hendricks would regret that she still worked at the drugstore. He would begin to behave coldly and find fault. He would act as if what he had done had been her weakness rather than his, as if the very fact of having a woman's body had been an encouragement. He would search for pretexts and excuses, just like Josh, until eventually she would be forced to leave her job.

She had pardoned the two men; it had freed her from resentment, but she had no interest in forgiving them. In any case, neither wanted it. If they couldn't have her consent, they wanted her silence. Her forgiveness was for herself. It was a way of coming to terms with what had been and what had not been her responsibility. It was a way of getting past the event. Wouldn't it be better to leave now, to get out of Cortland? She imagined a great space opening before her and she wanted to explore that space, to touch its corners with her hands. She wanted to get her life moving again. Her forgiveness was a way of saying goodbye.

CYNTHIA, MY SISTER

Bryce sat on the sand and held the burlap bag open between his legs. When Eric dumped in a shovelful of sand, Bryce said, "Oooo, sexy!" He said it fifty times as Eric filled the bags. Eric was twenty-three and in his first year of graduate school. He had driven sixty miles from Iowa City to Muscatine to help sandbag because he was bored and because it was spring. Bryce had come with several hundred volunteers from Parsons College. A dead college now. These days, as Maharishi Institute, it is full of kids trying to levitate. What a simple, uncomplicated ambition. As Parsons, it was full of kids who hated their parents while wanting to love them or who loved their parents while wanting to hate them.

The flood of the Mississippi River around Muscatine, Iowa, in the spring of 1965 inundated most of the downtown. On his first day, when Eric was looking for a boat to take him downriver, he saw an old five-story brick hotel with water lapping against its second-story windows. Written on the wall in black lettering was THIS HOTEL ONE HUNDRED PERCENT FIREPROOF. The water that April rose twenty-two and a half feet, a height not surpassed till the flood of 1993. Beyond the hotel lay a network of pontoons and floating docks leading out to the small boats, which kept departing and arriving.

A motorboat took Eric downriver, and after an hour he was deposited on a spit of land where several hundred men and women were shoveling sand into green burlap bags. He was teamed up with Bryce, who said, "You know, I'm only here because my parents despise me." Then he gave a smile that showed a row of perfect teeth. He was nineteen.

"Oh?" Eric had said.

"Quite true. They live in Belgium and can't stand to have me around. I make my father upchuck." Bryce made a vomiting noise. He had beautiful blond hair, long and straight, parted on the right so it fell across his forehead in a wing that he kept sweeping back with his hand.

Bryce said the entire college had come to Muscatine. It was shortly before exams and they had nothing better to do. "Quite an adventure, don't you think? And if we could also have an earthquake, how sweet it would be."

Bryce's father worked for the embassy in Brussels. About a dozen of the Parsons students were "embassy brats," as Bryce called them. Eric later met several others and was impressed by their knowledge of the world: ski resorts in Switzerland, back streets in Amsterdam, villages in Egypt, an easy sophistication and detachment combined with a sense of being unwanted, as if at any moment their disinterest could change to tears. Yet perhaps not. They seemed to find their very unwantability amusing and not their fault. Some children are born with blue eyes, some are born unwantable.

Eric wanted to be a writer. He thought if he worked hard he might have a future, although he couldn't imagine what that meant other than publication and acclaim. The writing itself, at the moment, was too difficult to enjoy, too full of failures and small humiliations, and so this future—even though he couldn't define it—was at times all that kept him going.

When their conversation reached this level of exchange, Bryce said, "A future? What's that? You mean the day after tomorrow?" Bryce sat on the ground and squinted up at Eric as he closed the top of the burlap bag. He said he would like to be an angel or a sugarplum fairy or a wealthy old woman's companion. "I would tweak her nipples and make her squeal," he said.

When it was Bryce's turn to shovel, he said he would prefer to take a walk instead. Eric and Bryce wandered off together. Bryce wore a beat-up brown leather jacket, gray wool pants, and a white silk scarf. He was slender and several inches shorter than Eric. The sandy area was hilly, but Eric couldn't decide if they were natural dunes or man-made because trucks kept bringing in more sand and a yellow Caterpillar was pushing it into heaps. There were Iowa national guardsmen looking shiny and muscular, convicts in blue denim work clothes, miscellaneous volunteers like Eric, and a lot of Parsons students, who seemed intent on having fun no matter how much they might work. Three were throwing a Frisbee. One could tell the Parsons students because they were well dressed and had careful haircuts. Other than muddy shoes, they showed little sign of wear and tear. Many wore dark glasses. One used an ivory cigarette holder. And they kept laughing, but their laughter had a shrill quality that made it abrasive. It was the laughter of people who wanted others to know they were laughing.

Eric had known a boy in high school who went to Parsons. He applied because he had been turned down everywhere else and because his parents had money. It was a party school where little work was done and degrees were available. The boy had been quiet and never studied. At parties he sat in a corner and got drunk as fast as possible. Passive resistance and obliteration of consciousness: at that time in Eric's life it had seemed a reasonable philosophy.

Eric and Bryce climbed to the top of the levee. Away to the west stretched a shallow lake spotted with houses. A narrow road cut across it and three green dump trucks moved slowly toward them. The only trees were saplings. The houses were ranch houses with swing sets in their flooded backyards. Six formed an arc in a small subdivision. All appeared deserted. Then Eric saw two young men climb out a living room window and splash back the two hundred yards or so toward the levee.

"Several of my classmates," said Bryce. "They've found a nice dry place to fuck the girls. In their intellectual natures they are idiots, but in their sensual natures they are veritable Einsteins."

A moment later Eric saw two women in bright crew-neck sweaters also climb out of the house. Their hair was mussed and they were laughing. When they saw Bryce, they waved.

"Well-traveled roads," said Bryce. "Parsons girls have skin like chamois cloth from overuse. Personally, I tend to slip a lot on a wet deck. Whoops! That's me." Bryce swept back his hair and turned toward the river. His eyes never seemed entirely open. "The whole idea of being washed has a moralistic tone," he said. "Washed up, washed to one side, washed away."

An old car ferry was puffing upriver toward the landing point. It was a flat barge with a small wheelhouse and a black stovepipe rising above it. Two snakelike chains of men were passing bags of sand down to the water. The sun was very bright and the sky cloudless. Far across the river was a line of trees. Logs, crates, clumps of straw, even broken tables and chairs floated down stream. A pair of ducks flapped away overhead.

"Care for some chili?" asked Bryce. "I'm feeling peckish."

This bowl of chili was the first of many that Eric had over the next few days. It was supplied by the Red Cross. Salvation Army chili was best, but a Methodist church in Muscatine also made a good chili with chunks of meat. Sometimes there were crackers. Red Cross chili was watery and had no meat at all.

They stood at the end of the road on the west side of the levee. A middle-aged Red Cross fellow ladled the chili into Styrofoam cups from a tub set in the back of his jeep. He wore khakis and shiny black shoes spotted with mud. Several dump trucks were parked between him and the levee. Moving slowly toward them was a third dump truck loaded with sand. Water stretched away on both sides, and Eric saw the tips of fence posts. About twenty men stood around, some eating chili, others waiting to be served.

Bryce gave Eric a white plastic spoon. "You might want to protect this," he said. "There're never enough."

"How long have you been here?" asked Eric.

"It feels like several years. Today's Wednesday? We got here on Monday."

"Where do you sleep?"

"There're cots in the Methodist church social hall. It's quite nice, actually. They're arranged on the same principle as a cemetery: row after row. It gives one philosophical thoughts." Bryce accepted a cup of chili. "Did you make this yourself?" he asked.

"Take it or leave it," said the Red Cross man.

"Ah," said Bryce, "would that life were so simple."

By now the dump truck had reached the Red Cross jeep. Although the jeep was pulled to the side, only about a dozen feet of space separated it from the water. The driver of the truck leaned out the window. He had red hair and freckles. "You going to move that jeep?"

"The others got around." The Red Cross man had an impatient air, as if nothing was quite enough.

The driver put the truck in gear. There was a clunk, then the low labored groaning of the motor. The sand rose up over the cab in a pyramid.

"I love tense scenes," said Bryce, "they make one think that life is actually taking place."

The truck eased itself past the jeep. Only a few inches divided the two vehicles. When the truck and jeep were side by side, the truck began to tilt. Eric realized the bank was giving way. He saw this awareness enter the driver's eyes: first suspicion, then wonder, then dread. The truck slid sideways so ponderously that there was never a splash. It was like watching an elephant lie down sideways. When the truck was at a 45-degree angle, the driver tried to open the door but it was too heavy to lift. He sat gripping the wheel as his face grew redder. If it hadn't happened in slow motion, someone might have shouted. Little waves surged outward and the truck came to rest in about seven feet of water. Its underside was muddy and crisscrossed with drive trains and exhaust systems and cables. The water came up to its middle.

"Hold this a moment," said Bryce, giving Eric his chili. "I see a chance for action." Sprinting across the road, he jumped onto the truck, scrambled over the front tire, and stood up on the door. He reached down to help the driver from the window. Two other men joined him, grabbing the driver's arms and hauling him up. Streams of water ran off his clothing. The four men balanced on the door of the truck, then jumped back down to the road.

The Red Cross man kept saying, "It wasn't my fault."

"Poor fellow," said Bryce, rejoining Eric. "I've said that my entire life and it's never done any good."

Once the dump truck came to rest, it looked absolutely permanent. The driver stared at his load of sand oozing into the water. Eric was impressed with the speed with which Bryce decided to help, though he seemed driven more by whim than by valor.

Eric and Bryce walked back up the levee. "To see that truck go plop was a happy event," said Bryce. They climbed through the sand and paused at the top of the levee to catch their breath. Bryce took off his white scarf, then reknotted it around his neck. "And why do you want to be a writer?" he asked.

Eric had many answers for this but none he could settle upon. He tried to determine from Bryce's eyes the degree of his seriousness, but the question had seemed offhand like everything else about him, as if Bryce meant his whole life to be a casual gesture. "To capture the world," said Eric at last, feeling foolish as he said it.

"And what does that mean?"

"To capture an event and make it real to someone else."

"Ah," said Bryce, "you'd like to capture the world and I'd like to set it free. If not that, then to forget it exists. So troublesome, the world. It never stays where it's been put."

The ferry had reached the landing point and men were loading the sandbags onto its deck. Bryce and Eric made their way toward them. "You'll like passing sandbags," said Bryce. "It's like an embrace but not quite like an embrace."

One passed the sandbags with arms partly folded, catching the sandbag on the left arm, then heaving it off to the right. The sandbags came as quickly as they could be passed until Eric felt nearly hypnotized. Several of the Parsons students liked to play a little joke. Someone would toss a sandbag; then, instead of passing it on, the student would toss it back, causing his victim to fall or drop the bag or drop two bags, so that for a moment the line would come to a halt as the student laughed.

It seemed that Bryce had invented this joke, or at least he was accused of inventing it. That afternoon as they loaded the car ferry, Bryce tossed a sandbag back to a national guardsman, a burly fellow with black hair and the name FLETCHER stenciled across the shirt pocket of his green uniform. Fletcher grabbed Bryce by the lapels of his leather jacket and lifted him a few inches in the air.

"This is ill-advised," said Bryce.

Fletcher took a few steps to the edge of the car ferry and dropped Bryce in the river. The sandbag passing stopped as Bryce floundered about in the water.

Other Parsons students cried out, "No fair, no fair!"

"Asshole," said Fletcher.

Two students hauled Bryce out of the water. He shook himself like a dog, then raised an eyebrow at Fletcher. "One must hold the world lightly," said Bryce, "or not at all."

Eric and Bryce dropped out of the line. Bryce took off his jacket and shook it; then he took off his shirt. He was thin and his flesh was very white. "The trouble with being wet is that it always lasts longer than one wants. At first I was refreshed; now I am simply cold." He shivered.

"I've a sweater in my backpack," said Eric.

"That would be kind of you." Bryce hung his shirt on the branch of a small tree. He took off his loafers and socks. He raised the shoes, emptying out the water. His blond hair was plastered to his forehead. "My impulsive nature bears its own punishment," he said. He took out his wallet, wiped it off, then set several burlap bags on the sand and distributed the contents of the wallet across the bags: ten-dollar bills, identification cards, and pictures. One picture showed a blond woman standing by a crumbling pillar. Her hands were on her hips and her expression was a mixture of exasperation and good humor.

"That's Cynthia, my sister. She's three years older than I am. She married a Frenchman and escaped the parental yoke. Our English nanny called her 'trouble on a biscuit.' " Eric's sweater was gray with geometric designs. Bryce drew it over his head. "I like how it itches," he said.

A Parsons student gave Bryce a towel and another gave him a pair of socks. Nobody had any extra pants but somebody said he would take a look in one of the empty ranch houses.

"I'll bask here and consider my sins," said Bryce. "Call me if they want us to take a trip on the ferry. I adore voyages."

Eric went back to the line of men passing sandbags. A student named Henry went with him. Henry was overweight and breathed heavily. He had black horn-rimmed glasses that made his eyes seem oversized.

"He's only here because of his parents," said Henry. "He thinks if he does everything they say, it'll make his life better. Sounds like a crock of shit to me. Parents always want more."

It took another hour to load the ferry. The students told jokes, laughed, whistled at girls. The guardsmen hated them. Fletcher in particular liked throwing the sandbags hard at whomever he was passing them to; then he would grin at his buddies. The day grew warm and Eric tied his jean jacket around his waist. When the ferry was full, he went to get Bryce, who sat on a pile of burlap bags playing poker with three other students. He wore only his undershorts, Eric's sweater, and a pair of pink socks. His clothes were draped on the tree behind him. Money was scattered on the burlap bags and Bryce was winning.

"How sad to win money when there's nothing to spend it on," he said. He pulled on his gray wool pants, which were still wet, put on his loafers, and left his jacket and his other clothes on the tree. "We'll be back," he said to his clothes cheerfully, "don't worry." Bryce and Eric walked over to the car ferry. The engine had started and black smoke puffed out of its smokestack. They scrambled onto the sandbags, where about fifty men and a few women were already sitting. "If I feel tempted to toss a sandbag at another soldier," said Bryce, "make sure you tell me to stop."

The trip downriver took about thirty minutes. Eric had expected the river to be turbulent but it didn't even seem particularly swift: flat brown water that kept getting deeper. Eric couldn't see the bank on the other side—just trees and sometimes the roof of a house. The trees were getting their leaves and looked feathery. The ferry made its way through a wood, then through a farm, passing between a half-submerged house and barn. Bryce lay on his back and talked about Europe. Chickens were perched on the branches of some of the trees. Eric felt they had forlorn expressions. Many of the guardsmen were sleeping. Parsons students were playing Rock, Paper, Scissors.

"There was a bar in Berlin where I taught everyone to do the Bunny Hop," said Bryce. "We had a wonderful time."

"Why'd you go to Parsons?" asked Eric. He had been to Germany five years earlier and had spent a week in Amsterdam. Given the choice between Fairfield, Iowa, and Amsterdam, Eric felt there was no contest.

"Trust fund pressures." Bryce had carefully combed his hair so the blond wing again cut across his forehead at a 45-degree angle. "And I try to be culturally egalitarian and believe all places are equal. Besides that, my father needs to have an ocean between us."

"Why do you say he hates you?"

"Because I'm living evidence that his sperm isn't as potent as he'd like it to be."

"What does he want you to be?"

"Something other. Taller, shorter, darker, blonder. He likes everything around him to enhance his vanity. I, sad to say, detract: hence Iowa."

"Can't your mother do anything?"

"She means well but she's his little echo, a living ditto mark. He barks and she obeys."

"And your sister?"

Bryce sat up and wrapped his arms around his knees. "Ah, she's the one they're trying to keep me away from. My father sees himself as a sort of Christian Moses, except where Moses had ten commandments, he has five hundred."

"What if you just did what you wanted?"

"Then it would complicate the trust fund, which says I must graduate from college. Parsons at least accepted me. It makes me fond of them."

Eric felt that if he didn't work hard, he would disappear, as if hard work gave a person substance, as if it were the energy that engendered three-dimensionality. He couldn't imagine living like Bryce: casting himself loose, falling backward, and expecting to be caught or not caring if he wasn't.

The levee that was their destination seemed made entirely of sandbags, although they only formed the top layers. On one side, the water was a foot below the bags; on the other was a slope of more than twenty feet. There were trees and fields but no houses. About a hundred people waited for the car ferry. A Salvation Army tent stood at the bottom of the levee and three workers passed out cups of chili. Eric later learned the place was considered dangerous because of the weight of water against the levee and that the Red Cross had refused to come in. Indeed, the next day the levee was abandoned and the sandbags were washed away. But Eric only learned this afterward. He never had any sense of where he was or what was being done in other places. He filled sandbags, passed them, waited to be taken someplace, and ate quantities of chili.

At one point he found himself next to the guardsman Fletcher, who looked at him suspiciously. "Where're you from?" asked Eric.

"Ottumwa," said Fletcher, turning away.

"I'm from Iowa City," said Eric. "At least at the moment."

They stood on the levee waiting for the sandbags. Down below, Eric saw Bryce chatting with two of his friends. When the bags started to move, Fletcher threw them to Eric harder than necessary and Eric dropped several. After a while Eric said, "Do you have to throw them like that?"

Fletcher grinned. "I guess I'm just strong." He wore a green cap with the visor tilted jauntily across his forehead.

Eric took himself out of the line and went to have a cup of chili. The sky had turned gray and the wind was blowing. It was past six o'clock. Eric's boots made sucking noises in the muddy ground. Bryce was talking to a Salvation Army woman. "She says it might snow," he said cheerfully. "I love variety."

In two hours they raised the levee six inches. The man in charge always seemed to be throwing up his arms and pointing at something. He never laughed. Eric's arms ached and he wished for a dry place to sit down. It was dark when they got back on the ferry to return upriver. There were bales of straw, and the men nestled among them to stay warm. Bryce and Eric sat near the wheelhouse. Bryce piled straw over his legs. The engine made a thumping noise and they had to raise their voices.

"Are you going back to Europe this summer?" asked Eric. He himself planned to go back to Chicago and write.

"I might slip into France but I can't let my father know."

"Is it that bad? What did you do to cause it?"

"He feels I behave in an un-sonlike manner. What indeed *is* sonlike? That's what I'd like to know. Surely it's more than saying *Aye, aye, sir* and dressing smart. In any case, I was in my sister's room one night before she was married. We were both drunk. My father walked in. He felt we were behaving in a manner inappropriate for brother and sister. He slapped me."

Eric felt Bryce leaning against him. The ferry had a spotlight that swept over the deck and across the trees. The shapes of the men sprawled across the bales of hay looked like casualties on a battlefield. Going upriver the ferry was moving against the current, and the trip took much longer. It began to drizzle.

"Have you ever had what's called 'a homosexual experience'?" asked Bryce.

"No."

"Are you interested?"

"No."

"Don't think badly of me, will you?"

Eric didn't say anything for a moment. He tried to imagine Bryce with his sister. "I won't," he said.

"If you knew how much I hate things," Bryce began. Then he stopped. He got to his feet and threaded his way between the hay bales. The spotlight swept across him, illuminating his blond hair. His body was a thin silhouette. Eric saw one of the guardsmen get to his feet. He guessed it was Fletcher. Then the man sat back down again. Eric walked to the front of the ferry. He sat on some straw and let his feet dangle over the edge. His hair was wet from the drizzle and he wished he had a hat.

The trip upriver took an hour. As they were moving through thick woods the ferry passed an elaborate houseboat that somebody said belonged to the Coast Guard: a white colonial house on a barge. It didn't look like a houseboat at all: a three-story house with dormers, window boxes, green shutters, and a front porch.

Curtains hung in the windows and the lights were burning. It seemed completely deserted.

Bryce sat down beside Eric again. "It resembles my child-hood home."

"It's like an apparition," said Eric.

"Just like my childhood home," said Bryce. "I'd give my shoes and socks to see it sink." He turned away. "You know, I love my sister, but I don't love her like a sister. When we were growing up, we were only together at Christmas and maybe a week or so in summer before we were shipped off to camp. I wrote to her and sometimes she wrote back. That night I was in her room was the first time I'd seen her in two years. She asked if I was gay and I said I didn't know. She'd already been with lots of men and described their bodies, how their hair was different, how their penises were different. She told me the different things they liked. Since then I've only seen Cynthia once, very briefly, in a room with other people. She won't answer my letters. To be away from her makes me feel that my whole body has been cut up with scissors. At times I still feel her skin against my fingertips."

Eric realized he was digging his fingernails into his palms. He straightened his fingers. The engine sounded like a drum pounding over and over. When they rounded the next bend, he saw the lights of the landing stage where men were stacking sandbags.

Bryce put his hand on Eric's wrist. "Look at me."

Eric was surprised to see tears in Bryce's eyes. He had an impulse to put his arm around him, to comfort him, and the thought of even so innocent an embrace alarmed him. Instead, he patted Bryce's shoulder. "It'll be okay."

"Dreamer," said Bryce.

The ferry docked and the men began loading sandbags. The yellow Caterpillar groaned as it heaped up piles of sand. The drizzle became a fine mist that hung in the air. The lights were powered by generators and their engines made a roar. Parts of the sand hills were brightly lit, other parts were in shadow.

"My clothes must be dryish," said Bryce. "I'll return your sweater. You must be cold."

The clothes were still damp but Bryce put them on anyway. Eric put on his sweater. It was warm from Bryce's body. Bryce zipped up his leather jacket, then handed Eric his silk scarf.

"Here," he said, "you need this. You lack panache."

Eric started to put it in his pocket, then tied it around his neck instead. "What are you going to do about your father?"

"Sometimes," said Bryce, "I think I might kill him." He pushed back his blond hair and smiled. Eric was struck by how sweet it seemed, how it made Bryce look about six years old. "But if he's dead, I remain unforgiven. Unblessed and all the rest—none of that changes if he's dead. It's a substantial problem. I hate him but I need him to keep taking his vitamins." Bryce gave an artificial laugh, a high twitter. "Who says the world's not a comical place?"

For the next two hours Eric filled sandbags; then around 1 A.M. he went back downriver on the ferry. He didn't see the white house again. He and Bryce had become separated. At first he thought Bryce was on the ferry, but he didn't spot him. Eric slept a little, making himself a cave with straw. Reaching the levee, he joined the line unloading the sandbags. Even the most rambunctious Parsons students had grown quiet.

Henry began to follow Eric around and stood next to him in the line. Every few minutes he would pause to wipe the drizzle off his glasses. "You like cars?" he asked.

"Sure," said Eric.

"My dad's got two Jaguars and a Maserati but he won't let me drive them."

"Does he let you drive anything?"

"My old lady's Ford," said Henry. Then he laughed. "Did Bryce tell you the story about having sex with his sister?"

"He didn't actually mention the sex part. You think it's true?"

"He wouldn't tell it so much if it weren't true. He's fucked up, but who isn't?"

Eric wanted to say he wasn't fucked up, but he wasn't sure he could prove it. "He says his sister never writes."

"He's got a big picture of her in his dorm room. A wedding picture with his sister in a white dress. It's like a shrine." Henry nodded toward the white silk scarf. "He lent you that?"

Eric had nearly forgotten the scarf, which was dry by now. "He gave it to me."

"He used to have it draped around his sister's photograph. It matched her dress."

When they finished unloading the ferry, it was nearly four in the morning. Instead of riding back upriver, they were told to wait for trucks to take them to Muscatine. They clustered around the Salvation Army tent, trying to stay out of the drizzle. Several people lay down on the ground on ponchos and tried to sleep even though it was wet.

"I'd like to be a writer," said Henry, "if I was certain there was money in it. These things are always a gamble. Maybe I'll raise show dogs instead."

When three dump trucks arrived, they crowded in the back. Most of the men in Eric's truck were from Parsons. "I wish we'd have a flood every week," said one. The sky was gray in the east and Eric could see the shapes of trees. Whenever the truck hit a big bump, the men were flung together. Eric had to hold on to the side to keep from being thrown out. As it grew light, Eric saw fields covered with water and flocks of ducks.

The trucks dropped them off at the Methodist church. Eric

followed Henry, who already knew the routine. In the church dining hall more chili was being served, this time with bread. It was
half past five and about fifty people were eating. A few Parsons
girls came in from the dormitory wearing dresses and makeup
and with their hair nicely brushed. They looked as neat as if they
were on their way to a dance. All the men were muddy and wet.
Several men whistled.

Eric wandered around, looking for Bryce. He asked several
students but they hadn't seen him. He went into the dormitory,
which was in the gymnasium. There were rows of army cots with
blankets. Eric took a blanket and put it over his shoulders but he
didn't feel like sleeping. About fifty people were sleeping or trying to. Bryce wasn't one of them. Back in the dining hall, Henry
came up to him. "We're supposed to get a tetanus shot."

"Where do we go?"

"Some guy said we should ask at city hall."

"Have you seen Bryce?"

"No one's seen him."

Eric's car was parked two blocks away. Henry and another Parsons student came with him. All three wore blankets over their
shoulders; they looked like Indians. It seemed that one third of
Muscatine was on the top of a hill, one third on the hillside, and
one third at the bottom. It was the bottom third that was flooded.
City hall was on the top. The drizzle had stopped and the sun was
poking above the trees. Eric parked behind city hall between two
police cars and they went inside.

The mayor's name was Bosch. He was a dark-haired man who
kept a jar of jellybeans on his desk. "Take as many as you want,"
he said.

He didn't know anything about tetanus shots. He seemed
befuddled but probably he was exhausted. "I've been trying to
call someone over at your college. Don't you have a dean or some-

thing? We had to arrest one of your students. A guardsman brought him in."

"Who was it?" asked Eric. He never doubted that he was talking about Bryce.

The mayor stood behind his desk in his shirtsleeves, picking up one piece of paper, then discarding it for another. "I forget his name. He was wrecking a house. I don't know the details."

The police station was in the basement of city hall. Eric, Henry, and the other student went down to the front desk, where a sergeant was filling out papers. A radio by his elbow played pseudoclassical music, Mantovani or someone similar.

"Bryce Cramer," said the sergeant. "He's sure got himself in a heap of trouble."

"What did he do?" asked Eric.

"Is he a friend of yours?"

"Yeah, I guess so."

"He was wrecking houses down at Sandy Point. Like he had a baseball bat. He smashed the furniture, broke the windows. As if the people don't have a bad enough time being flooded, without a crazy guy wrecking their house as well. A guardsman heard the breaking glass and stopped him. Had to beat him up some. Trespassing, vandalism, maybe even theft—he's in hot water."

"Was the guardsman's name Fletcher?" asked Eric.

The sergeant nodded. "That's right, William Fletcher."

"Can we see Bryce?" asked Henry.

"Nobody can see him but his lawyer. But he's through there." The sergeant pointed back over his shoulder to a window. Eric went up to the glass.

Bryce sat on a bench with his elbows on his knees. When Eric tapped on the class, he looked up. Bryce's face was bruised and there was a bandage at the corner of his mouth. He looked at them without expression, then he raised his left hand, holding out the palm, and slowly raised and lowered his four fingers in a childlike wave. Bryce's leather coat was ripped and his pants were muddy. After a moment, he stood up, turned around, and sat back down on the bench with his back to them. He leaned over again and cupped his face in his hands. Eric stood there for a few more minutes but Bryce didn't move. Touching his fingers to the white silk scarf, Eric tucked it into his jean jacket.

Eric drove back to Iowa City that morning. He got home at ten and slept until six. His muscles hurt and his body felt as if he had been flung down a flight of stairs. He had no dreams, but he kept feeling the motion of heaving the sandbags. He had dinner, tried to read for a while, then went back to sleep. In the morning he drove to Muscatine. He was still wearing Bryce's white silk scarf. A dump truck took him to the sandpile. The driver said the flood could wipe out the whole fuckin' state as far as he was concerned. They shouted over the roar of the engine. The sky was cloudy and a wind was blowing.

Eric filled sandbags for the rest of the morning. He found something soothing about a task with clear goals and measurable accomplishments, a task that didn't defer its rewards to an indefinite future. At one point when he was getting a cup of chili he asked a Parsons student what had happened to Bryce.

"The school lawyer bailed him out and drove him back to Fairfield. He busted up two of those houses." The young man pointed across the water toward the half circle of six ranch houses.

Eric thought about Bryce and his sister as he filled the sandbags. Eric didn't have a sister himself, only a younger brother. He had had a friend in high school who supposedly had sex with his sister but that was only hearsay. The girl had been a tall, beautiful blonde and it seemed crazy not to want to have sex with her.

Early in the afternoon the ferry came back upriver. Most of the men on board were national guardsmen. Fletcher was one of them. Eric didn't think he wanted to talk to him, until he saw him joking with his pals and smoking cigarettes. Even so, it took about ten minutes before Eric could get up his nerve to approach him.

"How come you beat up Bryce?" Eric asked.

Fletcher had been walking back from a military jeep carrying about half a dozen shovels. He looked at Eric as if he couldn't quite determine what language he was speaking. "That crazy guy? He was busting up the furniture."

"You didn't need to hurt him. He's half your size."

Fletcher set the shovels down on the ground. "He tried to kiss me."

"I don't believe it," said Eric.

"He did. He said, 'I'd like to kiss you.' So I hit him."

It occurred to Eric that Fletcher was probably eighteen or nineteen and this whole experience must be very strange to him. "Was he drunk?"

"No, he was crazy, that's all." Fletcher didn't seem to grow uncertain but there was a pause in his delivery. "He'd been smashing everything with a baseball bat; then he said he wanted to kiss me. I could've beat him up worse than I did. That's his scarf, isn't it."

Eric touched the scarf at his neck. "He let me have it."

Fletcher picked up the shovels and turned away. Eric had the feeling that he had already been forgotten.

Eric drove back to Iowa City that afternoon. He thought how Bryce had said the deserted houseboat reminded him of the house where he was raised. He thought of him smashing up the ranch houses cold sober. He thought of himself as a would-be writer and how he imagined writing could make sense of the world. But it didn't do that. At best it took a jumble of information, arranged the pieces, and turned it into a mystery. It didn't solve the mystery but made it seem capable of solution. It claimed that meaning existed. And sometimes it didn't claim; sometimes it whined and wheedled. How much more comforting was Fletcher's position: Bryce was crazy, Bryce was perverse.

Parsons students had been fucking in those houses the previous day and perhaps during the night as well. When Fletcher had caught him, it was just dawn. Bryce had been smashing the furniture in the dark, hitting what he couldn't see, breaking the windows. Fletcher had waded out through the water with a flashlight. "What the hell you doing?" he had shouted. Bryce had looked at him and pursed his lips. Probably he had brushed the blond wing of his hair back off his forehead. "Would you like to kiss me?" he had asked. And Fletcher beat him up. Hadn't Bryce known that would happen? Hadn't that been Bryce's intention? Eric thought how he had looked in the police station on Thursday morning: the little wave goodbye, then how he turned and showed them nothing but the curve of his back, as if he were saying no to them, no to all the world.

Four days later Eric called the college to find out what had happened to Bryce. He had flown home to Belgium two days earlier. Bryce's father had paid for the damage to the houses.